# RUTHLESS ENF(

## VAMPIRES OF BATON ROUGE: BOOK 2

Roxie Ray and Lindsey Devin
© 2022
**Disclaimer**

This is a work of fiction. Names, places, characters, and events are all fictitious for the reader's pleasure. Any similarities to real people, places, events, living or dead are all coincidental.

# Contents

# Chapter 1 - Kyle

I glanced at my tablet, where I had it propped against my headboard as I packed. Nic's face filled the screen, and I made sure to be a constantly moving figure, in and out of the shot, I was too busy to sit down, and I fucking hated video calls. But the king was the king, and when he requested one... Well, I didn't say no.

No matter how much I wanted to.

I glanced inside the small duffle bag I was packing. I didn't need a lot of shit. Hell, I didn't *own* a lot of shit in the first place and didn't see the need to surround myself with *stuff.* I'd never be one of those vamps with homes full of meaningless crap and so-called *treasures.*

My needs were basic and simple. The bare minimum to keep surviving, because that was the only guarantee in an immortal life, after all.

Well, one lived well.

Without unnecessary risk.

And I wasn't exactly following that last part just now. I threw another balled-up pair of socks into my bag.

Would my actual survival really be in the balance after all this time? I paused for a moment, disliking the uncertainty that filled me after that thought. It had been a long time since I'd had to consider no longer existing.

"You okay, Kyle?" Nic's voice startled me, but I hid my flinch.

I had years of practice at concealing my reactions, and now I barely reacted to anything. I remained perfectly still, so that I was the only one who knew how I felt when others spoke.

"I'm fine." I didn't need to use excess words, either.

Nic wouldn't expect them after all this time, nor would he demand them.

I glanced up as he nodded.

"You sure? I'm not entirely happy about this project you've volunteered for." He drew his eyebrows down, creasing the skin over his nose as he looked thoughtfully into the camera at his end, like he could actually search my face and learn something about how I felt.

He knew better than that, though, and I nearly laughed in response.

Instead, I bit back a sigh. "You know how much rests on this," I kept my words fairly light as I grabbed my toothbrush and added it to my bag.

Nic didn't bother to conceal *his* sigh. "Yes, I know. This faction could bring my whole reign down. They're in New

Orleans now, but we know from what Temple has said that they won't stop there. They'll be in Baton Rouge soon enough."

I nodded. "Yes, and I can stop them." I'd fought enough wars and knew enough about tactical attack to be certain that I could infiltrate a rogue gang and bring them down.

The crease between his brows deepened. "Everything is so precarious, Kyle. I don't know if Sebastian has said quite how much."

I grimaced. Sebastian hadn't fucking shut up about how unstable the politics still were in Baton Rouge and New Orleans, and how new this power switch was. If he hadn't told me what Nic thought was so important by now, I really was going on a fool's errand.

But Nic wanted to enlighten me anyway, and I wasn't about to interrupt my king. I could get away with giving Sebastian shit, but I wasn't even going to try with Nic. Apart from anything else, he didn't actually deserve it. His morals and instincts were generally on point, and although Sebastian was improving in that area, I didn't usually hesitate to remind him which of us was the better man. I didn't let the prince get away with crap, anyway.

"If we don't bring these Blackbloods under control, they'll spark a revolt in our vampire population — either of vampires who want what the Blackbloods offer and defect to join them, or others who are scared that we can't provide them with adequate protection and rise up against us in fear. Simply put, we could end up fighting more than one war."

I nodded. I'd considered that, but I couldn't get lost thinking about what-ifs and maybes. I'd leave that kind of broad strategizing and theorizing to Nic and Sebastian and keep my focus on dismantling the Blackbloods from within. I couldn't afford to be distracted or have my attention scattered across the wider issues.

"And the deal with the wolves is…" Nic hesitated, and his thoughtful expression increased. "Shaky, you could say."

I nodded again. That much made sense. Relations between vampires and wolves had never been easy, and Nic had been unusual when he'd reached out to Conri, the local wolf alpha, to ensure safety for his newly found human mate, Leia.

The deal Nic had brokered at the time had been further reaching than he'd anticipated. Conri seemed to have kept nosing around, and now he and his wolves had a power-sharing agreement in New Orleans. They had land and we had rule. Allegedly. But that deal wasn't any of my business, and it would amount to no more than a distraction now if I let it.

I hoped Leia was worth all this additional effort and stress. Nic seemed to think she was, which was maybe all that mattered. I couldn't imagine that any human was truly worth that much, though—and that was all Leia had been when Nic first met her. All Kayla had been when Sebastian met *her*, too. These bastard Duponts and their sudden urge to mate.

Regret was sharp through me, but I pushed it away before it could form an actual thought or an image.

I shook my head and scoffed.

"Everything okay, Kyle? You think of something?"

In truth, I'd almost forgotten Nic was still there, watching me. "Just thinking about these bastard Blackbloods." The lie tripped easily from my tongue. After all, why wouldn't my displeasure be about them? I was focused. In the game.

Nic nodded and smiled, but his smile was pinched at the corners. "You'll be fine."

I didn't know who he was trying to reassure—me or himself. "I've been undercover before," I reminded him, and the most recent time really hadn't been too long ago. I'd come to scope out the situation in New Orleans before he'd sent Sebastian to manage his new territory.

"But this is a little different," Nic said, and I wished he'd kept his damn mouth shut because I was trying to stay in the right headspace. "You'll only have limited contact with us."

And I knew that. It was the reminder I didn't need when I was trying to narrow my focus on the job. All contact with my friends—practically my fucking *family*— would have to be very carefully managed to avoid arousing suspicion. I glanced around my room in Sebastian's house again. It was spartan, but it was a space that was completely mine. I had my whole life in here and in my office at Nightfall, Sebastian's high-end club and the center for the Dupont rule in New Orleans.

I didn't even know how long I'd be away. But maybe the change would be a good thing. I'd lived with Sebastian and Jason since they'd arrived in New Orleans, and now I needed to try to be anonymous.

Luckily, I tried to live pretty much under the radar, anyway. I avoided contact with humans and tried to stay on the outskirts of vampire society. Made life easier when I only had day-to-day survival to consider.

Hopefully, I could manage to remain anonymous now. I didn't exactly doubt myself, but it did depend on whether anyone had noticed me in the Dupont camp since we'd arrived. I wanted to believe no one would have been paying enough attention, but belief was a long way from a guarantee.

"Temple will always be around, of course," Nic continued, and I tuned back in to his words. "But really he's too well known by everyone in New Orleans."

I almost smiled at that. The idea that Temple, a veritable shadow, was too well known bordered on ridiculous. But of course, it was true. He had eyes everywhere and everyone knew he was watching. Anyone who wanted to know anything reached out to him. To be seen talking to him regularly would definitely arouse suspicion from so many of the wrong people.

"Jason is less obvious as your contact. He's been more involved with the wolves, and they don't care for our politics as long as it doesn't affect them." He nodded as he referenced his sireling. "I'll tell Jason to keep in touch. In the meantime, you take care. These aren't good people. Watch yourself around them."

As Nic signed off from our call with his unexpected caring last words, I shrugged off a sudden sadness. I'd reinvented myself plenty of times in the past and mixed with a whole host of people I never wanted any more experience of. I could do it again. Nic had saved my life in the past — literally dragging me from the brink. This mission was the very least I could do.

Besides, I wouldn't truly be alone. Jason would still be here if I needed him. And Sebastian.

And, despite Nic's decision, Temple would probably be around more than I needed him to be. He really did thrive in the murky gray shadows of anything that shouldn't be happening. Anything that wasn't on the up and up. Still, he was good at what he did, and he was an invaluable source. Thank fuck he was on our side, to be honest.

He'd be a formidable adversary to have if he wasn't.

I needed the break away from the inner circle of the Duponts, though. I'd been on the verge of losing myself to the momentum of the family interests and the grinding wheels of their reign, and I wasn't a lackey or a yes-man. I was a soldier. A loner in many ways. I was used to having an agenda of my own and using my wits to meet it.

This assignment was more my speed, regardless of any unfamiliar flutters of anxiety the thought of being so deep undercover brought. But that unease meant nothing. It had just been a long time since I'd done something so big, so important, and with so much risk. That was all.

I slung my bag over my shoulder and exited my room quietly, clicking the door closed softly behind me, the noise strangely final.

Kayla's perfume lingered in the hallway even here. It scented the air all over the fucking house, actually, and that was another reason I was glad to be taking some time out. I was over all of this mate shit. First Nic, then Sebastian. If it was contagious, I didn't want to be anywhere near a source of infection.

We'd functioned as a family, a *powerful* family, for hundreds of years, and then two humans had wandered a little too close to the king and the prince and suddenly everything had changed. I shook my head. That kind of shit wasn't about to happen to me.

Not again.

I was a soldier. I fought. I didn't love.

Machines never loved.

***

I traveled quickly to my new place on the other side of town, sticking to the shadows, moving silently along streets where I only saw the odd drunk or the flicker of a curtain as it twitched back into place as I passed.

The odor of rotting garbage and stale piss filled the alleys I walked down as I searched for the address I'd memorized. I climbed rickety metal exterior steps to a narrow metal platform that seemed barely pinned to the wall by large, rusty metal bolts that moved easily in holes that had become too big over the years.

Just as I pushed the wooden front door open, my burner cell rang in my back pocket. It could only be Temple—only he had this number until Nic spoke to Jason. I dumped my bag on the box that seemed to double as a coffee table in the room that smelled of damp and mold spores and spilled beer, and shoved the door back into place, wedging the swollen wood closed more than truly shutting it.

"Yeah?" I wasn't up for a cozy chat just now. I had too much to think about.

"It's me," Temple said unnecessarily, and I glanced at the glowing screen for a moment, looking at the number displayed. It seemed safer not to assign a name. "I just wanted to run through the stuff one last time."

Also, unnecessary. I'd done nothing but run through everything in my head as soon as this mission had been confirmed. If I'd forgotten a piece of information, it hadn't been worth knowing in the first place.

"I know my job," I bit out, the words short and cold.

"Humor me." Temple's tone held anything but humor, and I gritted my teeth against another curt reply. His neck was also on the line, and maybe he preferred to be over-prepared. "Backstory." His word was a direction. A command for me to tell him who I was.

"Kyle Durg." I forced out the last name. What the fuck kind of name was that? What the hell was a durg, anyway? Just sounded mindless. Maybe that was for the best. Anyway… "From the Midwest. Nothing special in my family history. No vampire nest attachment. Turned by a rogue — not my decision. Hate all vamps. Happier to see them destroyed. Loner by choice. Happy to join the Blackbloods as long as their objectives match mine." I could almost hear Temple nodding when I finished talking. He'd probably been mouthing along.

I'd memorized his fucking script almost word for word.

"It'll be a story they've heard a couple of hundred times before." Now he sounded distracted like his attention was already focused elsewhere.

I rolled my eyes. "It'll do. It keeps me vague enough that no one will do any more searching."

"Agreed. And you have all the details for your meeting tonight?" He was back to business.

"Esmé, second-in-command to the boss."

Sebastian knew comparatively little about what I was doing to secure his place, but that was because ignorance was his best defense if anything went wrong. I could just be a rogue member of his family. It kept him distant and gave him plausible deniability if my cover was blown.

"Okay." Even Temple's breathing was quiet. "Don't forget to be at the bar at the right time tonight. You won't see me."

But I had no doubt he'd be there, skulking in the darkest corners like he usually did, keeping a watchful eye on everything. I had no idea why no one had taken Temple out yet. He knew way too much about everyone's business, but maybe he just didn't look threatening enough. Nothing about him screamed *danger*.

Oh, but it really should have. Information was always power and that much power made Temple a very dangerous man indeed.

He hung up without saying goodbye, and I slipped my phone away. Standing in this room hadn't improved the atmosphere in here, and I shivered as the chill in the air worked through me. That would probably be the last I heard from Temple if Nic was switching my contact to Jason. Temple would probably still be pulling strings in the background, though. He'd never step away entirely from a project he'd created and where he had stakes in the outcome.

There was a dive bar I could still meet him in an emergency, though. If anyone saw us there on an odd occasion, they wouldn't care. They were too busy living under the radar themselves to pay attention to who else met up and traded information.

***

I was early for the meeting. *Esmé*. Her name ran round and round my head. But what the hell was someone with such a delicate, feminine name doing so high up in the hierarchy of the Blackbloods? I shook my head. Stereotypes aside, I didn't give a fuck about how her name made her sound. She was obviously ruthless enough to have made it into a position of power.

And according to Temple, she was my in.

I just wanted to scope this place out first, get the lay of the land. I never walked into a situation without knowing *exactly* what I was walking into—that was how I'd fucking died the first time, and even back then, I'd thought I was a careful guy.

Now I was careful times two. Sebastian and Jason laughed at me sometimes, but it was different when you'd expected to be turned. Out of all the elements of my backstory, being turned by a rogue while I was all but dying in what had passed for a hospital back then was the one true thing.

Nic had saved me when he'd found me. Or when I'd found him. I'd already done a lot of damage... Too fucking much damage. Things I'd never forget or forgive myself for, but Nic had set me straight and kept me moving in the right direction. *That* was why he had my loyalty.

The place where I had to meet Esmé was hopping. Loud honky-tonk music blasted from outside speakers and motorcycles took up most of the space outside. It was like the looking glass version of Leia's bar. Where Ben had created a wholesome, welcoming atmosphere there, this place was seedy and shadowed, and the obvious copper tang of blood made the air heavy.

But although the bar was crowded, the clientele looked mostly human — human with a heavy side of biker. It didn't seem the most obvious place for two vampires to meet, but I didn't detect any immediate threat, so I entered and made my way to one of the empty booths at the back. The vinyl was sticky as I sat down and slid farther in, and the tabletop in front of me was stained, chipped, and greasy. A frayed paper menu, splattered with ketchup and fuck knew what else was the only thing on the surface, and I studied it for a moment before pushing it away. I rarely ate, even for appearance's sake, and I didn't need to know the tired dishes this bar's kitchen cranked out. I could smell the burned oil anyway— and the stale meat fat that turned even my stomach.

I tapped my fingertips briefly on the table as I waited and resisted the urge to check my watch. It was casual here. I needed to be casual, anyway. Carefree. Anything not to draw attention to myself. I accepted a beer and marked the passage of time by the changing tunes on the outdated jukebox.

The waitress stopped by again, her hand on the notepad just barely sticking out of her apron pocket.

I shook my head. I wasn't making an order.

"You been stood up, hon?" Her smile was big and forced as she snapped her gum. "That girl don't know what she's missing." Her gaze skimmed me assessingly, but I wasn't worried.

She wouldn't remember me after she'd clocked off her shift. Making myself unmemorable was almost my superpower.

After she wandered away from the table, probably in search of a customer where she could actually earn a decent tip, I did check the time, and I *had* been stood up. Esmé hadn't shown for our meeting.

But I didn't move. I could have gotten up and headed back to the grungy apartment where I lived now, but then what? Instead, instinct kept me nailed to the spot. There was something in this bar… Something I needed to know. I just wasn't sure what it was yet.

I narrowed my eyes, studying the shifting bodies in front of me, the barflies propping up the bar, the bikers hooting and hollering back and forth, and the women tottering on mile-high heels to the bar before returning, full of giggles and cheap, colored alcohol, back to their tables.

Gradually, the crowd started to thin, and the door banged open and closed with increasing frequency as people left alone or in groups. The night was drawing late. I didn't check my watch again.

I didn't need to.

"Last call." A voice rang from the bar, an instruction to anyone who hadn't finished drinking or who wasn't drunk enough yet.

A few people made their way to talk to the bartender, and as they did, a woman slid into my booth, sitting opposite me and resting her shaking hands on the table between us.

After a moment of seeming disinterested where I kept my attention apparently focused on the rest of the room, I turned my gaze to her. She had dark eyes, a brown so deep it was almost black in the low light of the bar, and cherry red, wild hair that reflected a riot of color when one of the constantly moving spotlights shone on it.

But she wasn't Esmé. Gut feeling told me that much before I'd even studied her properly. My nose twitched. No… She smelled human. Except not. Her scent was tainted. She was something other. Human but not.

As she smiled at me, the movement stiff and almost blank, her eyes a little dull and glazed, I almost snapped my fingers as I realized exactly what had joined me at my table.

Fuck. She was human but she was also a thrall. She was addicted to vampire venom, and she'd be completely lost if someone didn't turn her soon. I shifted away. I didn't want anything to do with a fucking thrall. They were trouble with a capital T.

She glanced at my drink and licked her lips, drawing my focus to a lip gloss the same color as her hair. I pushed the beer toward her, the foam head sloshing over the side as I did. If that was all she wanted, she was welcome to it.

She looked at me expectantly, like I might start talking, but she was probably just hoping to be my next meal — or one of the courses, anyway. It certainly didn't seem like a coincidence that a thrall had chosen to sit with the only vampire in this place.

I couldn't help the bitter taste of pity as I looked at her, though. Her life was very much currently on the line, and there was very little she could do about it.

Nothing *I* cared to do about it, either.

# Chapter 2 - Sam

Fucking Esmé. On days where she wasn't ravenous, there was always one more job before she'd give me a decent hit. One more thing I needed to do for *her* before she'd give *me* the one thing I craved, even as I loathed myself for craving it. Even now my skin itched, and my blood burned as it raced through my veins. I needed Esmé's venom to take the edge off. It no longer cured the withdrawals for long, but nothing beat the flood of ecstasy after her fangs ripped into my skin.

The thought alone made me antsy, and I picked up the beer in front of me, chugging it as I studied the guy I'd been sent to meet in Esmé's place. He was… interesting. Well, would have been interesting to me once upon a time.

I'd been watching him for a while from across the bar, and I was just biding my time to approach. Waiting for that perfect moment where I'd have his undivided attention and it wouldn't matter that I wasn't the contact he expected.

He looked like a killing machine. I shifted, rubbing my thighs together as I imagined all the places I'd let him press his fangs into me. My fingers would curl against his scalp. There wasn't much hair to hang on to, and even from here, the raised ridge of a scar was visible on his head. There had to be a story behind that.

And, as had become my habit, I assessed the newest target. Fresh blood. Could he help me?

He had an air of boredom, but he was anything but bored. He hadn't stopped watching people coming and going since he sat down — almost like he was doing some kind of customer survey or his life depended on giving an accurate headcount or description of everyone in the bar.

His narrow-eyed gaze appeared to miss nothing, and I tilted my head. This was the guy Esmé had said wanted to be brought into the Blackbloods on some sort of mission? He didn't seem like their usual type. He didn't seem… mindless enough. Brock tended to like good little soldiers. Not anyone who could actually be a match for him.

He liked unquestioning minions. Everyone he accepted into his army was expendable. Except this guy didn't look like he thought he was expendable. He looked… trained. Like he knew what he was doing.

I sucked in a breath. Damn. He looked like a threat. Maybe it was a good thing Esmé had sent me tonight— given my take that he wasn't the usual type to try to join the Blackbloods, which made him so much more interesting. Useful maybe, too. I wanted to hear his story. What had brought him here? Why did he want to be a Blackblood? What was this top-secret mission? *Could he help me?* How many times had I thought these same words over the years? How many times had I flipped and flopped between desire to escape Esmé's hold on me and resignation to my fate? It was exhausting. I was exhausted now. Things were just relentless.

But the idea that this man could help me was important. Esmé wouldn't have wanted me to wonder or think about his suitability beyond what she'd already told me to consider when taking this on for her, but I was applying my own criteria. Criteria Esmé didn't know about — could never know about. She was only interested in a deal with some guy she'd made to get *this* guy in.

I didn't concern myself with those details. But Esmé would forever lean on how much I owed her. That and the addiction she'd created in me when I saved her life by almost letting her drain me of blood.

I studied the vampire a little more from where I perched in the lap of one of the motorcycle club prospects, ignoring the weedy guy I was sitting on while he nuzzled my neck with his lips, scraping over my skin with his too-scratchy whiskers. His erection dug against my hip, but I ignored that too. It wasn't like I had any further use for this guy than providing cover while I watched my target.

And the guy I was watching was clearly still waiting like he sensed I was here or some shit. Like he knew his meeting wasn't off.

And that was weird. Any other guy who'd been stood up by Esmé would have left by now. Most likely anyway.

The prospect's hand drifted across the front of my top, but I batted away his unwanted attention. I didn't care about a lot of shit these days, and I certainly didn't care about casual sex. My attention was on my next fix, and I'd only get that if I met with the mark across the bar.

My time was nearly up. I could literally feel myself dying, the craving inside me replacing my will to live, but maybe that was the kindest way. I wouldn't know the end when it came, and I wouldn't care.

As the bartender sang out the familiar words of *last call*, I stood abruptly, pushing the prospect gently against the back of his chair, and attempted to sashay toward the vampire. Then I dropped my approach to a saunter when it was clear his attention was nowhere near me, and I was too wobbly to pull off anything remotely like a sexy walk anyway. If Esmé had just given me a damn small hit before making me come out here, I would have walked straight and tall, but oh, no. She preferred her little lapdog hungry.

This guy couldn't have been sending out clearer vampire signals if he'd tried. He was sitting almost in the darkest area, barely drinking. I'd never seen someone nurse their beer for so long while hardly taking a swallow. The server had visited his table a couple of times. On both occasions, he hadn't even cracked a smile.

My body tightened just imagining the fangs lurking beneath his gums, and I paused, resting a hand on the chair in front of me to steady myself. The intense sexual desire inside me receded, and I grabbed some stranger's leftover beer from the table where I'd stopped. Throwing it into my mouth, I wished it could be Esmé's venom instead.

I shook my head, sickened at myself and my need for the woman I'd accidentally tied myself to. Then I revisited the fantasy I'd had earlier where I'd chopped her head off and her blood had spurted high into the air, covering me and taking complete care of my Esmé problem.

The idea of Esmé dying barely bothered me these days — especially if she went out in a river of blood that I could drown myself in. That end almost seemed better than merely fading away while still in thrall to her. And I didn't want to be turned, either. I didn't want to be one of these fucking bloodsuckers. Especially not a Blackblood.

Esmé had me as her virtual prisoner. I literally needed her to live, but I'd be damned before I became like her. I almost laughed, suddenly giddy.

I was already fucking damned.

Of course, Esmé also believed *I'd* damned *her.*

I refocused my attention on the vampire in front of me. He was my mission tonight. Then Esmé would be pleased with me, and she'd feed from me. We could all win tonight. The guy would get his meeting, Esmé would get her blood, and I'd get my venom.

Short-term goals.

But I didn't care.

In this life, they were all I had left.

He wasn't looking in my direction as I approached him, but he knew exactly where I was. I could almost see him tracking me, working out my trajectory, planning his answering defense or attack… He really was a fucking machine.

But his face gave nothing away. Not a muscle twitch or a flickering eyelash. There was no reason for me to be so certain of him and his thoughts, but I was. *Interesting.*

I settled into the booth across from him, the vinyl sticking to the backs of my thighs as my skirt rode up higher than was proper. I didn't care. I was too busy studying this guy, a vampire who held himself so stiff he could have been carved of stone. Except his biceps flexed as I sat down, like his fingers had just curled around something under the table.

I wasn't even sure if he knew he'd moved but I noted the small reaction. The part of himself he probably hadn't intended to show me.

I waited, studying him, a smile fixed to my lips as I watched him. His eyes were brown. A warm kind of brown that brought to mind liquid chocolate. *Hot* chocolate. Something I used to love. Something I could only remember loving now. But his eyes brought me a warm feeling I'd long forgotten.

I could have drowned in them.

His hair was dark too but cropped close to his scalp, and my fingers itched to trace their way over the scar I'd observed on his head. And he was dressed like he expected trouble — a tight-fitted black tee that showcased more muscles than I'd known existed, and black cargo pants tucked into shit-kicker boots.

If he wasn't military, he wanted to be.

He was also hot as fucking Hell. And if I wasn't exactly what I was… And he wasn't just another leech… I'd go there in a New York minute. Less time than that, probably. I wouldn't exactly wait for an invitation. Well… even virgins knew what to do really, right? I read. I watched TV. I knew how my body functioned and what a guy could bring to this particular table.

"Who are you?" His voice startled me out of the smutty direction my thoughts had ventured.

It was deep and mellow. Another reminder of the hot chocolate I no longer drank.

A sound that surrounded me like a hug. But I didn't want that right now.

I had a mission.

I had a fucking mission.

My grin widened. "I'm your way into this shit show."

He tilted his head, just the tiniest evidence of curiosity, and his watchful gaze from earlier returned as he met my eyes. "And you are?"

Ahh, a man of few words, then. I nodded. Maybe he'd do fine in the Blackbloods after all. "I'm Sam. Esmé sent me." Her name was like a password. Surely, he'd hear me out now?

But he was a cool customer, and he didn't react to the name he should have known. It really was like talking to a rock. A good-looking rock, but a rock nonetheless.

I hadn't intended to fill the silence, but I did it anyway. His quiet was very… compelling. "Esmé couldn't be here." Shit, I sounded more desperate than I'd intended.

He nodded, but the gesture could have meant many things. Perhaps the idea Esmé couldn't be here was obvious from the fact that I was. Or maybe he already knew. More likely, he didn't care, but I didn't expect this guy wasted even one muscle twitch of his body if he could help it. The nod had meant something. I wanted to keep talking to find out what, but I pressed my lips together instead, afraid to overplay my hand now, afraid to let more of my need show.

He half stood. "I came here to see Esmé. Not her…" His lip curled and I tried not to recoil at the disgust the small movement telegraphed my way. "Pet."

I forced a laugh, and it was loud and fake, but hopefully, the discordant sound hid the tremor present in my voice. "Well, I'm all you've got, pal."

He was a stiff, good-looking rock with an attitude problem. In short, he was a bastard. But I could shrug that shit off. Vampires were all fucking bastards. Humans were beneath them. Hell, we were food. No one was nice to their actual *food*.

I nearly laughed again, and it was almost genuine.

He didn't sit back down, instead pulling out his billfold and snatching a couple of bucks for the table. Shit. I was losing him.

I held out my hand, stopping short of actually touching him. He looked like he definitely operated on a hair trigger.

"Wait. I mean it."

He looked at me, his eyes like hard stones now. As cold and stiff as the rest of him.

I stifled my shiver. "I really am your only shot. You can either accept that I will take you to Esmé or I can walk out of this bar right now and your opportunity to get in with the Blackbloods disappears." I held his gaze, but it was difficult.

As much as something about him drew me in, I wanted to look away.

There was too much there. Too much intensity. Too much pain.

And there was too much I wanted.

I needed him to come with me. I needed to make an ally on the inside, and it had been too long since there was anyone new, someone I could maybe use to my advantage.

Although looking at him, he wouldn't be used by anyone. He'd do the using — and the throwing away at the end.

Still, I didn't have a whole lot else going for me but hope these days. And sometimes not even that.

I held my breath and waited. Almost crossed my fingers for good measure.

"If this is a trick—" His voice had taken on a hard edge, but then he softened it. "I'll kill you."

His last words were almost seductive, and again I nearly laughed. Homicide or a rescue? I couldn't decide which he'd offered me.

But I forced a casual shrug. "It's not the first time a vampire has offered to end things for me." Then I stood and walked out of the bar, not checking to see if he was following.

I could sense him behind me, though. And he should have been cold like his stony façade, but the heat from his body sent a buzz of awareness right through me. I wanted him to wrap his arms around me and hold me like he could put me back together through sheer force of will, like he could hold me in one piece when I was falling apart in slow motion.

But I shook that wild impulse off. I didn't need anything from this guy but his help to get out of my current situation. And first, I had to take him to Esmé.

"My car's over here."

He didn't say anything when I turned to face him, but he did lift his right eyebrow just enough that he almost looked amused. I got in behind the steering wheel and waited. He seemed to almost fold himself into the passenger seat, but he didn't complain. Served him right for being so stiff and muscled in the first place, anyway.

I pulled out of the parking lot, squealing my tires just a little as I watched the last of the lights in the bar flicker out for the evening in the rearview mirror. I gripped the steering wheel, my knuckles whitening as my anxiety increased. Damn, this needed to go well.

"So, you know what you're here for?"

He nodded; the movement short. My question didn't open the conversation I'd hoped for. I wanted to know more about him, to find out his story. Esmé hadn't told me shit. Perhaps if I volunteered part of myself first, he'd say something.

"I'm Sam." I'd said that part, but it was always worth repeating. "When I first met Esmé, I was looking for a job. My brother introduced us." My laugh rang dangerously close to hollow because I could do without the sudden memory of Sean. I couldn't imagine any other job hunt that led to a slow death like mine. "Are you looking for work, too?"

He didn't say anything, and I sighed.

"Look, you don't have to tell me if you don't want to. My only job tonight is to get you to Esmé so you two can work out all your secret squirrel shit." Yeah, and then collect my venom. My pulse sped up at the thought of a hit. "You don't have to confess your deepest, darkest secrets to me."

He made a noise that sounded like a snort, and I shot a quick glace in his direction, but his face was as expressionless as ever. If I'd conjured either amusement or annoyance in him, it wasn't on display now.

"Esmé is going to vouch for you with Brock and then…" I paused as I told him the only things I knew. "Then you're on your own." My stomach twisted, and I almost felt bad for him.

I was kind of abandoning him to the Blackbloods. I'd never felt personally responsible for one of the new recruits before. Maybe this was different, though, because he had some sort of ulterior motive, and I had an ulterior motive for wanting to know more about him, and that made us kind of kindred.

It almost made me want to turn the car around and tell him to run while he still could. But that was a ridiculous thought. He wasn't a helpless human. His story wasn't like mine. He was a vamp and all vamps deserved to burn. Nothing would ever shake me from that belief. I'd seen the worst of them when they'd killed Sean and now…Now this life with Esmé was my penance.

I turned into the driveway of the house where Esmé kept me holed up. It wasn't much to look at from the outside, with bits of siding hanging clean off, and it was even worse on the inside. But it was home, and I guessed my final resting place at some point, so it was good enough for that.

There was one lamp burning in the living room. The glow shone through the window, and that meant Esmé was already there. I shivered. Part in fear, part in anticipation. If she was already here, that meant she was hungry, so what happened next wouldn't be pretty.

Sometimes, it was like she forgot she was also denying herself when she sent me off to do her bidding using her venom as the reward at the end. There really were no bounds to her control freakery.

I opened the door. I didn't unlock it first, because it was never locked—there was no point. No self-respecting burglar would waste their time in here. Inside, Esmé was pacing like a crackhead jonesing for his next fix, her white-blonde hair flaring behind her like a fine mist every time she made a turn to walk back the other way.

She faced me, her fangs already extended, her nostrils widening. Her eyes shone the red of hunger, and her cheekbones were prominent, making a monster from her normally elfin face. Without even waiting for me to step over the threshold, she grabbed me, dragging me against her and pinning me with her superhuman strength.

I caught sight of the guy's expression as Esmé's fangs sank slowly into my neck, and I nearly startled out of my bliss state from the intensity of it. Far from his face being his usual blank slate, he looked murderous, like he wanted to kill Esmé. His own fangs grazed his lower lip, and his eyebrows were drawn over dull red eyes.

But then I was gone. Sinking into the waiting warmth of Esmé's arms, listening to the steady rhythm of her sucking as she drew mouthfuls of blood from me, the slowing of the blood racing through my ears. I surrendered myself to the familiar sensations, to walking that tightrope that could tip me into death.

But Esmé was an expert. She wasn't ready for me to die yet, and she groaned as she released me. She wiped the blood carelessly from my neck with her fingertips and left me to crumple to the floor.

I lay there for a moment before strong arms lifted me and I rested my head against a chest of hard muscle. I was placed with surprising gentleness on my ratty old couch that smelled like too much sweat and stale blood. Then I closed my eyes as he faded from my view.

The high would only last twenty minutes, but it would be the best twenty minutes I'd had in days.

# Chapter 3 - Kyle

My gums ached from my fucking fangs pressing against them as I watched that ice-queen bitch drink from the thrall. She'd pushed her hunger to the edge and was on the verge of losing her control. But she pulled back just as her thrall went limp — right before she went too far.

I almost admired her self-control.

Almost.

But I'd never truly admire anything that bitch did. She was a Blackblood. There was nothing to admire in any of them.

I'd never had a thrall. Never wanted someone who wasn't in control of themselves, but the taste of human blood straight from the vein… Fuck. My balls tightened just at the thought, of the memory of that beautiful coppery warmth filling my mouth and coating my throat.

It had been years since I'd allowed myself to drink in such an uncontrolled way. I always controlled myself now, in everything.

The thrall fell to the floor and Esmé threw herself into a nearby chair, her chest heaving and blood still sliding down her chin and dripping onto whatever delicate thing she was only half wearing. It shone in the light like satin.

But I couldn't leave the human there like that. I'd left too many humans scattered in my wake like worthless pieces of garbage. Between being turned and meeting Nic, I'd only known bloodlust. An intense raw need to take… to take so much… and sate my hunger. Aside from when I'd known love… But that had ended in carnage, too.

For a moment, Esmé had looked like she might succumb, like she might ravage her thrall, but she'd pulled herself back and left her alive, a glazed, smeary expression of bliss spread over her human's face, the blood still glistening on her neck almost a perfect match for her ridiculous shade of red hair.

But I couldn't leave the thrall —Sam —like that. Too many images assaulted me. Camille. I'd loved her. But I hadn't been able to stop.

My fangs retracted at the memory, the ache in my gums becoming the thrum of guilt instead, and I bent to gather the thrall to me. She needed to rest. Her bliss would be short-lived. She was too far gone to feel the effects of the venom for any length of time that mattered. Her body was emaciated, little more than a pile of bones held together by the skin stretched over them, in my arms.

"She'll sleep now." Esmé surprised me when she spoke, and her eyes were calculating as she watched me draw away from her pet. "Come with me, and I'll show you around."

I glanced at the inside of the hovel where we were, and Esmé laughed.

"Oh, this is only Sam's quarters. I live downstairs." She stood and held out her hand, a sexy twist of a smile on her lips, and I clasped my hands behind my back.

I didn't want to even touch her. There was something evil about her. Something insidious that seemed like it might infect me the moment I made contact.

"What's wrong?" Her lips formed a small pout now.

No doubt, she usually had guys falling over themselves to correct that small expression of unhappiness.

"Nothing." I offered her a small shrug as I grunted the word.

She arched an eyebrow. "All right. Well, maybe nerves are to be expected. It's healthy to be anxious. Keeps you on your toes." Her throaty chuckle was like fingernails on a chalkboard, and pain shot through my fangs at the sound. "If Brock doesn't like you, he'll kill you. Regardless of what I say, right?" She frowned. "So, he'd better the hell like you. My neck's on the line, too."

Maybe I couldn't do this job after all. I wasn't sure I could cozy up to Esmé and make it look real. Everything about her repulsed me. There was nothing sexy or admirable at all about sucking a human dry for years and never turning them. Oh, some vampires collected thralls like jocks collected notches on their bedposts, but I had no time or taste for it.

It was cruel and left us at risk of discovery. That was another reason Nic had my support. He protected us and made sure we blended with humans in a way that kept everyone safe. The Blackbloods threatened not only Nic's rule but also our continued survival as a species.

And that was why I was here. It made no difference whether I wanted to touch Esmé or not. It had no bearing on the wider picture. Sooner or later, I'd bring them down.

She walked across the room and into a small kitchen that smelled like rotten meat.

"Excuse the aroma," she murmured. "Sam appears to have been off her food."

I nodded. She clearly thought she was funny, but I couldn't agree.

The apartment was small and basic until we reached a door that looked like it led into a garage. Esmé slipped a key from her pocket, unlocked the door, and then pulled it open to reveal a steep flight of stairs.

"The house is appropriately warded and spelled for a basement," she said. "My quarters are down here."

I followed her down the steps, every sense on high alert. Anything could be down there, including enough vampires to bring about my final death if they ambushed me. As we arrived in an almost exclusively white living room, the scent of the house changed to something vanilla-based. Or marshmallows. Esmé inhaled, her smile appreciative.

"Ah, civilization." She blew out an exhale. "That's more like it."

I glanced back upstairs.

Esmé shook her head. "She'll sleep for a while now. Won't be any trouble." She sank into the soft white sofa and curled her legs underneath her.

The blood on the front of her clothes looked out of place in such a pristine room and on such an elegant female.

"I expect you're wondering why…" She left her sentence to trail off like I might jump in and finish it for her, and when I didn't do that, she laughed. "A man of few words." Then she tapped her chin. "Perhaps that's wise. But aren't you the slightest bit curious?"

I decided to play her game. "About what?"

She lifted her chin. "Crack house upstairs, home and garden magazine downstairs?"

I shrugged. "I don't care about interior design."

She laughed. "Good answer. But it never serves to keep the humans too comfortable. They need to remain… disposable."

More revulsion threatened to choke me, but instead, I forced my lips into a tight smile. She could read that any way she wanted.

Abruptly, she moved, not bothering to conceal her vampire speed as she stood. "Come on, I need to show you something else." She stalked from the room, her renewed strength after feeding on her thrall obvious.

She walked down a hallway toward a closed door at the end before throwing it open with a flourish. There was a large table in the middle and a couple of desks set up around the edges with computers and various bits of technology. It wasn't dissimilar to Sebastian's meeting room, but it clearly doubled as an office.

My attention wandered to the walls. Pictures of New Orleans and maps of the local area were tacked to every available space. There were street views and even blueprints of some of the more well-known local buildings. Some of the maps had threads leading to the pictures of the street facades and buildings or even to people. Nic was there. And Sebastian. I glanced at the remaining faces, anxiety a tight twist inside me until I ascertained I wasn't there. Neither was Jason, but… shit. They had a lot of information.

I gestured to the walls so there was no doubt about what I was referring to. "What's all this? Takeover plan of some sort?"

She didn't respond immediately so I just watched her. People usually answered me eventually. Staying quiet was often my best intimidation tactic.

She met my gaze and nodded tightly. "Yep." Her gaze tracked back to the walls of surveillance and information. "Brock wants to destroy the Baton Rouge King and take everything he has."

I didn't react while I digested that information. It didn't really mesh with what we knew about the Blackbloods. They moved from area to area, decimating local vampire populations and turning humans at will to boost their numbers, but this… I scratched my chin. A normal movement, to set Esmé at ease.

"Sounds kinda like a revenge plot." I leaned heavily into the drawl I rarely used these days.

She shrugged. "Honestly, I have no idea. There are things Brock doesn't tell even me." Her mouth twisted then she tossed her hair. "Not sure if I care, though. After all, he's only my sire, right?" Her follow-up laugh was brittle, like something was broken inside her, before she drew herself up to stand tall and her eyes turned cold again. Game eyes.

"What's your deal, Esmé? How do you know Temple?" Something really didn't sit right. This woman was ruthless and had no morals at all. Who the hell was she even working for?

"Just following the money, honey." Her eyes narrowed as she studied the pictures on the walls, stepping closer to pick out a figure in the shadows on one of them.

Holy fuck. Temple, too? Barely recognizable in the photo, but that was his usual position in any room.

"Temple has promised me a shitload of money and a position in his spy crew. A place to settle. A life. I think I'm ready for that." Her voice turned wistful before hardening again. "Brock might be my maker, but he's never cared for me, and I'm sick of bending to his will."

I scoffed and my thoughts wandered to the poor, abused thrall upstairs before snapping back to Esmé. I couldn't afford to be distracted around her if she was happy to be so duplicitous. *All about the money, honey.* Her words echoed in my head. I'd need to watch her. Money could pour in from any direction, after all.

She dropped into one of the chairs around the meeting table and patted her palm against the smooth wood surface. "Sit. We need to get a few things straight."

I stood for a moment longer. I didn't take orders from anyone but Nic. So, I waited a few beats longer. Then, when it was my choice, I deliberately pulled out a chair and sat slowly on it.

"So, how are we going to do this?" She tapped long, manicured fingernails against the wood now, like she had too much excess energy.

I shrugged. She wanted a reply, but surely, she already knew exactly how she was going to introduce me to the Blackbloods? If not, what the hell was I doing here?

Temple had vouched for this chick, and it wasn't like him to pick flakes.

But no. Esmé wasn't a flake. Her eyes were too intelligent for that as she watched me, like she was trying to turn the tables, force me to respond.

I shrugged again and redeployed my drawl. "Lookin' for a job?"

She nodded. "Yeah. Yeah, that will work. It's how I find all my best people, anyway." She glanced meaningfully in the direction of the stairs leading to the upper floor where we'd left Sam. "So many towns where folks are looking for jobs. And what good fortune to come across a vampire, right off the bat, right?"

She tinkled out a delicate laugh this time, and I tensed against the sound. She gave off fragile vibes with her tiny frame, white-blonde hair, and huge blue eyes, but I couldn't afford to underestimate her.

But I nodded. "Just lookin' for a job," I confirmed.

"I'm going to propose you to Brock as an enforcer." She flicked a glance over me then returned for a slower perusal. "You certainly have the build for it."

Her tongue flicked over her lower lip and her pupils dilated, leaving her with a hungry look and me with no doubt of what images might be playing out in her head.

Before I needed to ensure I'd adequately concealed my disgust, there was a noise to my left and Sam stumbled through the door, wobbly but smiling as she sipped on a glass of orange juice.

"Hey, guys," she exclaimed, her voice too loud, her tone far too jolly. "Thought I might find you down here."

I stood and offered her my chair, but she shook her head. Disappointment crept into my chest that she'd refused my chivalry. But damn, why was I even being helpful? This woman meant nothing to me. She was a thrall. A *pet*. A fucking human. I just had to remember that.

Only it felt like it might be easier said than done.

Worse, she was the enemy's pet. A human under Blackblood control and being so beautiful that my cock jerked with awareness every time I looked at her only made Sam more dangerous, not less so.

"Are you ready to go? I can drive you back to your side of town in my car," she asked.

I glanced at her, hardening myself to see only the venom-drunk thrall. Did I really want that behind the wheel?

"Well, she's woken up quicker than I expected, but she's fine. She drives all the time." Esmé gestured expansively with her arm, the movement lazy as she seemed to know exactly what I was thinking. "Her reactions are still good enough to brake when she needs to. Besides, what are you worried about? You might *die*?" Her laugh was less fragile and tinkling this time, but no less hideous for that.

I wasn't used to people reading me or my hesitations, which meant Esmé was probably even more dangerous than I'd given her credit for.

I nodded at Esmé. "I'll see you in the morning." Then I turned to Sam. "Good to go."

"Wait." Esmé's voice was suddenly cold as steel. "I've just had an even better idea as to how I found you." Her lips curled up in an unpleasant smile, and she waved a hand. "I mean, sure, you want a job. Who doesn't? And who *wouldn't* want to work with Brock? He has power, influence…" She ticked off the words on her fingers, but her tone said *blah blah blah* as she continued. "But what if you have a more *personal* connection?"

She glanced meaningfully between Sam and me before clasping her hands together over her heart and tilting her head.

"I think my little Sammy just got her first boyfriend." She spoke in a sing-song voice she might have used with a baby, and my insides all curled at the edges. "What a gift I'm giving you, Sammy. A *guy*. You want to experience *love*, right?"

"What?" Sam's eyes widened and she almost seemed to avoid looking at me. "Esmé, no. I can't…We…"

But she didn't finish her sentence. She just shut her mouth with a click as Esmé's expression hardened.

"You'll do as I say. And if you brought this stray home, it makes a lot more sense why I'm helping him. And *I* think you need a guy. The life you took from me."

"But Brock thinks you found him on your own, and you don't share credit…" Sam sounded like her throat had dried and her tongue had stuck to the inside of her mouth as her voice emerged the smallest of croaks.

"And as long as you remember that, we're fine." Esmé smiled coldly at Sam then at me. She focused back on Sam. "A swansong performance, Sammy. Hell, I don't care. Lose that fucking V-card. Go out with a bang." She laughed cruelly then stalked away, deeper into the luxuriously appointed quarters, a cold breeze seeming to swirl behind her.

After a moment of hesitation, Sam turned, pivoting to her left without a word and led the way back out of the strange underground wing and into the part of the house that smelled like a BO-stained T-shirt from lost and found. We left through the front door, and I squashed myself back into the front seat of her car. It was like we were a pair of robots on autopilot.

"Give me directions, okay?" She tossed the instruction to me as she squealed out of the driveway.

She didn't actually look at me, though, and her unease permeated the interior of the car, the tension likely a result of Esmé's instruction that she was to pretend to be my girlfriend.

I shook my head as Sam revved the engine. This woman didn't do anything stealthily. She didn't talk much as she drove along, responding only to my directions, and I didn't push her to say anything.

Being a thrall must be tough, and I couldn't imagine anyone choosing it. Still, if she was stupid enough to stay human after all this time, that was her own fucking fault. There were ways to avoid the long, slow, humiliating death, after all.

But a tiny part of my heart couldn't stay hard as I imagined the agony that awaited her.

Still, she had to have gotten herself into this mess somehow, right? And it wasn't like I had the time or the headspace to start worrying on her behalf or thinking how to get her out of it… Yet as I stole sidelong glances at her, gears that hadn't cranked in my brain for a long time started turning.

Even though her situation was absolutely none of my business.

Sam stopped the car and climbed out when I did. I cast her a quick glance. Where the hell did she think she was going? But I didn't ask the question. The answer was obvious as she followed me up the steps.

My apartment was as shitty as I remembered but if Sam noticed, she didn't say anything. It was probably a step up from where she called home. It didn't smell like a hobo's sweaty crotch, at least.

She stopped just inside the doorway, her face still that strange mixture of venom-induced animation and worry. She nibbled her lip for a moment before speaking. "It wasn't always like this," she started, using her hands to gesture to everything and nothing as she spoke. "Esmé used to be my best friend."

"Not my business." Each of my words was short and bitten off at the end. I wasn't here for some sort of girly or heart-to-heart chat, regardless of the image Esmé had decided we should project in public. Besides, no one could see us inside this tiny hellhole, so whatever Sam thought she had to do to follow Esmé's orders on our status was null and void.

I had a mission. I looked past her, out of the door, inviting her to leave. She glanced behind her like I might have been focusing on something in particular but when she looked back at me, her eyes had lost some of the excitement they'd had when she'd started to talk. She took one step backward before glancing behind herself again. Then she lifted on tiptoes, and pressed a fleeting kiss to my cheek.

"In case anyone can see," she murmured.

I closed my eyes as her perfume lingered in the air around me, and I kept my lips flat as she seemingly waited for something else. She didn't move, and I could barely hear her breathing. When I opened my eyes, I nodded and gestured quickly at the door. She took the hint and left, disappointment fleeting in her gaze.

If I felt bad, it was only for a moment. Only for as long as it took me to wedge the door closed behind her. I wasn't here to make friends. I had shit to do.

Speaking of shit to do… I reached for my burner phone and contacted Sebastian on the burner phone number of his I'd memorized.

He answered right away but didn't identify himself or me. "Hello."

"Hello," I replied, but that was probably all I could get away with and stay neutral. We didn't have a code for passing unexpected information. "There's something else going on besides the usual chaos and destruction." I just needed to make this fast. "I'm not sure what it is yet exactly, but I'll keep you posted."

Before he could reply, I hung up, disconnecting our call as quickly as I could. For both of our safety. Plus, it gave me great pleasure to hang up on him. Could've been a legitimate security concern but could also have just been me being a dick.

Yeah, I was a dick.

A dick whose official duties for the day were all done. Except... Part of me almost *wanted* to talk to Sebastian for a little longer. I wanted that connection. Only I couldn't.

But I could talk to Jason. And I was hungry, anyway. I needed to find a bar. A vampire one. Preferably with a good stock of O Neg.

I dialed Jason's number next, and he answered in a gruff voice. "Rusty Nail," he grunted, as if he'd just taken up mind-reading, before hanging up.

I almost wondered why I'd bothered. Didn't sound like he was going to be a great conversationalist. But at least he'd given me the name of a bar. Hopefully, vampires were welcome there and it wasn't a hangout for dogs. I shuddered at the thought. At this rate, Jason was spending so much time with the wolves, he'd wind up with fleas. Or whatever worse parasite they carried.

With another shudder, I headed out the door, strangely happy that I'd be seeing a familiar face. Hopefully, this Rusty Nail place would be easy to find. I'd already done a bit of reconnaissance, so I was pretty sure I knew the direction to go in.

The streets were as quiet as they'd been earlier, but there was nothing peaceful about the quiet at all. It was a poised silence. Sinister, like something was about to happen. A lot of the buildings were boarded up in the direction I walked, but there was still a prickle at the nape of my neck, the sense of being watched. Something was out there or in one of the buildings.

Nothing that could harm me, but this wasn't exactly a neighborhood awash with humans. It was like they'd all moved out at once and just never returned.

I found the Rusty Nail bar two blocks from my apartment and there were a few vamps hanging around out in front. They stepped toward me as I approached, and I raised my hands, palms outward, in the international gesture of goodwill and peace.

"No trouble," I said. "I just want a drink." I glanced around for Jason, but maybe he was already inside.

The vampire closest to me snorted. "No trouble," he mocked, his voice falsetto, and I stiffened, each of my muscles tensing. "Well, new guy, you have to pay to get in."

A second goon stepped up alongside his friend. "Yeah, this is our bar."

I almost relaxed. Their bar, was it? "Oh, yeah? We back in high school now, too?"

The first guy barked out a laugh and swung for my right cheek.

"For fuck's sake." I sprang into a defensive position, ready to take all three of them. I didn't want to maim or kill… Well, maybe maim, but I settled for just making sure they were all quiet. When they were all laid out on the ground in front of me, their eyes wide and their bodies still, I spoke again. "You three remember your manners, now?"

The leader nodded, his pale face almost translucent under a flickering streetlamp.

I strode over him and yanked the door to the bar open. Holy fuck, it was gross in here. The floor was sticky with spilled blood, and its stale scent lingered in the air — death and decay. Something rotten. I wrinkled my nose.

This was sure the fuck a long way from Nightfall and the designer drinks Sebastian made sure were on hand. A vampire could get poisoned in this fucking dive.

"Drink?" The bartender looked at me expectantly, and I nodded.

"O neg."

He slid a bottle down the bar, and I grabbed it before turning to survey the place. Looked like it was about to be my local, so I should get to know it. If I had to compare it to anything, it would have been Leia's place, The Pour House, before Ben got his hands on it and directed the renovations there. Except I could almost guarantee no one had drunk blood at Leia's place.

Everyone in here was staring at me, and I stared right back. They'd get used to me. Or not. I didn't give two shits.

I grabbed the bottled blood — I hated this shit, but it was better than losing my mind from the vein — and took a seat at the bar, although I deliberately faced the room, propping my foot against the stool next to me. An entire bar full of Blackbloods, because that was definitely what these guys were. There wasn't a familiar face among them — not one Dupont supporter among them. I was in the lions' den... Swimming with the sharks. Whichever animal analogy I most preferred.

Only, I could be a shark, too.

The women in the bar watched me, blatant curiosity in their eyes, and some of the humans shuffled closer to me, almost offering themselves as some sort of sacrifice.

I wasn't interested in any of that subservient shit, and I hadn't come here to hook up. I tilted the bottle to my lips and hid my grimace as the slightly coagulated low-quality blood slid down my throat. Shit, this was my life until I was done here.

I swallowed. This fucking mission needed to be over quick. At least I'd made a good start here. All of these vampires now knew I was in their space. They knew my face. By morning, I'd be the talk of the Blackbloods. A newcomer built for a fight. That should make Esmé's introduction between Brock and me easier.

A movement in the corner of the room caught my attention. Some guy stood up then sat back down. No reason at all. Crazy old fucker. Then I looked closer. Holy hell. Jason? He looked grungy. Dirty, even. Like he'd robbed the nearest homeless guy's clothes and left him naked in his cardboard box. But maybe the new look was for the best. Brock knew a lot of our faces and Jason sure the hell didn't look like Jason right now.

I approached his corner and hooked out the chair on the next table over. Then I raised my bottle to my lips to disguise their movement. "Hey. You look like shit," I greeted him.

He muffled a chuckle as he gave the smallest of shrugs. "Better than looking like final death." He swigged from his own bottle of blood, and my stomach turned as he smacked his lips together like he appreciated the taste. "Sebastian said things aren't good."

I shook my head, the movement also small, my lips pressed together. "They know a lot more than we thought. And their agenda isn't the same as we thought — with the mindless amassing of bodies and moving on. They want New Orleans. Maybe BR too. They want Nic gone. Taken down entirely." I leaned back, shifting my pose to casual and alone, in case anyone was watching, and drank again.

Sebastian inhaled then exhaled slowly. "They got a solid plan?"

"I aim to find out." My voice was quiet and grim. Hopefully, no one could see the pair of us over here, talking to ourselves in a corner.

"If you need me to get Conri onside with a plan to get rid of the fuckers, let me know."

I stayed still. I wasn't convinced that involving the wolves further in vampire politics was a good idea. But I wasn't one to say never, so I didn't say anything at all.

"You good?" Quiet concern laced Jason's tone, but I didn't look at him.

Instead, I nodded thoughtfully. Where would I start? The shithole I was living in? The shithole Sam lived in while Esmé had some sort of underground strategy room downstairs? The fact I'd just acquired a pseudo-girlfriend, completely off any kind of Dupont plan? That part, I truly didn't know if I could cope with.

Being so close to a human woman again? I'd avoided them all since Camille. I just didn't go there. It wasn't worth the risk, the inevitable loss of innocent life.

"Well, I'm here if that changes, or you just need a friend."

I nodded abruptly again before shoving my chair back and started striding from the bar. I'd see him again soon, no doubt.

But as I pushed through the creaking door and stepped onto the deck that was so soft it could only be rotten, he spoke softly behind me, and I almost jumped. Damn Jason for being so quiet. Or me for being so lost in my thoughts.

"I'll give you a ride, dude."

# Chapter 4 - Sam

Kyle closed the door in my face and suddenly, I only wanted one thing… I wanted my mom. Even after all this time as a fucking thrall, I still couldn't escape the instinct to return home, to seek protection. But that was an entirely selfish impulse.

Mom had no idea the supernatural world existed — let alone that I was inadvertently part of it, and it was killing me. I wanted to keep her in the dark. It was safer that way.

She'd been compelled back to peace after Sean's death at the hands of vampires… and now she didn't even recall she'd had a son. I'd been complicit in that, removing any evidence of his existence, and the guilt from that added to my torture, gnawing at me.

But the urge to go home, to a place of safety and comfort and a mother's love, was stronger than my reason and common sense… and I couldn't ignore my guilt today.

Besides, I didn't know how long I had left. At some point, Esmé's venom would stop feeling good and it would simply overwhelm my system. How close was I treading to that edge? The highs were already shorter. Long gone were the days when I could stay blissed out for close to a week after one short feed.

The venom would take my mind first, though, and I wanted to see Mom while I was still lucid enough to appreciate her. While I could still leave her with some good memories of me. I didn't want anyone needing to wipe me from her mind as well.

I drove to her house almost on autopilot, muscle memory taking me there more than any of my other senses. It was a small home. Pokey almost, but it was perfect. It was nestled back from the street behind an overgrown front yard, and neighborhood children used to whisper about the witch who lived there.

That was laughable these days. If only she *had* been a witch. Maybe she could have helped me now.

I knocked on the old door. The gloss paint on it shone in evidence that Mom took care of her property, and the inside would be neat and tidy and smell like fresh baking and laundry detergent. My childhood rushed at me as Mom opened the door, and memories wrapped me in a warm hug even before she did.

It was pretty late for an unannounced visit, but Mom only smiled at me. "Samantha."

She held the door open, and I followed her inside, basking in the warmth and the cleanliness. After the rancid smell of my own home, this one mattered even more.

I wanted to turn the clock back to a time where Sean had never died, and I'd never left. But I'd always been headstrong and thought I knew the ways of the world. Well, hell. I knew them now.

When it was too late.

What was that thing they always said about hindsight? Hindsight could suck my ass. That sounded about right.

I glanced at Mom. Had she aged a little more than the last time I saw her? Was she walking a little slower? Living around immortals messed with my brain, and it was almost like I expected everyone's aging to be halted in the same way. I lived in a very unnatural world.

A world that shouldn't have existed. It defied natural order. Even I was evidence of that.

I was going to die before my mom and that definitely wasn't the natural order.

But I'd fight to keep all of my knowledge from her. Aside from anything else, it was so much safer for her this way. The less she knew, the less she had to worry about and the fewer monsters she'd have to worry about hunting her. Not that Esmé or Brock seemed to worry about human discovery, usually. Esmé had probably only agreed to help remove Mom's memories of Sean because she was so grief-stricken herself. That had probably been the last act of kindness Esmé had ever done. She'd taken Mom's memories of Sean, and that had been exactly what Mom had needed.

And if I was going to die, Mom deserved to just lose me clean. An unfortunate death. Not one caused by vampires, one that would rip her whole world apart. Not another one, anyway. And I couldn't see her mind wiped again.

Yes, for so many reasons, Mom needed to stay in the dark. Even though part of me wanted to tell her every single thing. I was tired of the secrets and living with Esmé because she owned me now.

I followed Mom into her small living room. It was crammed with furniture that she and my dad had collected over the course of their life together. *Wheel of Fortune* blared away on the television, and Mom automatically sat back in her usual chair. I perched on the edge of a couch that was both careworn and overstuffed. Lumpy in some places and patchy in others, it conformed to me pretty quickly, offering a ready welcome to my ass.

Since Dad died seven years ago, Mom had followed pretty much the same routine each day, and she'd left the house exactly the same as it was on the day Dad left home for the final time. When I died, Mom would be all alone. First Dad, then Sean… next me. Guilt churned in my gut, and I edged closer to Mom's seat, taking a look at the latest puzzle on the screen as I did so.

"How has that guy not asked for an *E*?"

Mom turned to me and smiled. "Not enough money to buy it. Sucks to be him, I guess." Mom nodded sagely as she passed her judgment and I laughed.

The contestant asked for a couple more letters before Mom turned the volume down, signifying her boredom with the show, and turned to me. "How are you getting along with Esmé? Still like having her as a roommate?"

I nodded, already anticipating the next question.

"Any man on the scene yet?"

Luckily, I'd had lots of practice deflecting this line of inquiry, but before I even needed to trot out some well-worn phrase, Mom spoke again.

"I expect you're too busy at work to find a man of your own, right? Being a private detective must make you pretty jaded, too, I guess. Know too much about the male of the species?"

I nodded again. I didn't want to speak and dig my lies any deeper. One day, caught without a decent story, I'd just named a local law agency and said I did some freelance work for them. But I tried not to add to my lies if I didn't absolutely have to.

Luckily, Mom stood. "I'm just heating up leftovers, but can I get some for you?"

I rarely felt hungry anymore, but I nodded. "Sure, Mom. That sounds great." Because it did. Nothing would match a moment of normalcy with my mom.

"So, how's the work going anyway? Any exciting cases?"

I almost sighed. Looked like I was going to have to do some more lying after all. I forced a smile to my face, but it felt tight and maybe a little too wide.

"Oh, there's a guy who's been cheating on his wife." I waved a hand like it was the most casual thing in the world. "I've been digging up what I can on his history and getting pictures so his wife's lawyer can get more alimony." At least I hoped that sounded right.

Mom didn't question anything. She just bit gently on her lip as she transferred the lasagna from the fridge to the microwave. "I don't know what the world's coming to these days," she said. "Your dad never would have…" She didn't complete her thought, but I knew.

Their marriage had been perfect. Genuinely perfect. And now she was without him.

She'd be completely alone soon. I couldn't shake that repeating thought from my head or the guilt that washed over me every time I thought it.

The guilt from earlier returned with a vengeance, and I touched her arm briefly. "I know, Mom."

I couldn't say all the things I wanted to say. I wouldn't get to say goodbye or put my affairs in order, so I needed her to know I cared.

"And you're still enjoying it?" She ushered me to the small table as she passed me a plate.

I nodded. "Sure." Then I laughed. "My job pays the bills, I guess." That part almost wasn't a lie, anyway, if I considered that my job was feeding Esmé, and she paid all my bills.

Mom's face creased into a frown, and it looked like the movement was an effort—it probably was. She didn't usually find a whole lot to frown about, and the expression was unnatural for her. "You need more than just a job, honey. You need—"

"It's great. Really." I cut her off before she could launch into all the things she thought I needed in my life. We were growing dangerously close to the man-and-children conversation I'd thought she wasn't going to have with me today.

She nodded as she served a portion of lasagna onto my plate. "As long as you're sure."

"I really am." I forked a bite of the pasta dish into my mouth. Food didn't hold the same enjoyment these days, but I could eat to make Mom happy.

As usual, the lasagna was homemade and perfect, the blend of herbs just right and the meat sauce rich. By the time I'd scraped my plate clean, Mom was handing me a wedge of apple pie.

Apple pie accompanied by a meaningful glance.

I knew exactly what that look meant, too. The man-and-children conversation had only been waiting until dessert. I shoveled the apple pie in as fast as good manners would allow, keeping my mouth full so I wouldn't have to do any talking.

"Have you thought about trying online dating?" Mom said, and there wasn't enough innocence in her voice for this to be the first time she'd considered advising me to wade into a virtual swamp of strange men.

From what I'd heard from friends before my life went to shit, there was definitely something a little primordial soup about swiping.

I chewed and nodded anyway — but it was only a nod to acknowledge her words, rather than a nod that meant I agreed with them.

"And I'd really like to meet someone you're seeing… maybe even see you settled before…" She faltered. "Before, you know." She waved her fork, her piece of pie just barely clinging on. "Before I go." She loaded the last word with additional meaning, and my heart squeezed.

I'd go first, and I was never going to meet someone. Those dreams — of boyfriends and love and marriage and forever — those would remain dreams. Regrets, really. The things I'd never done.

I forced a smile. "Sure, Mom." I'd never made false promises to her before, and I wasn't sure what made me do it now.

There was no way I was ever going to bring a man back here to meet her. But it suddenly seemed like the less cruel option, to extend that hope, to pretend my life could be that normal. That I lived in the light instead of the shadows. I wanted all of those things that Mom wanted for me, and maybe we could both believe it. Just for a few minutes.

Until the pretense pricked my eyes anyway,

"Esmé's waiting on me to start movie night." I offered a pretty shitty explanation for my speedy exit as I stood and tucked my chair back under the table before loading my plates in the dishwasher.

I really didn't want to eat and run but I didn't want Mom's focus on her future as a grandmother, either. That would hurt both of us way too much.

***

The streets were quiet on the way home, so the lights reflecting in my rearview made the car following me stand out. But picking up a tail while just going about my normal business was nothing new.

I was Esmé's property and the Blackbloods kept tabs on me. Probably Brock had ordered it. Even if he didn't actually care for Esmé, she held value for him, so he kept an eye on her walking blood bag to keep her happy.

The reminder of my situation chilled me, but there was nothing I could do about it.

They didn't even hang back or pretend like they weren't following me, and I had kind of a wicked, spiteful urge, so I led them all over New Orleans. Riding through fancy neighborhoods where I pulled a three-point turn outside huge, gated properties and down winding alleys and backstreets lined with boarded -p buildings.

After two more U-turns, I headed home, glancing in my rearview one last time. "Hope you enjoyed the tour, boys."

But I didn't quite reach home. Something gave me pause just before I made the final turn. Now that I looked closer, beyond the simple presence of the headlights, I didn't recognize the car as one of Brock's usual goon mobiles, and the guy in the driver's seat looked unfamiliar, too. The passenger seat was shrouded in darkness, and Esmé would kill me properly if I led anyone to her home.

I stopped at the curb and turned the engine off then just waited. The car that had been following me pulled up behind me, and I drew in a quick breath, holding it until it burned in my chest. What was worse? Being killed by Esmé if I led unknown people to her or being killed by the unknown people because I wasn't even attempting self-preservation? I didn't really have time to decide.

I focused straight ahead, my gaze unblinking and out through the windshield. Someone tapped at my window, but I didn't move, steeling myself against the flinch, turning on my capacity to tune out my surroundings — maybe that was in part to do with the constant distraction of being in thrall to venom. There was another tap, and I'd expected it, but I was unwilling to look my potential death square in the face. After interminable seconds, I finally turned my head.

What the fuck? *Kyle?*

He made a motion to the window, and I leaned forward slightly and actually *rolled* the fucker down inch by dramatic, jerking inch because my car was so old and beat up.

The car behind us was still idling.

"What are you doing, Sam?" His voice was hard, cold, like I owed him an explanation, but my damn chest still tightened when he said my name, like it mattered that he knew it and how it sounded on his lips. "Where the hell are you driving to?"

"Home." It was only one word, and it was the truth.

"Through every bad part of town you can think of?" He made a scoffing noise, but this was really the most I'd heard him say in one go.

He left my window and as I rolled it up again, the passenger door opened. "I'll ride with you then catch my other ride back to my apartment."

I would have argued. Probably should have argued, but suddenly his scent filled the interior of my car, and I was a little dizzy from it. Instead of asking him to leave, I simply nodded before pulling away, watching in the rearview mirror as the car behind me moved in synchronicity with mine.

"Even with Esmé's protection, you're not safe in some of those places." Those were the last words he spoke, and when I glanced at him, he wasn't even looking at me.

We rode the rest of the way in silence, but there was something reassuring about his presence. A warmth I'd been lacking for a long time, although I very much doubted that Kyle wanted to be anyone's warmth.

I pulled up on the cracked slab of a driveway in front of our house and before I could cut the engine for the final time, Kyle spoke.

"You didn't answer before. What were you doing? Driving around like that."

I didn't intend to answer now, but I did anyway. "Shaking a tail."

His lips twitched like I'd amused him.

"But what were *you* doing? Why were you following me?" I held my breath, unsure what I wanted his answer to be. Vampires never did anything for a good reason, in my experience.

Was I also just food to him? Had he been looking for a late-night snack? Was I the closest thing to a twenty-four-hour diner he knew of in New Orleans? The questions I asked myself sent a chill through me, and I risked another glance at him.

He could be very dangerous to me, but maybe not in the usual way vampires were dangerous to me. This one... this one I wanted to know.

He made me wish and want and hope.

All the dreams Mom had just awoken in me rushed to linger in my mind, of a future, of a man, of love, and I saw Kyle in them, and I looked away from him. I was being ridiculous. That wasn't my future. Vampires would be my downfall, nothing more.

And this vampire was here for work, and I was part of his pretense. That knowledge lodged bitterly in my gut, but maybe pretending to love was better than not ever experiencing it.

He shifted in his seat and his scent swirled around me afresh. It was all I could do not to press my nose to him and breathe him in until I couldn't hold any more air. I'd burst for him. That knowledge hit more like a sledgehammer, and as if he'd read my mind, he moved again, edging a little farther away.

"Just be careful where you go. It's dangerous out there." His voice was gruff.

Then he pressed a quick, surprise kiss to my cheek and slipped from the car, before taking the shadowed sidewalk back in the direction of the one that had stopped following us about a block from my place. My cheek tingled and I touched it, almost in danger of swearing to never wash again.

I wanted someone who wanted to kiss me. I'd never dared admit that to myself before, and I wasn't sure I wanted to admit it now. I didn't need the tidal wave of hope and sadness such an admission threatened to unleash.

But the unexpected display of affection was definitely all about appearances. So, my tail on the drive back had been Kyle and whoever, but I was being watched by others now that I was home. I flipped the bird to a car parked across the street as I sauntered to the front door. Yeah, I'd been right. Two of Brock's usual minions sat in the driver and passenger seats. Still, if they had time to waste watching me, I was happy to greet them with the respect they deserved.

The strange triumph at my unexpected interaction with Kyle faded as soon as I stepped inside the house, and it was all in such stark relief to Mom's place. The unpleasant odors were stronger here again now that I'd been home, somewhere clean and filled with love, and the ratty furniture in my space was anything but welcoming.

A chill hung in the air, and I made my way slowly toward Esmé's wing. She didn't really like me down there very often, but I tried the handle anyway. The door was locked, which meant she wasn't home.

That was happening more and more often, and Mom's lasagna curdled in my stomach as I remembered how our friendship used to be. There'd been a time when Esmé and I had really been friends. Inseparable, even. Those were the moments I called to mind whenever I discussed Esmé with Mom. I was able to borrow from the actual truth.

Esmé's absence now, though, proved how little I meant to her. And that was pretty ironic considering the thing that had changed everything in our lives was when I'd saved hers.

In that split second, the worst decision I'd ever made, I'd saved Esmé's life and damned my fucking own.

Sean had already been dead —beyond saving —killed by a fledgling vampire on a rampage, and Esmé had been beside herself and taking more risks than usual when she'd taken on that vampire in retribution. She'd underestimated the strength of the newly made, though, because what they lacked in experience, they sometimes made up for in enthusiasm.

And when she'd had her throat slashed open, I'd been the one to provide the blood to keep her alive.

I couldn't lose both Sean and Esmé in one night. I just couldn't.

Except, if I'd truly known the future consequences, I would have. I'd have watched Esmé's eyes turn glassy and empty if I'd known it would save me now.

She couldn't even be bothered with me anymore. I'd changed my status from friend and equal to underling and food, and… I laughed, the sound dry and cold. Food was never a friend, apparently. At least not in the world of the Blackbloods.

I shivered as the chill of the house seeped into my skin and closed around my bones. Perhaps a hot shower would fix things. Of course, the nicest shower was in Esmé's quarters, but the one with the cracked tiles and unreliable water pressure in my bathroom still got hot enough to warm me up.

I stood under the spray until my skin was red and wrinkled. I didn't want to leave the cocoon of water cascading over me, but it would start to cool off soon and it was better to get out with the memory of the shower still being hot.

Besides, there was only so much standing in the shower I could do. Standing there with my eyes closed allowed my mind to wander too much, and I imagined… Suddenly, I was joined by a large man with close-cropped hair and a scar I wanted to trace as it worked over his head. He had eyes I wanted to gaze into, lips I wanted to taste, and I—

I shook my head. That train of thought was dangerous. Heat had prickled in my breasts and flickered between my legs, and I didn't need that. I just had to get through this and keep Esmé happy.

I wrapped a thin towel around me and rubbed my arms briskly over the rough fabric to dry myself off and keep the heat in my body that the water had introduced. I yanked on my fluffiest pajamas and shoved my feet into thick socks. Really, I probably needed a warm drink to wrap my hands around too, but I settled for some fingerless gloves, even though they made me feel like a bum in my own home.

I sat on the sagging couch cushions and tried to imagine I was back at Mom's as I turned on the old TV. Only certain channels worked, and most of them flickered, but there was still something comforting about watching the minutiae of the lives of fictional people and hearing them interact.

I glanced at the clock. Hopefully, I'd have a while to catch up before Esmé returned home from wherever she was. She was probably somewhere doing something for Brock, anyway, and that meant she'd return home hungry.

As much as I craved Esmé's venom, I resented the increased frequency of her feedings. It was like she was speeding through my slow death, using me all up before she found herself a replacement.

And what did her needing so much more of my blood so often say about Esmé? It was like she craved me too. I shuddered. I'd never wanted to be anyone's drug. I'd never wanted to be *on* drugs either, but with the way my system needed the venom these days, I was as good as.

The thought of venom coursing through me sent a shiver of anticipation through my body, and I grimaced as I tensed my muscles and waited out the surge of desire. I rubbed my hands over my upper arms again, trying to chase away the feeling. I didn't want to *want*. I didn't want to chase that high, that bliss, all the time.

Every day, there were times I considered running away from New Orleans and going cold turkey. But that wouldn't help me. I'd still crave. I wouldn't ever recover.

I'd still die.

There was only one way I'd ever escape this life, and that was if Esmé turned me — or someone else did. But I didn't want to be one of those. A bloodsucker.

And Esmé had never mentioned it as an option. She probably hadn't even considered it. She's grown steadily more selfish since the night everything had changed. It was another sign I'd lost my friend to being her food source.

She'd stopped caring for me, her attitude growing increasingly cold even as my need to reclaim the old Esmé and our friendship grew. I craved our old attachment, and I wanted reassurance that I was something more than a handy fresh blood supply.

Of course, some of our friendship had faded when she and Sean got serious, when she'd started calling him *mate*, but she'd still had time for me, still hung out with me, still laughed with me.

That Esmé no longer existed.

I'd just started to relax, my breathing steadying, warmth returning to my body when the front door burst open and rebounded off the dry wall. Or nearly rebounded. It pulled a huge chunk of the wall away with it, leaving a gaping hole.

Esmé stumbled through the doorway. "Hellooo, Sham." Her words were slurred, and blood dripped from the tips of her elongated fangs and down her chin.

I would have rolled my eyes at the caricature she presented, but every one of my movements was frozen as I watched her.

She must have attacked some guy or girl in the quarter — maybe many someones — because the only way she could have gotten drunk like this was to have fed on alcohol-laced blood. And this was a very drunk Esmé indeed.

She wobbled farther into the room, shoving the door closed with all her vampire strength behind the movement. The house shook as the door slammed into the frame.

I lifted my chin, determined not to show her my fear. When she was like this, it felt like anything could trigger a feeding frenzy. "Why are you so drunk?"

She shrugged and cackled out a laugh. "Because we're both toast."

I flinched a little. She never openly admitted my status as a dead man walking.

"How do you mean?" I almost challenged her to admit my fate now.

But she threw herself dramatically into a chair. "We're both going to die for shiding with the Dupontsh. There's no way we can shurvive letting a traitor into the organization. Brock will find out. He'll know. He'll read me. Shomething." She stopped talking, her voice cutting out abruptly as she focused on a fly crawling up the wall opposite where she sat.

I sat quietly for a moment, unpicking Esmé's words from the slurred syllables. I'd been aware that her activities worked directly against Brock, but I didn't know she feared discovery. That wasn't the kind of thing she usually confided in me, so I'd learned not to question it.

The person I'd been most worried about was Kyle, in case he didn't know what he was taking on. Not Esmé. I'd assumed she could protect herself. But her assertion that I was *also* toast? I could barely bring myself to care. I was dying one way or another, anyway.

Still, my mouth engaged before my brain did as I considered what she'd just said.

"Why did you agree to getting Kyle a position on the inside then?" I cringed inwardly, hoping she wouldn't notice the belligerence in my tone — or if she did notice it that she mistook it for curiosity.

I never questioned her decisions, not since we'd become less than friends anyway, and I wasn't sure why I was doing it now... Except I didn't have a whole hell of a lot left to lose.

Maybe my visit to Mom had made me resentful. I'd already lost so much, and now I could see my entire life slipping away.

Esmé barked out her strange laugh again, and it sounded like metal scraping against metal. "To put us both out of this misery." She closed her eyes suddenly like she'd slipped into an instant sleep before blinking them open again and focusing intently on me for a moment.

I started to recoil, but she stood, the movement lacking her usual grace but almost blurring with speed. She reached out like she might grab me before she swayed and turned the involuntary movement into a wide spin as she staggered off toward her wing.

I sat still, expecting her to remember that she'd forgotten to feed from me. But maybe I'd gotten lucky. Maybe she'd sated herself at the same time as getting drunk.

Only part of me didn't feel lucky. Part of me felt disappointed... cheated of my high.

Esmé's key scraped around the lock on her door before the lock mechanism finally snapped open and the door slammed to signal she'd passed through it.

I breathed a sigh, and it was mostly relief.

# Chapter 5 - Kyle

My eyes sprang open, and I was wide awake. I never needed time to adjust. From asleep to being awake in a moment. That was just the way it was and had been since I'd turned. For a second or two, though, I had no idea where I was. Then I drew in a deep breath of damp air and groaned.

Hell. I was still in the same shithole Temple had arranged for me to live in. It was rare that I actively longed for Sebastian, but I missed his lifestyle right about now, even if my version of his appreciation for luxury didn't have so many bells and whistles. At least I'd always enjoyed somewhere clean.

This place was far from fucking clean. But maybe Kyle Durg wasn't a clean kind of guy. I groaned and kicked my blankets off. Time to start the day.

An unfamiliar scent lingered in my nostrils, teasing me with something I couldn't quite put my finger on. An image of red hair came to my mind. *Sam.* She certainly didn't belong in my head. But she'd lodged there somehow, and when Jason had driven past her, I'd made him follow her so I could ensure she got home safely.

Of course, that was only because any thrall was like a beacon for a vampire in need of a quick snack in this town, and I needed to keep Esmé sweet as my way in. So, protecting her food source seemed like a good way to prolong that sweetness.

It had nothing to do with Sam at all. And absolutely nothing to do with the way my balls tightened when I thought of her or the way my hand was lingering near my dick now.

I shook my head, trying to shake loose those thoughts. What the hell had I been thinking when I kissed her cheek yesterday? Sure, theater, performance... But really? Nothing to do with the softness of her skin or her scent at all?

She was a temptation I didn't want to explore.

With another head shake of self-disgust, I got out of bed, then showered, dressed, and grabbed an emergency blood pouch from the fridge. I hated living like this, but the ends justified the means in this situation.

When I swung my front door open, an unfamiliar car was idling at the curb, Esmé in the driver's seat and Sam in the back, hunched over, her focus on her phone. Purple shadows darkened the skin beneath her eyes, and I frowned. Then I steeled my emotions. I'd already decided I wasn't concerned about the well-being of a human, hadn't I? Especially not someone else's pet. Even if I'd entered into the uneasy pretense of caring on Esmé's instructions that Sam and I *date*.

I huffed out my disgust at what Esmé was forcing on me. But I certainly didn't have to care in the privacy of my own thoughts.

My focus was on my mission, anyway. Securing Nic's reign and bringing New Orleans back under Dupont rule. Even I could see that Sebastian was the city's best hope over Blackblood control. Sebastian and I didn't always get along, but he had some good ideas regarding establishing and maintaining a good rule, and he was also loyal to Nic now that he seemed to have his head screwed back on straight after all the Leia shit that had gone down between them.

"Time's a wastin'," Esmé greeted me as I settled into her passenger seat. But she didn't say anything else as she drew away.

Perhaps she wasn't a morning person. That was fine. I wasn't up for conversation with her, either. I just needed to keep her close enough to watch her and make sure she didn't double-cross me the same way she seemed to be so happy to do to Brock.

At least her ride was bigger than Sam's. I wasn't twisted like some kind of immortal pretzel in the front of this one.

The journey to Brock's house didn't take long at all. He was almost in the same neighborhood as me. *Almost* being the operative word of that sentence. He was close enough to keep an eye on his budding army but far enough away to be making plans to expand. And he wasn't exactly in the thick of it if it all went wrong one night and violence spilled over to the human world.

Yes, he'd clearly planned his location quite carefully. The streets widened a little as we rode, and became leafier, the trees lining the road older and more majestic. After a few minutes, Esmé slowed, pulling up to a solid metal gate.

No fancy filigreed wrought iron, here. Brock was clearly a guy who valued his privacy. After Esmé spoke quietly into an intercom system, the gate rolled silently open to reveal a huge house — bigger even than Sebastian's — and several outbuildings.

I shook my head as I skimmed a glance over them. I didn't even want to know what went on in those. I'd probably find out at some stage — well, if the mission went well, I definitely would — but I wasn't looking forward to that moment.

"We're here." Esmé rolled to a stop inside the gate and at the foot of some stone steps. The stone was cracked and old, and armed guards stood at the top. There was no real reason for them to be armed — particularly not with the automatics they cradled like babies. They were all vampires, but the guns went with their pseudo-military aesthetic of tight T-shirts, cargo pants, boots, and sunglasses.

Esmé smirked as she glanced over at me. "Looks like you fit right in."

I huffed but didn't reply as I ran my fingers over the raised scar on my head. Then I opened the door as Esmé got out and I walked around the car before climbing the steps.

One of the guards jabbed his gun toward me. "Halt!"

I stopped, my hands raised in front of me. This wasn't the bar from last night. I wasn't about to fight my way in, and I wasn't going to say anything that might antagonize them, either. I'd play my role exactly the way I was supposed to.

"What are you doing, Danny?" Esmé looked the guard dead in the face. "He's good. I say so."

Danny shrugged, but the movement was small, like he didn't want to make it. "But Brock said —"

Esmé waved a hand. "Go ahead then." After she spoke, she stood to the side, arms folded, tapping her foot.

"It's just a weapons check," the second guard offered almost apologetically, as if Esmé scared him, as the first guard stepped forward and patted me down. "Can't be too careful, I guess."

"I guess." Now Esmé was examining her nails, her spine ramrod straight, her entire being radiating that she was pissed. "Can I take him through now? Brock *is* expecting us."

The guard, Danny, stepped away from me and nodded, although he looked disappointed not to have found anything on me.

"Come on." Esmé opened the door and beckoned me forward, seemingly perfectly at ease to leave Sam sitting in the backseat of her car.

I still didn't talk. I had nothing to say, and God only knew who was listening within these walls. Esmé all but speed-walked through the property, barely giving me chance to look around. I remembered what I could of the layout, glad the Blackbloods were so transient. They hadn't exactly brought a lot of shit with them. The rooms weren't crammed full of treasures and valuables, and that would make these spaces easier to navigate if we needed to bring our army here.

Holy Hell, I hoped it wouldn't come to that. We didn't need an all-out vampire war because one jumped-up little fuck couldn't keep himself in check. Still, soon I'd have the measure of Brock Saxton and know what we were dealing with.

Esmé pushed open a door at the back of the house, and we stepped out onto a wide deck that overlooked a big, fenced yard. Several pairs of men were sparring in what looked like it was supposed to be an organized training session.

But my gaze caught on the biggest of all the men there. It was like he was a beast and a vampire all at the same time. Some sort of hybrid, almost. He was all muscle and mean attitude under a lowered brow and ridged forehead.

There he was.

Brock Saxton. It couldn't have been anyone else.

He hesitated for the briefest of moments as he sniffed the air before pulling his fist back and smashing it into his opponent's jaw. There was an audible crack as the bone broke and the guy hit the ground, sending up a plume of dust from the surface, his eyes already rolled back in his head.

Brock didn't waste any time checking on the guy he'd just knocked out. I stood and waited for him to come over, my stance my usual one — loose enough to look at ease but poised to fight if I needed to. Esmé had brought me here to meet Brock, so this next part was a test, and it was one I intended to pass.

He grabbed a towel from the railing of the deck and climbed up the steps to stand beside us, watching me the whole time as he moved the towel slowly over the back of his neck, even though he looked like he'd barely broken a sweat. I didn't flinch, but I did move to stare just beyond him like a good soldier. He wiped the towel over his face and the back of his neck again then slung it over his shoulder.

"This him?" He looked at Esmé now as he jerked his head in my direction like I wasn't there or couldn't understand. He was reminding me of my position straight away.

I maintained my forty-yard stare out past him.

"Sure is." Esmé nodded and kept her voice hard. "Sam brought home a little boyfriend, and I figured he's perfect for an enforcer."

"That so?" Brock's voice held a touch of derision, and Esmé didn't reply. "You're allowing a boyfriend?"

I couldn't tell if he was genuinely curious or simply needling Esmé with that question.

This time, she seemed to withhold a sigh, and her voice held a deliberately casual air. "Figured it can't do any harm now, right?" She shrugged and sounded almost bored.

Brock chuckled. "Harsh but true. All good thralls come to an end eventually."

I sneaked a glance at Esmé to discover she'd developed a forty-yard stare of her own, looking beyond Brock and focusing on nothing in particular across the training space.

Brock studied me, his gaze narrow as he worked it up and down my body, sizing me up. "Well, he dresses like a play soldier, anyway." His tone was dismissive. Then he took a swig from a water bottle some little minion of a fledgling offered him before he rammed the tip of his forefinger into my chest. "You fight every one of my enforcers in this yard right now, and if you come out on top, you're in."

I glanced at him but didn't say a word and a slow, evil grin twisted his lips.

"You're either in or you die," he said with a lazy shrug. "No skin off my nose either way."

"No problem." I tensed my jaw.

Hell, if this guy wanted to see me fight, I'd fight. If I destroyed half of his workforce, that shit was on him, although the idea of the lengths he'd go to so that he could replace what I wasted twisted my insides.

Brock gestured down the steps, a smirk twisting his lips. "After you."

I resisted flipping him the bird and nodded instead. "Of course." I scanned the men in front of me as I walked down the steps. My boots knocked against each tread, the echo sounding like a rapidly firing gun.

A young vampire swaggered forward and took up an immediate position that looked like something he'd learned from watching TV or playing a video game. I almost laughed. Street fighters presented no problem. And I preferred arrogant ones because they made mistakes.

He crooked a finger. "Come at me," he said, and this time I did allow myself a smile.

Oh, yeah, this one would definitely make mistakes. He was both cocky and stupid. The best of combinations.

He lunged at me, and I threw my fist out, striking his jaw and taking him straight to the ground. It wasn't even a contest. I didn't have time to return to Brock, though. Or even look at him to see if I could read his expression. Four guys detached themselves from the larger group and strode toward me, like this whole thing had been planned and practiced for days. Maybe I'd give them points for choreography.

Their faces changed as they came closer, taking on enhanced vampire features. Their cheekbones became more prominent, their fangs elongated, and their eyes glowed a dull red associated with high emotion. Aggression in this case, most likely. Like that might scare me and gain them an advantage. They hadn't yet learned how not to rely on the fear of humans to give them their win. I was bigger and I was scarier — any day of the week.

That was also something I could use to my benefit, that they were essentially behaving like I was a human who would buckle under fear alone. My usual team under Nic legitimately trained like Navy Seals. Hell, half of us were ex-military, some from special ops and various missions we couldn't even discuss. We had skills that would make these new vampires look like the children they were.

Was this really how Brock intended to train his army? In a yard with no real structure or leadership to show them the techniques of battle and war?

In the end, I almost laughed as I took them with military precision, using them against each other as they moved in their uncoordinated attack, getting in each other's way and forgetting to function as a team. Clearly, they'd never been trained that way in the first place.

The first guy swaggered over. Wait… What? They were actually going to take *turns* to fight me? Like some sort of polite cast of extras in a movie? I shrugged, my initial confusion at their tactics probably just looking like I was loosening up. He feigned rushing at me, making himself as big as possible, his arms held at an odd angle at his sides like he thought he was some sort of boogeyman. I slammed my fist into his gut when he danced a little too close and he doubled over, earning himself a knee to the face.

Blood spurted from his nose, and he howled in pain, rage almost visible, shimmering in the air around him. Before he could move, and before any of his friends could think to come to his aid, I grabbed him and threw him against the wall, calling on my superior strength and ability.

Bones cracked and the vampire lay still.

I turned to the next three and they looked at each other like they were counting themselves in.

They rushed me as one, and I swept to the side, grabbing the two closest and cracking their heads together. The resulting sound was squelching and wet, and gray matter oozed through the splits in their skulls. Their eyes dimmed immediately, and I threw the bodies off to the side.

Only one vampire from this group stood, watching me now. Momentary confusion flitted over his face, at odds with his vampire features, and pity knotted inside me.

Then enthusiasm for a fight overcame his good sense, or maybe he simply had no choice, and he charged at me.

I darted to the side, using the wall in supernatural parkour and jumped off, landing on him and taking him to the ground.

He flipped, surprising me, and reared up, his fangs bared.

Instinct and adrenaline flooded me, and I punched through his ribs before withdrawing his heart. It beat one last time, bugling between my fingers, before I threw it to the ground, my disgust in equal measure at myself and the man I'd killed.

Brock too. He'd set up this fucking circus.

I clenched my jaw. Brock was failing in his duty to his fledglings. That carelessness with his responsibility only further strengthened my resolve to bring him down.

The sixth guy approached me, but I'd become a little complacent in my anger. I stood quickly, but he swiped my feet from under me with a fast-moving roundhouse kick to my legs, and I landed hard on the ground, but I sprang back up before he could gain any traction from laying me out.

Brock laughed but I didn't even glance at him before I took his man out with a combination of moves at vampire speed. It was gratifying to have a worthier opponent to use them on. But he still didn't last long, his head snapping back and his body landing hard on the ground. He'd ache when he came around. At least I hadn't killed this one.

They all deserved it… but *the waste* grieved me.

I almost didn't see the seventh guy venture closer. He'd obviously been watching and planning his moves accordingly, and he was a blur as he crossed the yard. I side-stepped him and he paused to reassess before turning straight into my fist, but he wasn't a one-shot guy. He wobbled but answered me with a slam to my ribs.

He definitely knew what he was doing.

I defended against him as I moved forward, trying to get within striking distance of his throat. I just needed one good throat punch and he wouldn't be a problem anymore. Not that I wanted to give away all my moves to anyone watching.

As his great weight landed on the ground with the other vampires who had yet to get back up, I waited. Turning my back immediately was risky, but I faced away from the vampires I'd just taken out anyway, and all that happened was a low groan from one of the bodies on the ground and a slow, sarcastic clap from the deck.

"Started you off easy, boy," Brock declared. "Things get tougher now." He shoved Esmé's shoulder. "Get down there and show him how we really fight."

Panic flickered through Esmé's eyes for a moment, and her mouth thinned, but then she straightened her shoulders and tipped her chin up, steel in her blue gaze. Now, this was a soldier, despite her almost fae-like appearance.

"You show him, Esmé," Brock said again. "Decide if he's good enough to be one of us or if you're going to kill him."

The determination in her gaze flickered again at the position Brock had just put her in, but I didn't think she was about to let me have an easy fight. I didn't fight many women, and it wasn't an activity I sought out, but I needed to be accepted into this group. And I could make an exception for a bitch like Esmé.

After what she was putting Sam through, especially. I brushed that thought away. Sam didn't belong in my head.

Whatever Esmé dished out, I could match. Hell. I could better it.

She met my gaze and smirked, sudden confidence seeming to blaze from her. I shrugged. There was only one way this was going to go, regardless of how much faith Esmé put in her own skills, but I had time to play first. I let her get the first hit because it was the quickest way to judge her strength and speed.

It also lulled her into a false sense of security. She threw back her head and barked out a gleeful laugh.

"Maybe you *were* wrong about this one?" Brock called from where he was resting his forearms on the railing surrounding the deck.

"Maybe," Esmé conceded, her eyes bright with amusement. "First time for everyth—" But she didn't finish the word as my fist connected with her chin and the force of the blow sent her whirling away from me.

She recovered quickly, though, and sped around me to land on my back. "I'm not young like they were," she murmured in my ear.

"No, but you do get yourself in some stupid positions," I answered as I grabbed her shoulders and yanked her forward and over my head before slamming her onto the ground.

I couldn't help but see Sam again as I gave Esmé what she deserved for treating a human so badly, and I pushed her out of my thoughts a second time.

This fight had nothing to do with the human thrall or how Esmé saw fit to treat her pets. This fight had one purpose only.

It was my way in.

I stepped toward Esmé again, to where she lay on the ground, but she was more twisted than I'd expected, and she groaned.

"Serves her right." Brock laughed from his position. "Still, forget her now. I saved my best for last." He straightened and turned toward the house. "Demon," he yelled. "Get out here."

The door slammed open, and a guy walked out. Big and cocky. Not as big as Brock. Maybe about Jason's size, and he looked like he'd be at home as a center on a football team.

He thundered down the steps, but they held up under his huge stomps. I rolled my eyes at the showmanship even as I prepared for the inevitable hard hit of his first tackle. This guy had something to prove. He had a name to live up to, after all.

And he tried to prove it from the very first moment, when he crashed into me full on, our chests colliding. A crack sounded, and pain wound itself in a tight circle around my chest. Shit. He'd broken one of my ribs.

I readjusted my position to ease the pain and gave thanks that vampires didn't need to actually breathe to stay alive. I didn't need the agony of dragging air in and out of my lungs while I put this guy out of his misery.

Every blow I tossed out toward him, he matched. And every one he threw my way, I did the same. It was like fighting my own fucking reflection. If I hadn't known better, I'd have thought he was a defector from Nic's loyalists.

But something must have distracted him on the other side of the yard, and he glanced to his left. Not for long, but it was enough. It was my in.

I didn't waste any time or tip him off by drawing my fist back. Instead, I slammed my forehead forward, cracking it against the bridge of his nose then following the move up with a flurry of punches designed to take advantage of his disorientation.

It worked, and he suddenly fell sideways, despite having given no sign he was losing consciousness. One moment, the lights were on, the next they were all the way out.

He had the heaviest landing so far, the loudest thud, and I half expected the ground to crack beneath him. Wiping blood from my cheek with the back of my hand, I turned to face the deck, my heart speeding at the sound of an unexpected cheer.

The tone was familiar, it spoke to me. I wanted to linger and listen to the owner of the voice. I sought her out, my gaze roaming the porch until it landed on the blaze of red hair. My chest tightened.

Sam was no longer captivated by her phone or sitting in the backseat of the car, but how the hell long had she been there, watching the fights? She certainly played the part of quiet, obedient human pet well. She grinned wide, and for a moment my heart lifted, and I almost smiled back.

It was like part of me remembered another lifetime. A moment when I'd been carefree… when attraction could be answered, when love was possible. Happiness filled me at the sight of her, before I clamped down on it, regaining control of myself in an emotional change of direction that almost gave me whiplash.

I redirected my gaze to Brock, staring him down, deliberately not even glancing at Sam now. There was a thoughtful look to Brock's expression, like this wasn't the outcome he'd expected, and his fingers tightened around the railing, his knuckles almost sticking out as shiny, white, raw bones.

More warm blood oozed down the side of my face, but I resisted the urge to wipe it away this time. "Am I in?" I all but growled the words.

I'd passed every single one of his fucking tests.

He glanced at Esmé, where she still lay on the ground, apparently waiting to heal enough to get up. Then he shook his head like he couldn't believe it. It wasn't straightforward denial, anyway. He let out a low growl but finally nodded.

Esmé made a noise that sounded partway between a sigh and another groan, and Sam returned to looking down at her phone, her face pale before she cast another nervous glance in Esmé's direction.

I turned and surveyed the rest of the damage I'd wreaked. Looked like I was going to fit in just fine.

# Chapter 6 - Sam

Holy fuck, Kyle was good. I'd known he probably would be — he just had the capable vibe. Although, the more I thought about it, *of course* he had a capable vibe. He'd been chosen by the New Orleans king to infiltrate the Blackbloods. Not just any man would be sent out for a job like this — not if they'd done their homework and knew what Brock was capable of.

My blood chilled a little. What Kyle was doing was so dangerous. What Esmé was doing was dangerous. I had no idea of her endgame, but she was certainly playing with fire by acting against Brock. It put me in danger, too.

But watching Kyle fight just now had given me the first real hope I'd had in a long time. He was clearly a vampire who knew how to get shit done. He didn't like Brock or the Blackbloods. So, what if he could help me? I'd always wavered over whether it was worth the trouble. But if it *was* worth it? Was Kyle the one who could help or knew some way to get out of my situation? Maybe I needed to bide my time and wait for a moment where I could at least find out.

In the meantime, watching him kick all that vampire ass was the best thing I'd seen in… Shit, I couldn't remember how long.

But I'd also tried to stay fairly quiet about my enjoyment. Brock had been standing way too close for me to telegraph my shifted allegiances. I'd mostly watched my phone and stayed still, under the radar, obedient. I hated drawing attention to myself, but I couldn't help the cheer when Kyle won his final fight. It was only one whoop for a job well done and a congratulations to the newest enforcer. One who was supposed to be my boyfriend. Forgivable, surely?

I'd been worried about the fight against Demon when he'd stepped out of the house. Demon usually beat everyone.

The ass beating Kyle had dealt out, though, was the least the Blackbloods deserved—they all deserved so much more—but I'd take watching any beatings doled out to them that I could get.

I moved from the deck to the kitchen inside pretty much as soon as the fighting stopped. I didn't want to be in Esmé's line of sight in case she beckoned me right out into the yard in front of everyone. I didn't want Kyle to witness another of my humiliations. That thought surprised me.

Really, Esmé's needs had nothing to do with Kyle. But something had shifted inside me without my having realized it, and it mattered what he thought, what he *saw* when he looked at me.

Still, Esmé would need a feed once she grew a little stronger, so I needed to stay close by.

For once, the idea of a feed didn't fill me with the same thrill it previously had. I felt cheap. Humiliated. Prostituted.

I didn't turn as the door behind me opened. I'd known Esmé would come inside eventually, after all. Except, it wasn't Esmé at all.

"Hello, Sam."

I flinched at the way Eddie spoke my name. It was creepy and slimy, and I needed an immediate shower. I still didn't turn, but he slid onto the barstool next to me, his proximity making me shudder.

"I said, *hello*."

"Hello," I mumbled, not looking in his direction.

It was always easier to behave as they wanted. They were stronger than I was, and most of these vampires wouldn't think twice about killing me if I displeased them for any reason at all.

Kyle had kicked his ass early on, and Eddie had fallen quickly. Also recovered quickly, it seemed, because here he was. Bothering me.

Cold seemed to radiate from him, and my body chilled in response. I closed my eyes and swallowed my revulsion.

He leaned over — *too close. Too close* — and took my phone from my hand before setting it on the table nearer to him than to me, somewhere I couldn't exactly grab it back from. I was powerless against these vampires, especially in this house, although I was a second-class citizen to any of them all the time, the whole city over. Maybe not even classed as high as *second*.

"Saw you cheering for the new guy." His tone was nonchalant, but I'd have been stupid not to take note of the steel bass note to his words. "Do you think that was wise?"

I forced a shrug. "A new enforcer is always good news, right?" I aimed for hopeful innocence. Maybe something stupid but harmless.

His lip curled and his eyebrows lowered, turning his expression mean. His eyes became hot, that dull red that always signified high emotion in one of them, and I fought the urge to shrink away from him.

Eddie was the kind who got off on fear, and he leaned closer as he hissed out his next words. "Well, don't go getting above yourself and thinking you can fuck him. Makes no difference if Brock lets him in or not. There's only one guy here who's going to fuck you. Even if I need to wait until you're almost gone, and you can't talk, can't do anything but scream inside your head while your body loves everything I do to it, that guy is going to be me."

I started to shake my head, but he reached for me, going for my hands or my wrists. I couldn't tell. Didn't care. I didn't want him to touch me at all, so I shoved my stool back, unable to hide my reaction this time. I had to get back outside. Forget my phone — Eddie could keep it. It wasn't like I'd have use for it for much longer, anyway.

But he was fast. They were always so much fucking faster than I expected. He hauled me from my seat and pinned me against the refrigerator, the long handles digging into my back.

I squirmed uselessly because I had nowhere to go. I couldn't escape his strength. Kyle had made defeating Eddie look easy, but I had no chance at all.

Kicking my legs, I tried to wriggle loose but he only grinned, the stretching of his lips malevolent. When I opened my mouth to yell, he covered it with his huge hand, twisting my head to one side so my cheek pressed against the cool metal of the refrigerator door.

Panic froze me. I stopped moving entirely, my eyes focused on the window on the other side of the room. The faded, flowered curtains there didn't fit with the rest of the house, and it was like the vamps had forgotten to remove the last reminder of someone else's previous cheerful existence here. I didn't want to know what had happened to the owners, but I doubted realtors had been involved in the acquisition of this place.

Eddie smelled bad. He wasn't fussy where he got his blood from, and his breath turned my stomach.

He leaned closer until his greasy hair brushed against my skin, and he ran his tongue slowly up my neck. This time, the shiver that claimed me was due to something else as my body betrayed me at the anticipation of a hit of vampire venom. Adrenaline coursed through me, followed quickly by unwelcome desire.

Eddie paused and took a long drag of air through his nostrils. "Good girl," he muttered approvingly. "I knew you'd want this."

The tip of his fang dragged over my skin, and I hitched a breath, excitement fizzing in my chest even as I tried to fight it.

But before his fangs could pierce my neck, he was gone. I gasped for air as I focused on Kyle's hand wrapped around Eddie's throat as he pinned him to the wall next to me. Eddie's feet dangled about six inches from the floor, and his eyes bulged as his tongue flicked over his lips like he was about to say something.

Kyle growled, the noise ratcheting up to a furious roar.

Color bled from Eddie's face, leaving him almost chalk white as he rolled his eyeballs, seeming almost desperate not to meet Kyle's gaze as he looked everywhere but my unlikely rescuer.

"Never. Put. Your. Hands. On. Sam. Again." Each word was its own sentence and Kyle sounded like he'd gone full vampire, not a trace of humanity left. "Mine."

I wanted to run away but something about the scene before me held me captive, watching.

Eddie nodded, the movement immediate like he couldn't agree quick enough. He parted his lips as if to say something but only a breath huffed out. Kyle dropped him to the floor, and Eddie scuttled away, banging into a barstool and rebounding off the bar as he headed for the door that led to the rest of the house.

Kyle turned to face me, his fangs visible, his eyes red, in full vampire mode. I backed harder against the fridge, even as my heart raced and my pulse beat harder in my neck. I reached my hand to touch the spot where Esmé usually bit me. I had no way out again, no chance of escape from the vampire in front of me… But this time I wasn't even sure I wanted to.

I held his gaze, watching as the red bled from his eyes, leaving his usual brown color plain to see. So beautiful, and I could still drown in those eyes and die happy. He rested a palm on the refrigerator, beside my head, but I couldn't take my focus away from him, like he magnetized me. Then he leaned closer and the spicy scent of him, almost like bay rum, swirled around me. I closed my eyes and waited for his lips to meet mine.

I wanted that kiss. I could almost feel it. I parted my lips in anticipation, almost able to feel his soft breath against my mouth.

But nothing happened. Instead, there was a rush of cool air, and I opened my eyes again to find Kyle standing several feet away.

He looked at me for a moment, his eyes scorching me before he turned abruptly and strode from the room. I let out a shaky breath, and my knees buckled, sending me plunging to the cold tile. I sat there for a moment before Esmé's voice pierced my thoughts.

"Sam." It was just my name, but it was enough.

She needed that feed.

When I didn't immediately respond to her one-word command, she clopped closer to me in her mile-high heels, wobbling from where she still hadn't recovered from the damage Kyle had done.

"Get off the floor right now."

I nodded and climbed to my feet. I needed to get away, have some time to myself. It was too much to be at Esmé's side all the time, on call, being used like an animal.

Perhaps if she got what she wanted, I could chance a request to get away for a while. Sometimes she was more liberal with granting me freedom once she was sated. For that, I needed to be compliant now though.

She reached for me, and I drew away a little.

"Wouldn't you prefer somewhere more comfortable?" It would be a seduction to earn me the time away that I wanted, even though the thought of behaving this way turned my stomach.

She tilted her head and made a short humming noise of consideration.

"You don't want to be disturbed by someone like Eddie."

My mouth dried even speaking his name, but Esmé wasn't stupid. She'd seen the way he looked at me, and her face hardened. "Come this way."

She yanked my arm and took me to an out-of-the-way sitting room that no one had bothered to clear of the previous owner's furnishings. I'd never seen it before, but it was immediately clear that most of the softness in this room these days was supplied by the copious piles of dust.

She pushed me onto the sofa and fell on me, her fangs ripping into my throat before I could make another noise. I surrendered to the attack, thoughts of getting in the car and driving away sustaining me.

***

After I'd recovered from being fed on, the hit lasting a shorter and shorter duration these days, I went to find Esmé. She was sitting in the den watching something mindless on the TV.

"Can I take the car?" Because it was a question I rarely asked, she looked at me, her eyes a little wider than usual, her lips parted.

She didn't answer right away, and I twisted my hands together.

I needed to get out of there. I was so sick of simply surviving in a literal nest of vampires, but I couldn't let her know that. "The car," I repeated, like maybe she hadn't heard.

She nodded before turning back to the TV and waving her hand in a gesture of dismissal. "Take it. Brock wants me to hang around here and discuss something with him, but I'll have one of the others bring me home if you're still out."

I nodded to her back before leaving the room. Apparently, I'd been right about her being in a better mood after her feed. I didn't want to give her chance to change her mind or ask too many questions.

I hurried down the couple of hallways leading to the front door, trying not to be noticed as I left. No one else would care that I was leaving, but someone might care that I was here and roaming around unprotected. They'd smell Esmé on me, know that I'd been fed from recently, and want a snack of their own.

I held the car keys like I might fend off an attacker as I passed through the front door and by Brock's weird excuse for security. Danny dipped his head and sniffed me as I passed, but I ignored it. I couldn't get distracted now. I was leaving.

Breathing a sigh of relief, I slipped behind the steering wheel, but I didn't experience true freedom until I was through the gate and onto the open road.

Esmé was behind me, Brock was behind me.

The whole fucked-up morning was behind me.

This was freedom, or at least a taste. I was sure of it.

I headed toward the Quarter. A shopping expedition sounded good. It was part of a plan that I'd been formulating for a while. A long time before Kyle arrived, I'd thought maybe I could help myself, but I'd lost hope. Only now, he'd brought hope back… and if he couldn't help me himself, maybe I could still do something?

It suddenly felt worth a try, anyway.

I laughed. Esmé gave me an allowance to spend, although it was more a sick joke because where would I ever spend anything, and what would I buy? For her, it was like putting her money in a savings account — she'd get it all back after I died, right?

Not now, though. Not all of it, anyway, and it was unlikely she'd agree with where I planned to go to spend my money.

There was a shop I wanted to visit now that Kyle had reawakened me. Just a little tiny hole-in-the-wall place, but I'd heard whispers of witchcraft and maybe, just maybe, there'd be someone there who could help me.

Maybe even something to help me kill the cravings for venom so I could live a relatively normal life for however long I had left. One day, Esmé would probably bleed me dry anyway, if being a thrall didn't get me. But I couldn't believe there was simply nothing.

And I couldn't leave my fate to everyone else. Not my death, not my rescue. I needed to try to do something for myself, too.

The Quarter was busy with tourists and their chatter. It was also pretty. I always forgot how pretty it was here. I'd even almost forgotten what it was like to walk around with no responsibilities, no one to answer to. No person theoretically holding my leash. Well, Esmé was in the back of my mind like always, but the leash was a lot longer than usual right now.

The buildings here looked so charming and welcoming, and I shuddered at the memory of my home and of the rancid smell that permeated the entire upper floor of the house where I lived. Calling it a *home* was definitely a stretch too far.

Part of me kept waiting for that to not bother me anymore, the life I now led, the conditions I accepted as my normal. But the other part of me knew as soon as the smell of that house stopped being an issue, I was too far gone to save.

So, I needed to take this chance to save myself, no matter how small.

I slowed my walk as I reached the address I'd memorized. It really was only a tiny place. Looked old, too. A little bit crooked and definitely giving off witch vibes.

I cupped my hands around my face and peered through the window, past the jewelry and trinkets and beautiful tumbled crystals and gemstones laid out to entice passers-by. There was a woman in the shop, fixing something in the shelving display or adding more stock. I couldn't quite tell what her task was, but she looked busy. Satisfied. Happy.

She had the life I wanted. A simple life. A normal human one. I'd never aspired to much, and that hadn't changed. All I wanted was my life back so I could live it properly. Surely that wasn't too much to ask?

If only I could have walked away from Esmé when she'd been injured and needed all that blood. If only I'd been brave enough to let my best friend die. I'd met her first when I'd needed a job, but we'd become so much more than that. After I'd introduced her to Sean... Hell, that had been the biggest mistake of my life right there.

Well, I couldn't exactly decide the biggest mistake. If someone gave me a time machine, I would have chosen never to meet Esmé in the first place. All of my bad luck stemmed from her. Sean had died because I'd introduced them, and now I was her thrall because I'd saved her life by donating blood after the attack. Too much blood. Too much misery. Too much death.

And my own death would only compound it all.

I had to do something. Do *more*.

I laughed, the sound harsh. Yeah. So much more. I wasn't convinced I could change my future, but I had to try.

Taking a deep breath, I pushed the door to the tiny shop open, a little bell ringing above me to signal my entrance.

The woman at the display cabinet turned around, a welcoming smile on her face that froze only momentarily when she saw me. "Namaste. Can I help you find anything?"

I inhaled again then held the breath inside my chest while I made my decision about what to say and how much to reveal. But there was no point in beating around the bush about what I'd come for. Supernaturals came here, after all, so anything vampire related probably wouldn't shock this woman, even though she looked as innocent as any human without a clue usually looked.

"I need a spell or a charm to ward off vampire venom cravings." My voice was clear and neutral as I made my abrupt request, but the woman pressed her lips together and her gaze shot to my neck, lingering there as she seemed to examine me.

I raised my hand to the skin there, suddenly self-conscious. Esmé was pretty good at cleaning up after herself but occasionally she got sloppy and forgot to conceal her marks.

The woman scrutinized me for a moment longer then, apparently satisfied with whatever she'd seen, she nodded. "I'm Naomi." She crossed to the shop door, flicked the lock, and flipped the little sign from *open* to *be right back*. "Come with me through here." She gestured to a deep blue curtain sprinkled with silver stars.

"I'm Sam," I said, the revelation of my first name hesitant as I fell into step behind her.

We passed through the curtain and the scent in the air immediately changed, becoming much more herbal and intoxicating. losing some of the heavy patchouli from the front of store. The atmosphere was thick with verdant life and felt almost alive with electricity or something else that buzzed and hummed.

It was like we'd walked backward through time as well. The shop was quaint and pokey, but the back was like a kitchen from an English period drama — but some period way the hell back. The whole shop must have been a building original to New Orleans itself.

Herbs in various stages of drying out hung from hooks in the ceiling. So many herbs and shades of green I didn't even think I'd seen some of them before. There was a big sink and an old black range with a fire going. A pot sat on top of the range and liquid bubbled and boiled inside, changing color as new bubbles rolled to the top and burst.

A shelf ran around the top of the room and Naomi paused her stride and studied it from a distance, one finger pressed thoughtfully to her mouth. The books up there were thick and leather-bound, so old that the spines were cracked and peeling. Eventually, Naomi walked forward again before pulling a stool into position beneath the shelf and climbing onto it. Then she reached up to select a book and grabbed what looked to be the thickest one on display.

She used two hands to support it and I automatically stepped forward to grasp her elbow as she stepped from the stool. When she thunked the book on the wooden table in the center of the room, dust blew up in a small cloud and she waved her hand over the top of the cover to dissipate it.

The book looked older than the entire United States of America, and Naomi kept her movements slow as she began to turn the fragile pages.

Decorative calligraphy covered most of the pages, the writing almost art. I leaned closer to look at some of the wording —were they spells?—but the little I could decipher wasn't in English.

Naomi continued to move the pages slowly, occasionally pausing and leaning closer or biting on her lip. Sometimes she even ran her forefinger under a line and mumbled aloud, too.

Then she stopped turning the pages completely, and the book lay open and flat in front of her. "This is it," she said as she looked from the page to me. "A charm to help control venom addiction. It will take a little while to make, though."

I nodded, excitement a tight ball in my chest. Hopefully, I still had *a little while* to wait. There was no telling how long I truly had left. "But you can do something?" I tried not to let my hope show.

"I think I could make the charm into a ring?" She drew her eyebrows down as she scanned her gaze over the page again. "It will be small. Might look odd or be noticeable if I try to fashion it into something bigger like a bracelet. And you'd have to wear it around your neck if I made a pendant." She gestured vaguely to the area between her collarbones.

I nodded again, although I probably didn't need to agree quite so enthusiastically. I just didn't want too many questions from Esmé about any new jewelry. A ring was good and small. "Whatever you can do will be appreciated. I just need… I need *something*." There was no real way to express what I meant. Not without unpacking *everything*, exposing myself and my life to a stranger.

When Naomi met my gaze, there was a knowing look in her eyes. "Who are you in trouble with?" The way she said *in trouble with* definitely sounded like she actually meant *in thrall to*, and I sighed.

"It's a long story."

She gestured to one of the wooden seats. "I've got time."

I didn't know what to do with that reply. When I'd grown up, *it's a long story* had always been code for *I don't want to talk about it.* I glanced toward the curtain. She had a shop to open, surely? Not spend time back here just shooting the shit with me.

"Really." Her tone invited no argument. "And the more I know about your situation, the better I can help." When I still hesitated, she continued. "The better charm I can craft. If I can make it personal to you, it will work better." She smiled reassuringly as she looked meaningfully from me to the chair again.

Hell… It had been such a long time since I'd talked to someone… *Really* talked. Somewhere along the line, I'd lost myself, and now Naomi was offering me a part of myself back.

"It's the Blackbloods," I whispered, the words feeling forbidden as they left my mouth. In New Orleans, someone was always listening. It was like secrets carried on the wind here. "I mean, it's my… best friend." I still didn't know how to refer to Esmé these days. Then words emerged from me all jumbled and without order, "She's one of them now, one of the Blackbloods, and I saved her life in an attack—"

"At the expense of your own." Naomi didn't seem to need me to make much sense, and she wasn't judgmental. Just matter of fact, and I nodded.

"I didn't know that then."

"And she won't turn you?" There was curiosity there but nothing malicious.

It was easy to talk to Naomi while she was moving around the kitchen space, collecting things from various cupboards. Her apparent distraction gradually made my words flow easier.

"No, I don't think she will, and I can't imagine wanting that as my life, anyway. Who the hell would be a vampire by choice?" My lip curled at the word vampire, as it always did.

Naomi stopped then turned, one eyebrow raised. "Isn't that life better than this one?" She didn't mention it was the life I was about to lose completely.

She didn't have to.

We were both aware exactly what was on the line for me. That was part of what made her easy to talk to. I didn't need to explain my shit.

I shrugged. "I guess I don't know anymore." Then I giggled, but the sound was hollow. "Everything's a bit messed up."

"Tea?" Naomi lifted a teapot onto the range, and I nodded.

I'd lost contact with most of my human friends since meeting Esmé, and this situation wasn't one they could have understood, anyway. It wasn't even one they could know about.

While the water boiled, Naomi sat opposite me, and she let out a slow exhale. She lifted her gaze to meet mine. "I should probably tell you about my best friend, Kayla."

"Oh?" This conversation sounded like it could get interesting. "Is she like me?" Maybe this would be a story of hope.

But Naomi shook her head. "No, she's been turned. She was never a thrall." She said the word with almost no distaste, but I heard it lingering in her tone anyway. "She's a vampire — mate of Sebastian Dupont, the king's regent. They own this place." She looked around the space as she spoke.

A gasp caught in my throat and my voice came out thready when I spoke. "This shop? The king's regent? A Dupont?" My questions were asked with quiet but mounting horror.

She nodded.

"You can't say I was here." Of all the shops in all the world... Panic rose inside me, and I stood abruptly. "Vampire politics are crazy right now and—" I stopped. The last thing I needed was Naomi telling her friend that she'd met a thrall from the Blackbloods.

The whole situation was too fragile, too delicate. Kyle was supposed to be undercover. He was a Dupont loyal. I'd blurred the lines by mistake by coming here.

Esmé had gotten his position, but nothing under Brock was secure or stable. We all lived in a house built on a foundation of sand. Having me floating around between the two camps, between Brock Saxton at his place and Sebastian Dupont by coincidence here, put Kyle's undercover position at risk. Especially if Esmé found out where I'd been in her car and with my money. I wouldn't have come here if I'd known I was treading so close to the Dupont reign in New Orleans. Shit.

"I won't tell anyone. This will remain confidential." Naomi looked sincere, but I didn't know.

I had no idea who was even trustworthy anymore. Only myself most days, and not even me if I was craving venom.

But it had been a long time since I'd trusted anyone, and I'd wanted that back so badly. Still, I shouldn't have spoken so openly to this woman I didn't know. I fumbled some of my allowance onto the table. "Can we call this a deposit and I'll swing back by some time to collect the ring and pay the balance?" I barely waited for her nod of acknowledgment before I swept back past the curtain.

Shit. Had I just made a huge mistake by coming here at all?

# Chapter 7 - Kyle

I pushed through the door to the outside and stepped onto the deck that seemed to wrap its way around the whole building. There was a lot more exploring and mapping of this whole place to do before I had anything to take back to Nic.

The training yard was empty now, aside from the blood I'd spilled earlier. Every single one of the vampires I'd beaten in a fight had crawled away or dragged themselves off for a feed, but restless energy still crackled through me. My instincts were all on fire, and I didn't want to just maim. I wanted to kill. But there was no one out here to even take on.

Bloodlust claimed me. I wanted to spill it, to see it, to taste it. I drew a deep breath like I could extract the leftover coppery tang from the air.

A punching bag hung from one corner of the deck, and I wandered toward it before giving it a soft punch. A harder punch soon followed and one even harder after that until my fists blurred.

But it wasn't enough. The soft vinyl gave easily under my force, conceding easily, instead of cracking like bone or splitting open like skin. A sheen of sweat soon covered me, soaking my T-shirt, and I stopped.

Punching something wasn't helping, and I didn't have a change of clothes here. As far as I could tell, I didn't even have a way home. I hadn't seen Esmé for a while, and I hadn't seen Sam since I left her alone in the kitchen… for her own safety.

Shit. I wiped my hand over my forehead. I could have taken her then and there. Her eyes had been so innocent, her lips so… tempting. But that was wrong.

So wrong.

Humans shouldn't tempt me.

I could have drained her. I'd come too fucking close to her after I'd watched that fledgling nearly fucking do it. It could have tipped me over the edge. And now I was stuck here. Couldn't even get away and clear my head.

Still, I shook my head in a futile attempt to clear it anyway, but blood still pounded through my ears, and the noise made it hard to think, to focus. That fucking fledgling had been holding Sam against the refrigerator.

Panic had filled her eyes, and I'd… I'd…

I shook my head again. I'd *reacted*.

He'd been about to fucking bite her.

And I'd said she was mine. Only that was good, right? Made playing her boyfriend more real.

My anger level rose again as the memories crashed over me. But that wasn't right. My temper wasn't supposed to be spiking. I was supposed to be calming down.

None of this made any sense. Humans meant nothing to me. Well, except for the effort to keep them from finding out about vampires… Which had a lot to do with why I was here and was a reason I didn't need distracting from the mission.

It was too dangerous to let humans mean anything to me. Hell, I'd learned that lesson before. *Brutally.* I clenched my fists, dragging my thoughts from that past. I didn't even know this Sam girl. She didn't belong in my thoughts as a human or as a thrall, regardless of the wrench fucking Esmé had thrown into the works with her fake dating story.

As I turned from the punching bag, planning to find the quickest way out of the house and gate so I could at least go to where I was staying and shower the stench of Blackbloods off my skin, Brock stepped out from some nearby shadows.

I didn't jump at the sudden sight of him. I never flinched, but I should have known he was there. He shouldn't have been able to sneak up on me. I was too distracted and needed to bring my wandering mind back under control. I needed to remain alert. Especially given I was literally on enemy territory.

I glanced at the man. He'd looked like a monster before, but although he stood taller than me, there wasn't anything about him that was more powerful about his build or his attitude.

He looked me up and down, his gaze still the same assessing one he'd used earlier. "Impressive show today." He didn't sound particularly impressed. He almost sounded bored, but I got it.

He couldn't afford to sound too interested and still maintain his position as leader easily. These were not well-organized guys. Brock needed to rule by fear and lack of respect, so he couldn't afford to show me any of the latter.

I didn't say anything. Nothing was done to impress him. I wasn't like the others joining his little group. My purpose was different, and that was to get in so we could take him down. Instead, I waited, letting the silence stretch. He'd speak again soon.

People usually did.

"You might just work out as an enforcer," he said.

I nodded, still not willing to speak. This was me, exercising some power. Making him do the talking.

"And actually, there's some business I've got coming up that I need you to take care of."

Well, this was interesting. And very rapid progress. "Oh, yeah? What's that?" I allowed four words. Just enough to look engaged.

Brock slung an arm over my shoulders and pulled me uncomfortably close as he started to walk along the deck.

"We're taking out the Duponts, but we're doing it clever, right?" He stopped and loosened his grip as he looked in the direction of the nearest houses. "I like it here. New Orleans. Usually we'd rip through, but I think I'd like to stay. We've been watching this city for a while, keeping a check on ol' Frankie and his dad. We were about to move in when *boom!* Stolen right out from under us." He shrugged and his grin showed a hint of fang. "At least that's what that fucking king thinks. Now just gotta get rid of those fuckers who think they run the place."

"You got a plan?" I focused on running my fingers along the railing like I wasn't interested, but my plan to stay quiet had worked. It sounded like Brock had just told me a whole helluva lot more than he'd meant to.

He wanted New Orleans for himself, and he'd been planning to steal it out from under Francois and Émile. That would interest Nic.

He chuckled. "Full of 'em. Always full of plans, my new friend. The first is what I want you on tonight. You see, the Dupont king doesn't know everything that happens in this city, and his brother is too busy with his new mate to know shit either." He tapped the side of his head, his eyes bright with fervor. "I know shit. I've been watching and learning, and I know exactly how this place runs and who runs it."

I lifted an eyebrow. I wasn't surprised that Sebastian might be oblivious, but were there things that not even Temple knew?

Brock chuckled again before sitting on a swing seat, the old chain links creaking under his weight. "There are some businesses of the old king's that are still up and running. All very secret. Think it was the old regent, actually." He scratched his chin, and his fingernails scraping over the stubble there made a rasping sound. "Francois definitely had some fucking dodgy dealings, and the Blackbloods are more than happy to step in and take those over. It'll give us a foothold in Louisiana and start to erode the power of the new king. Wins all around." He grinned again.

"So, you want me on one of these hidden jobs?"

He shook his head. "Not yet, newbie. Slow your roll. You're starting on smaller jobs. Until I know I can trust you."

I leaned against the balcony railing and crossed my ankles. Total at-ease position to try to convey that he could also relax around me.

"We've got some spies in at that new club, and we've heard that there's a shipment coming in." Brock's gaze roamed across the yard as he spoke like he was always on the lookout for danger.

He probably was. It wasn't like he went out of his way to make friends.

I made a mental note to tell Jason or Sebastian to keep an eye on the Nightfall employees, although being able to distribute false information directly back to Brock was probably a reason not to weed out any moles. We could use whoever the traitor was now.

"A shipment of what?" I was still grunting questions.

"Liquor. For the club. We're going to steal it." He shrugged. "It's mostly a minor inconvenience but my plan is to keep fucking with them. Keep them busy with the small shit while I start to unravel everything else. Then I can watch them fall apart. Fuck. I'll take them apart and burn their little kingdom to the ground then keep the ashes for myself." His eyes darted to the side as he finished speaking, as if he was unwilling to meet my gaze head on. That seemed odd for such a big guy.

I shrugged. "I don't care about your reasons for the job as long as I get paid."

He exhaled and chuckled. "Money isn't an issue, believe me. You'll get paid." He leaned forward. "You just need to get yourself to the port at nine-thirty and watch the unloading of the *SS Atlantic*. Some of my other guys will meet you there and the rest is up to you." He stood, making it clear that was the extent of his instructions.

"Got it," I said as I straightened. Leaning wasn't as safe now that he was on his feet.

"Make sure you get it right." He walked away, and I went in the opposite direction, back toward the punching bag and the entrance to the house.

The training yard remained empty, and I pushed back through the door into the kitchen, mulling over the instructions Brock had just given me. It was a stupid mission. Not one even worth bothering with, and his reasons hadn't rung true. There was something else going on, but I had no idea what, and I wouldn't be able to find out unless I showed at the dock. It was risky to go in blind, but I hadn't taken this mission expecting it to be risk-free or easy.

This was either a test or a set-up, though, and I needed to be prepared for both.

I glanced up and found Sam making coffee. My body responded immediately, my cock twitching. I lingered by the door, away from her. She was... who she was. Human... way off limits and I didn't need the distraction.

I had one focus.

The Dupont rule.

"Kyle." Her face creased into a smile, and I took another small step away from her. "I hoped I might see you."

I didn't say anything, not wanting to encourage conversation. The less time I spent with Sam, the better. Except...

Fuck it all to hell. I needed to make this boyfriend thing seem real if I wanted to keep Brock's suspicions at bay. I forced a smile and stepped closer. Boyfriends didn't stand a room's length away from the women they took to their beds regularly.

She smiled again. "I wanted to thank you—"

I held up a hand. "No need."

She frowned slightly. "But you saved me. You rescued me from Eddie, and I—"

"It's fine." I cut her off again. "It wasn't a big deal. Not a thing. It just happened. And now you're okay."

She half smiled. "In a manner of speaking, right?"

I didn't acknowledge her allusion to her situation. It was better not to get drawn in to the matter of her being in thrall to Esmé, no matter my personal feelings about that.

The door opened and Esmé walked into the kitchen. She looked at Sam, her gaze hard before she spoke. "Oh, I'm glad you came back after all. There's no one else to give me a ride. I'm ready to go." Then she glanced between us. "It's always nice to see you two love-birds together, too." Her slight frown left no doubt that she was suggesting we should be a little closer to preserve her lie. "But now that I've found both of you, shall we go?" Her focus was back on Sam.

Sam glanced down at her just made coffee, the steam still rising from the mug, then at me. Then back to Esmé. "Can I just drink this? I was also talking to Kyle."

Esmé's lips turned down, her disapproval obvious. "And *I'm* ready to go. Bring your little boyfriend, if you want."

Sam's face tightened, the muscles moving just a fraction like she was irritated before she emptied her coffee into the sink and rinsed some water down after. "Come on then. I'll give you a ride, too," she said to me over her shoulder.

Her smile was gone now, and she looked a little defeated. But that irritation I'd just seen was pretty close to actual character, and in a thrall, that was interesting.

I quashed down the fresh anger that rose inside me. This time, the rogue emotion was for Esmé, and that really wouldn't do this operation any good. I needed to keep Esmé onside for all of this to work.

But couldn't she see the damage she was doing to Sam with her attitude? Did she even care?

Hell, why did I care? I shouldn't.

Esmé left the kitchen, her movement more of a commanding stride, and Sam fell into line behind her. After a moment of standing in the empty kitchen and drawing a couple of breaths that I didn't need to function, I followed. Deep breathing to calm myself was a habit, not a necessity.

Sam was already in position behind the driver's seat and Esmé was alongside her in the passenger seat when I reached the front of the house.

I bent and spoke through Esmé's open window. "I'm happy to walk." I didn't know the exact way back to the place where I was staying, but I'd find it. And walking always allowed me to think without distractions.

I wasn't worried about protecting myself on the streets, that was for sure. I still had a fight or two left in me.

Esmé shook her head. "Get in the back. You're my asset. I need to ensure you stay protected. Sam —" She turned to her left. "You can drop me off first, though, then Kyle and you can make things look *genuine*." She dropped her voice seductively on the last word, and her grin turned malicious, like she knew neither of us wanted this ruse. "But then come home so we can do the usual… night routine."

I froze for a moment as I climbed into the back seat. Esmé appeared to have been deliberately vague on that last instruction, but there was no doubt what she was referring to. Sam's grip on the steering wheel tightened, and the car filled with the scent of her desire.

It wasn't sexual desire… Not like *I* knew desire, anyway. This was tinged with the bitterness of self-loathing, but obviously, she'd find pleasure in the idea of Esmé's upcoming feed, even though she gave the definite impression she didn't really want to.

I climbed the rest of the way into the car, trying to hide my disgust behind a neutral expression. I mean, I got it. Who wouldn't react to the idea of an upcoming high? Esmé kept Sam like her own personal pet drug addict, ensuring she was always anticipating her next fix. The Blackbloods made me fucking sick.

We rode to Sam's place in silence, and the memory of the way Esmé made her live when she enjoyed luxury downstairs roiled in my gut. I watched her leave the car and walk toward the house, my gaze hot enough to light her on fire.

After she'd closed the front door behind her, and Sam shifted the car into reverse to back off the driveway, I leaned forward.

"Can I get you something for dinner?" It would make Esmé happy that we were going on a date, after all.

And it was also a sensible suggestion — it was better for her to have something inside her before Esmé fed from her, especially if Esmé was going to leave her nearly unconscious again.

It definitely wasn't anything more than that.

# Chapter 8 - Sam

His words sent a quiver of excitement right to my core. He was going to take me out? And I was hungry enough his reasons didn't even matter.

"Uhh…" I hesitated for no good reason at all. The answer was clearly *fuck, yes.*

I could tick off the main reason right away, and it should have been all I needed to say, yes. Esmé had told us to make it look real, right? Well, a date would do that.

But I wanted this date for more than the reason Esmé had provided, so I stayed quiet a moment longer. This was dangerous. But my stomach leaped in and cursed me, gurgling on cue, a rare indicator of a hunger that visited me infrequently these days.

But somehow, being around Kyle made everything so much more… normal.

Normal. Exactly the way Mom thinks my life is going. Maybe I could even… But did I dare?

No, best to not even think about it. Only… Mom would sure love to meet him. Okay, so maybe not meet *Kyle*. But meet a guy I took home to her. Just one time.

Before it was too late.

Kyle sat back and I watched him in the rearview mirror, trying to ignore the stream of words flowing through my head.

"You got anything you like to eat?" I tried to sound casual, and I nearly made it. I even added a small shoulder lift, as if I didn't care what he answered and I wasn't about to hang on his every word.

He grimaced. "You choose." Then he looked out of the window, and it was clear the conversation was over.

My excitement that he'd actually answered almost made me giddy, and the desire to word vomit my thanks was strong, but I pressed my lips closed as I also avoided happy dancing in the seat.

*Holy crap, Manny's, here we come.* For sure, Manny's. There was nowhere else I wanted to eat. If this turned out to be my actual last meal, I'd die very happy. I could almost taste the burgers and curly fries, feel the grease on my lips. I might have broken the speed limit a little getting there.

It was a proper retro burger joint out of an old train carriage, and I squealed my tires as I pulled into the parking lot.

"In a hurry?"

I hadn't expected Kyle to speak, and heat spread across my cheeks. I'd almost forgotten the huge, silent man was sitting behind me in the car. "Oh, uhh…" More unnecessary hesitation. I shook my head at myself. "Just that these burgers are great. The best in town."

He didn't say anything else and climbed out quickly when I parked. I followed a moment later and almost speed-walked to the hostess stand.

She arched an expectant eyebrow. "Table for two?"

That strange heat filled my cheeks again as I nodded. Table for two. Two of us. Almost a date. A date for everyone who needed to see to see. Shit. Maybe even my first real date with a guy. First in God knew how long, anyway. Had I dated? Like, properly? I could barely remember. The venom addiction sometimes fucked with my memory.

"Yes." Kyle's voice raised goosebumps on my skin, and I rubbed my upper arms to ward them off.

My mind moved straight from the idea of a date to tangled sheets in an oversized bed. So many things I'd never have now. So many things I'd never have, but I wanted. Holy shit. I *wanted*.

I looked at the menu after we were seated, and my mouth almost watered. I hadn't eaten a bacon cheeseburger in forever. I hadn't wanted to eat one in a long time. But now that I was here, with the scent of the food teasing me, and watching everyone else eating their food, I couldn't imagine anything I'd rather do than eat.

Well.

I glanced at Kyle's lips. Eating maybe came a close second to kissing. I wanted a proper kiss. Even a fake proper kiss sounded good.

Kyle's nostrils flared, and I squirmed in my seat, pressing my thighs together as I slapped my menu back on the table to distract myself from my thoughts. There was no point in studying the food list when I already knew it from memory, and when there was only one choice I was about to make.

"You already know?" He lifted an eyebrow, and I took the small change in expression as a victory that I had his attention.

"Yep." I couldn't hide my grin this time.

His expression never seemed to give away his thoughts, though, but maybe that was a vampire thing they developed as they aged. I had no idea how old he was, after all. None of them ever went around announcing it.

The server approached our table. "Coffee?" She extended the pot.

"No, thanks." I covered my coffee cup with my palm, and Kyle's lips quirked, but that might have been a trick of my mind, because this guy never smiled.

I probably looked very strange, given I'd just made myself a coffee at the house and now I was acting like I was allergic to it. "I'd like a malt shake, please." I sounded almost giddy, like a child. But a malt shake… It was the stuff of dreams right now.

This whole place was. I looked around again and sighed with happiness. Hell, awe.

The server sighed, but it was not a sound of happiness or awe. She set her pot down on the table before swiping wispy gray hair from her forehead and reached for her notepad and pencil from her apron pocket. "You got the rest of an order to go with that?"

I was too happy to care about her attitude. "You bet." I glanced down at the menu, but it was only for showmanship. I didn't need to look at anything at all. "I'd like the bacon cheeseburger, please, but hold the dill pickle, and replace the skin-on fries with curly fries."

"Yep." She wrote it down with the barest of scratches of her pencil and looked at Kyle. "And for you?"

I hesitated. He hadn't so much as looked at the menu, and the vamps I knew didn't really eat.

"I'll have what she's having." His reply was so smooth, I had no doubt he'd said those exact same words many times before.

But something about them sent a shiver up my back. *I'll have what she's having.* Tonight, I was his *she.*

The waitress nodded. "Good, now what kind of malt shake?" She turned her beady gaze on me again.

"Chocolate, please." She still couldn't kill my buzz, even as she tutted under her breath as she finished writing on her pad and turned and walked away to put our order through the till.

"Well." I put my menu back in the holder and rested my hands flat on the table surface, but Kyle didn't reply as we sat and waited.

Our food arrived quickly, and I opened my mouth to take a huge bite immediately as the server retreated. Then I looked across the table at Kyle and made my mouth small enough to be dainty about it instead. I hadn't been out to eat in so long, and this was nothing like eating at Mom's house, where I wasn't expected to be ladylike or impress anyone.

This was a guy. Okay, so he was still a vampire guy, but still... A guy and I were having dinner. I kind of wanted to impress him and look delicate and dainty. Hell, I just needed to look like I knew how to eat in public without stuffing myself with food. If I hadn't let Esmé feed from me when she'd been attacked, if I hadn't given my life for hers, I would've had a boyfriend by now. We might have done stuff like this.

This and a whole lot more.

So.

Much.

More.

I looked down at my plate and selected a fry. This wasn't a direction I wanted my thoughts wandering. *More.* The word wouldn't leave me alone.

"What did you think of your first day?" I asked to distract myself. I'd resorted to tearing bite-sized pieces of my burger with my fingers and popping them into my mouth. I narrowly avoided moaning after each one.

He nodded but glanced at the door. If this guy didn't have food in front of him, he'd be a runner, so I had no idea why he'd even suggested it.

"Well?" I prompted him for shits and giggles, mostly, kind of curious at what point he'd respond.

But part of me genuinely wanted to know. And another part just wanted to hear this man speak. He had such a nice voice and he so rarely used it. I wanted goosebumps again.

I looked at him expectantly.

He mumbled a reply so quick he could have passed a comment on the weather or asked about the health of my mother. I was no wiser about his day.

"What did you think of…" I glanced around and lowered my voice. "Brock?"

Kyle grimaced, the expression fleeting on his face. But he didn't comment. Instead, he picked up a curly fry and bit the end off, his movements slow and very deliberate.

His malt shake sat untouched at his side and he nudged it toward me. "You'll need your strength."

So, he wouldn't talk about his reasons for needing to be here in New Orleans and infiltrating the Blackbloods, although I could imagine most of them and where his loyalties lay. I never got much information directly from Esmé. But I'd driven her to enough sleazy bars in the middle of nowhere to meet a man who seemed to live in the shadows to know that she'd lose her head if Brock ever found out about her activities. They called that guy Temple, but I didn't know his connection with Kyle.

I'd gotten the impression Temple was connected with everyone, though… if he wanted to be. And he was working with the Duponts here in New Orleans. They were probably lucky to have him on their side, now that I thought about it.

He'd gotten Kyle in, and I could only think it was to bring Brock down.

That thought sent both a dart of excitement and a spike of fear through me. If Brock was gone, that would be amazing. But I had no idea what it meant for me.

Still, if Kyle hoped to bring Brock down, it lent weight to the idea he could help me. If my charm didn't work out.

"Where did you come from?" The curious question spilled from my lips before I could consider the wisdom of asking it.

His eyes widened just a fraction. "Baton Rouge." The words seemed to have just popped out because he grimaced. "Dammit. I mean… Some place out in the Midwest."

I waved a hand quickly between us. "Don't worry about that." I was committed to my original line of thought, not his cover story. "No, I meant before that." I put the final bite of burger into my mouth and watched him as I chewed.

He was quiet for a while then the faintest of smiles lingered on his lips. "I barely remember." A drawl that wasn't usually present in his speech colored it and gave a hint at some of his memories. "I don't remember a time I wasn't a fighter."

"Wars?" I didn't want to say too much in case he might finally speak of his own accord. I didn't want to interrupt him, to stop him. Even the chatter of the other customers seemed to fade, become muted background noise, as I focused solely on Kyle, willing him not to stop.

"So many wars," he confirmed.

"World War One?" I sipped at his shake after I spoke, trying not to give away my intense desire to know.

He laughed, the sound sharp and unfamiliar. Almost out of practice, like he didn't do it very often. "Civil." He leaned forward. "I was turned by a rogue. It was a messy, bloody time in my life." He stopped talking again and it was all I could do not to prompt him. "I've fought on the wrong side, I think, just as often as I've fought on the right one, but I lived for the fight. The strategy, the successes. I've learned a lot." Then he looked me in the eye. "And kept learning. Every battle, every war. New technology, better strategies."

"Military man even now?" I kept my questions brief.

He looked the part. He always had.

He nodded in confirmation. "It's what I do best." And he didn't even sound boastful. Just like he meant what he said, like he couldn't imagine doing anything else.

I could see that. "But so many wars…" It was like he'd lived lifetimes. Hell, the man sitting in front of me *had* lived lifetimes.

Actual hundreds of years. So much life.

So much fucking death.

He nodded. "A lot of war. And it seems like they don't stop." He shook his head, but he didn't add to his thought, and silence fell between us again.

I pushed my empty plate away. Esmé would be wondering where I was.

"Let's get you home." Kyle stood, and as I fumbled in my purse for money for the food, he dropped more bills than necessary on the table.

Like a proper date.

I looked up at him, but he didn't even glance in my direction as he strode toward the door.

He was waiting by the car by the time I reached it, by the passenger side this time, and I was kind of glad. He smelled nice and sitting next to him was a pleasure I hadn't really expected to experience again. It was bittersweet, considering how close I was to the end and how different everything could have been. Life wasn't fucking fair.

But maybe Naomi could help. I only had hope left, though, and sometimes hope hurt.

Kyle didn't speak at all in the car, and I glanced at him every so often, watching the play of streetlights across his face. He maintained his stare out the windshield, and it was on the tip of my tongue to ask what he was thinking, but that was too intimate for our situation. He didn't volunteer anything, and it wasn't my place to probe after all the things he *had* told me. It had almost felt like a connection, something I'd never expected with a vampire.

"Kyle?" I used his name like a question before I could stop myself. "Can you do me a favor?"

He glanced at me, his expression the usual neutral. He didn't invite any more speech, but neither did he prohibit it. That was probably as good as his encouragement got, to be honest.

"Do you mind if we swing by my mom's? I know she'd... she'd..." She'd love to meet him. Except I couldn't say that. We were only pretending to date, and to indicate I thought otherwise made me delusional. "I know she'd get a kick out of you," I finished.

I watched him, waiting for his reply, but I didn't hold my breath. I mean, why would I? That would only result in a much quicker death than I'd been anticipating. *Here lies Sam, who expired waiting for an answer from Kyle.*

Not the greatest epitaph ever written, but maybe it beat the one about me being a thrall.

But he nodded.

And the surprise that stole my breath anyway gave way to a warm glow somewhere in the middle of my chest. Around heart position. I rubbed my hand over it.

*You sure?* I wanted to ask him so badly, but I didn't dare. What if his head nodding turned into shaking? Instead, I didn't speak again. I just shoved the car into gear and peeled out of the parking lot.

The only way he could disagree now was to throw himself from a moving vehicle.

When we pulled up outside Mom's, I turned to him, about to give him a chance to change his mind, but he was already out of the door and making his way to my side of the car. This made no sense.

What guy in his right mind agreed to meet his fake girlfriend's mother after the first real fake date?

But maybe I shouldn't question it. Would meeting Kyle make Mom happy? Hell to the yeah. So, I just needed to suck up my doubts and make Mom happy the one last time I could. I owed her that much, right? After all the years and Sean… And she'd lost Dad. I could bring her Kyle and she'd be happy.

For me.

She'd be happy for me, and I wanted that. I wanted Mom happy.

I rang the doorbell and stepped back next to Kyle, who wrapped his arm around me, and I leaned against him, my body conforming to his as if I'd never belonged anywhere else.

The light above the front door flickered on, and the locks on the inside clicked open. Then Mom appeared, her face already wreathed in smiles as she looked at me.

"Sam!" Every time she said my name, she sounded so happy that I couldn't help but be happy too.

"Hey, Mom." I was suddenly shy.

"Sam and…" Mom looked at Kyle expectantly, not shy at all.

"Kyle, ma'am." His drawl was back, and I grinned just a little bit.

Mom opened the door wide and stepped back. "Well, don't just stand there on my doorstep. Come in."

I glanced at Kyle. Perhaps this was a favor too far, but he simply walked us forward, into the house I loved.

"We haven't got long, Mom." I had to get back to Esmé.

"Oh, I imagine not, a pair of young things out on the town. I remember those days." She blushed a little as if she really was remembering those days before looking at Kyle again. "Can I get you anything to drink?"

Kyle shook his head. "No, thank you."

"We've just come from dinner." I probably didn't need to clarify but Mom's smile widened farther.

"Dinner." She said the word on a breath like it was some sort of exotic event. "How truly lovely."

"Yeah," I agreed. "Yeah, it was pretty nice."

And it had been. It had been the most perfect glimpse into what my life could have been like if I hadn't thrown it all away when I'd thought I was doing the right thing by saving the life of another.

Kyle humored Mom for thirty minutes, and we sat together in her small living room, Kyle's hand reassuringly on my knee, his gaze affectionate and smiley. It was like spending time with a different guy. A very tempting guy. I hoped I didn't lose him when we left.

But I couldn't guarantee he'd stay.

So, for this moment, I chose to let this be enough.

Eventually, I glanced at the clock. Esmé could be raising hell looking for me by now. It was time to go.

I half rose and Kyle followed, mimicking my movements.

"We should go, Mom." I didn't need to fake the note of apology in my voice.

She took my hands in hers and squeezed my fingers meaningfully. "Come back soon," she said.

I hoped for soon.

Kyle leaned forward and kissed her cheek. "It's been lovely to meet you."

Mom simply nodded and opened the door for us, allowing Kyle out first. She took my arm gently. "He's perfect," she whispered, and I blinked back tears.

I drove Kyle back to his place in silence. I barely even heard his breathing, but I understood most vampires only did that out of habit, anyway, so maybe he wasn't bothering at all. Perhaps I should have thanked him, but I didn't want to interrupt his quiet, and I didn't know if I could find all the words I needed.

I stole a look at him as I drew up to the curb outside his crappy apartment. It was like we were having a contest to race to the bottom with how squalid our living conditions were. I'd barely rolled to a stop before Kyle had his seatbelt off and door open, one leg already outside.

"Thanks," he muttered then suddenly leaned back to press a fleeting kiss to my cheek.

But the door was closed again, and he was by his apartment before I could reply.

I shook my head. He made no sense. He'd spoken fairly openly earlier, and he'd been wonderful at Mom's... a model boyfriend. I couldn't have asked for better. No one could have made Mom happier. I thought we'd made progress... Only now, he was as distant as ever, leaving me with one kiss to savor as he acted out his part of our deception.

I touched my cheek with my fingertips, as if I'd feel a mark his kiss had left behind.

I sighed as I pulled back out onto the street. It was quiet back here. The kind of deceptive quiet that seemed peaceful but was only a finely balanced watchfulness. Like anything could happen. I shuddered. I was in a bad place all around, and I needed to find my way out from under Esmé and away from the Blackbloods. I was no longer in a position to be picky about how I did that.

I'd taken the first step by visiting Naomi. Hell, that was riskier than I'd intended. And now maybe Kyle would be willing to help me? It was definitely phrased as a question in my mind, but I was running out of options. Maybe he'd already shown he might have a small soft spot for me. No one had made him stop Eddie, after all? No one had tortured him into spending a whole evening with me. Yeah… it all fit so everyone thought he was really my boyfriend, but the kiss just now? Surely, there'd been no one around to see…

I grimaced. I was clutching at straws.

But men didn't just run around playing superheroes for women, right? Not without something more being at play. And it had felt bigger than just the act of warning Eddie off, bigger than playing to Esmé's demands, like somehow *something* mattered. At times, Kyle looked at me. Just a glance. And something else was there.

Enough to make me think I might be able to convince him to help me out, even though he owed me nothing.

I shrugged at my own thoughts. At this stage, it was worth a shot.

By the time I arrived home, I was pretty much resolved to needing Kyle as part of my escape plan. I just wasn't sure how I was going to get him. I sat in the car for a few minutes, gathering the courage to go inside. Something had changed recently, and I didn't feel as resolved to my fate at

Esmé's hands. I didn't want this stinky hovel of a place to be my last memory.

For tonight, I didn't have any choice about going inside though. Esmé would only track me down and drag me back here. I was her pet. That was her right. I sighed and grabbed my purse, throwing it over my shoulder as I left the car and slammed the door closed.

When I entered the house, Esmé was waiting for me as expected. Except she was drunk again, and humans littered the couch alongside her and the floor at her feet.

"Shit, Esmé." I said the first words through my mind.

But she just cackled her amusement as I rushed forward to check if the people were still alive and breathing. The last thing we needed was a clean-up request. Brock wouldn't like that at all, and it would place both of us under a lot of scrutiny — scrutiny I didn't need. Scrutiny I assumed Esmé didn't need if she was colluding with the Duponts, or at least their sympathizers.

I pressed my fingers to the wrists of each unconscious person in the room, leaning my ears over their noses as I felt for a pulse and listened for breath sounds. My final exhale was a sigh of relief as I dragged my cell from my back pocket and scrolled to the number for a couple of Brock's goons — the ones who usually followed me.

It didn't take long for them to arrive, and they laughed as they saw the people Esmé had fed from, but it wasn't fucking funny. Every time she did this without creating the soldiers Brock seemed to hunger for, she left us wide open to discovery. I couldn't even be sure how good Brock's men were at the compulsion to make people forget. They were all I had right now, though.

Hot damn, what a fucking mess. I looked at Esmé, contempt and disgust for her uppermost in my thoughts. When had my feelings become like this?

She'd been my best friend but now all she seemed to do was steal from me — the rest of my life, experiences, even the ability to think or feel.

She sprawled out on the couch now that she had more room without her discarded snacks, and her delirious noises increased as she yelled instructions to humans who were no longer there.

It seemed like this had been a growing problem since I'd saved her life — she'd taken to binging often, feeding on the inebriated, chasing her only way to get drunk — like she was attempting an escape from reality.

The one time I'd tried to speak to her about it, she'd swooped in and bitten me, feeding with a viciousness I never wanted her to repeat. My consent was always grudging these days, but that occasion, it had been absent completely. I touched my neck and the skin throbbed in response like I could still feel the violence of that attack.

I hadn't tried to speak to her again. It wasn't worth risking my precarious safety for.

"Come to the couch." Esmé lazily patted the cushion beside her as she issued the sleepy-voiced command. "I need this night to be over."

"Why not wait until you're sober, Es?" I sighed and watched her, but even that small question was too much to say.

Her attitude changed in an instant, her glazed eyes clearing as she narrowed her focus on me. The pale, ethereal blue bled to the deep red of her fury, and I froze as she flashed to stand next to me.

The atmosphere in the room changed, and helplessness bloomed inside me. This might finally be the night, the one where she drained me and ended this cycle of destruction we were both caught in.

# Chapter 9 - Kyle

If I'd expected the air to be fresher at the dock, I'd have been wrong. I tried not to breathe too deeply, to avoid drawing the odors of rotting fish, oil, and sewage into my chest. A small container ship had just arrived, chugging slowly to moor and unload. Water slapped against the sea walls and jetties.

I moved closer to the docking ship, staying within the shadows, skulking by the wall, to try to identify if that was our mark, and the two guys Brock had sent to meet with me seemed to wait a beat before following. They always waited before doing anything, and it was unclear whether that was because they didn't like working with me, they didn't agree with how I acted, or they were just stupid.

They were both young enough vampires to be stupid, though, so I went with that. And maybe they hadn't been all that bright before they were turned. Becoming a vampire didn't gift anyone with brains, and they looked a lot more like the hired muscle than the thinkers of any operation.

I drew closer to the small group of humans unloading the boxes and raised my fist in the universally understood signal for the guys behind me to stop before stumbling forward as the vampire behind me walked right into me anyway. I tossed a glare over my shoulder.

"Why didn't you stop?" My irritated words barely made a sound, but his hearing picked them up.

"You didn't say," he hissed back, and I shook my head.

Brock needed to get some proper training in place for the army he seemed to be trying to build.

Or maybe not. I needed to be careful what I wished for. Their weaknesses would make them easy to bring down, and certainly my group of men would run rings around them when the time came.

Luckily, the humans didn't hear me skidding around in the shadows as they banged the crates together and grumbled about the lateness of the hour.

"Michelle is going to fucking kill me if I keep getting home after midnight," one gruff voice said to the darkness.

"Pay's worth it, though." The lit tip of the second man's cigarette bobbed up and down as he spoke.

"Time to go, gentlemen. Night shift's arrived." A group of vampires — Nic's crew — approached from down the jetty, and the two men put the crate they were holding down like this was part of the normal routine.

"We've got it from here," a second vampire said, and the humans moved away without argument.

With the vampires in charge, crates were unloaded much more efficiently and quickly, and without any of the moaning and grumbling the humans had been doing. They worked with minimal chat — Nic and Sebastian's usual well-oiled machine — and I watched them for several minutes, trying to identify the patterns in their movements, trying to pinpoint their weakest moment.

We needed those crates. There was no way I could return to Brock without them.

I glanced behind me again. Brock had sent his two strongest fledglings, at least, which meant loading the crates into our transport wouldn't pose a problem. I had our truck driver's number on speed dial, and he could be here in bare seconds. The whole operation would go smoothly once I gave the signal.

I took a deep breath and lowered my ski mask over my head. I couldn't take the chance one of the Dupont vampires would recognize me and blow my cover. My undercover operation was only need-to-know information, and it was entirely possible these guys didn't know—or have any need to know.

Behind me, fabric rustled as the fledglings lowered their own masks.

"Move out," I muttered, and they were surprisingly stealthy for a pair of such big dudes.

We took the Dupont guys by surprise, and I hit both of them hard over the head, my gut clenching at the squelching noise the iron bar I'd grabbed made when it connected with their skulls.

They fell to the dock, surprise still evident on their faces, and I dragged them behind a stack of boxes. After a quick glance in the direction of my fledglings, I tipped some bagged blood into each of the unconscious vampire's mouths to try to stimulate healing.

"They're down," I called as I reemerged and grabbed my cell phone to get our truck on the scene. The sooner we left, the better.

We loaded up quickly and soon I was sitting in the passenger seat of a truck as it bounced over unexpected potholes on our way to the drop.

"Careful," I ground out. "We're not carrying cheap shit back there." I jerked my thumb behind me, to the trailer, where the fledglings were with the crates. Stealing from Sebastian was one thing, but allowing some dick driver to break all the bottles of his fancy-ass spirits? Sacrilege.

The vampire driving nodded and eased his foot off the gas as I ripped my ski mask off. Shit, it was hot in here.

We pulled off a quiet street and to a warehouse with most of the windows busted out. As I opened the door and jumped down from the cab, Brock stepped around the corner, his fangs glinting in the moonlight.

"All done," I said, and his grin widened.

"I knew you wouldn't have an issue," he said. "And the vampires who were there?"

Brock's fledglings emerged from the back of the truck.

"Kyle took care of them," one of the guys said.

"Yeah," the other confirmed. "And you should have heard the noise their heads made when he hit them. They won't be a problem again."

I kept my face blank. I very much hoped for them to be a problem again, although not immediately.

Brock walked around the truck and lifted a flashlight as he examined the contents. He whistled a low sound of surprise. "Well, fuck. This is the biggest haul so far." He clapped my shoulder when I joined him. "You done good, boy. Done good."

It was high praise indeed, but I didn't acknowledge his words. I never liked to interrupt people when they might speak without being guarded — and Brock seemed happy enough right now that he might just do that.

He clapped his hand against my shoulder. "Believe me. This is just one of the first steps in bringing the Duponts down. They'll notice us now. We'll be that irritating thorn just under their skin until I'm ready to attack properly. And if nothing else, they won't doubt our message now. They know we're here, and we're not going anywhere." He stopped and looked at me, his eyes both manic and searching. "And you…" He paused and seemed to make a decision. "We needed to make sure you were all in. With us." He cocked his head as he watched me, the gesture one of fake empathy and a plea for understanding. "You get that, right?"

I nodded and looked beyond him into the truck, my mind still on the two vampires I'd taken out. They should be healing by now… hopefully. "Let's get the crates out of sight." I signaled to the fledglings, and they began to unload the wines and spirits into Brock's warehouse.

They made quick work of the lifting and carrying, but I mostly directed. I'd done enough disrupting of Sebastian's business without dirtying my hands even more.

Luckily, Brock didn't notice that I hung back now that I'd passed his test. He approached me as the last box was left inside, and I was fixing a new padlock to the rusty old chain securing the doors. I tested the strength of it. We'd need to up the security if Brock wanted to keep hold of his contraband in a neighborhood like this one.

I could almost feel the eyes watching us. A prickle on the nape of my neck. Human criminals were no match for us, and Brock wouldn't tread carefully if anyone attacked while we were there.

"You coming back to the house?" He slung his arm around my shoulders like he was my new best bud. Like we'd officially started our bromance. "We have a bunch of bloodwhores you can take advantage of. Maybe I can make it a party." He lifted an eyebrow in suggestion.

My stomach roiled, bile clawing inside my throat. "Nah, man." I forced a grin as I leaned heavily on my drawl again. "Have my own at home." It was a lie, made about Sam at Esmé's direction, but there was no way I was going back to the Blackbloods' house and feeding from some unknown humans.

Hell, not even Sebastian and Nic knew I couldn't actually face the thought of feeding from a human since the night I'd killed Camille. Memories of her lifeless body in my arms, her blood coating my throat and clothing flooded my mind. She'd been such a pale corpse, her eyes wide, her lips parted as if in disbelief at what I'd done.

*My Camille.*

I'd killed her. And I'd never let my bloodlust take another human again — every person I'd killed since Camille had been an exercise in control, in strategy, on purpose. I never lost myself to bloodlust now.

I couldn't allow it.

But Brock shook his head slowly, and it was mocking. "Oh, Kyle. I think you've misunderstood my generosity."

My chest tightened as I waited for his next words. They weren't going to be good.

"It wasn't an invitation to the house. It was an instruction. You're one of us now, and you belong at the celebration." His words were heavy and laced with a meaning I couldn't fail to understand.

It was another test.

And he didn't add *where I can see you*, but the phrase was implied.

"Tell you what." His hold locked harder around me. "Get the warehouse opened back up and we'll take a couple of cases with us right now. Drunk humans are the most fun, right?"

His laugh was dark and almost sticky as I stepped forward to unlock the padlock once more.

"One of the guys will drive you, Kyle. I'll see you there with the booze." He yanked the door open and strode into the dark space.

I withheld my sigh and turned to face the two fledglings who'd met up with me at the docks.

"This way." The youngest one jerked his head toward a beaten-up car.

Without hesitation, I strode toward it, each of my steps purposeful and deliberate. Brock had made it very clear that he expected to see me at his house, and there wasn't a way out of this one.

Brock must have phoned ahead with his instructions to *make it a party* because the house was already hopping by the time we parked outside. A deep bass beat thumped through the air, and the laughter and drunken chatter spilled through the open windows.

I swallowed my revulsion. There was no control here. The Blackbloods didn't seem to understand the meaning of the word. Except Brock… There was something more to him. His hit on Sebastian had been minimal tonight, but I'd seen the room at Esmé's house. He was definitely masterminding something bigger, and if being here at this party was my way into that then this was where I needed to be.

I slammed the car door shut.

"Dude," the fledgling blurted as I caught the door before it fell off, then wedged it back into position and gave it a pat to secure it.

"Good as new," I said as I glanced at the house again.

I walked up the steps, my hands fists at my sides, and I approached the open door. Inside, humans lay like discarded candy wrappers on various couches. All of them wore the same blissed-out expression. Still more humans were being actively fed from in corners and up against walls. Forget an orgy. It was like an all-we-could-eat buffet, but how many of these humans were already thralls?

"What do you think?" Brock entered behind me and brought a meaty hand down on my shoulder. He directed the guys behind him to carry a crate of Sebastian's alcohol, clearly badged for Nightfall, to the corner of the room.

When they opened it, they revealed bottle after bottle of Sebastian's signature champagne, which was unexpected.

"We're drinking on the Duponts tonight," Brock hollered, and his war cry was met with a chorus of calls and whistles. "Can't stand around shooting the shit just now, but *you* should mingle," he instructed me, and his eyes took on a hard edge as he looked at me before turning sharply to approach two ancient-looking, pale-haired vampires. Everything about them was pale, and there was a distinct soft odor of decay, like rotting leaves when nature had finally given up.

Interesting… Higher-ups? Suddenly, my forced presence here didn't seem like such a waste of my time. I'd have something to tell Nic and Sebastian if I played my cards right, anyway.

I walked through the rooms downstairs, building a mental map of the place. Or that was what I told myself. I was also keeping a watch for Esmé… and Sam. But not actually Sam. Not like I was really concerned or anything. Just that someone had to watch out for her on an evening like this. She was completely addicted to vampire venom. This environment would be very bad for her indeed.

I shoved aside the sadness at not seeing her. That was a completely inappropriate emotion. I was happy she wasn't here. Happy she was spared this because it would only hasten her death, and I didn't think she was ready for that eventuality just yet.

"Kyle!" Brock yelled my name.

Fuck. I hadn't intended to wander right into his line of sight. I was only scoping the place out… *And checking for Sam.* I banished the unwelcome whisper from my mind again.

Brock chuckled and shoved a woman into my arms. I caught her on instinct and pulled her to my chest rather than let her momentum unbalance me. I glanced down at red hair and my throat dried.

"Sam?" I only mouthed the word, but she turned and looked at me.

*Not Sam.*

Of course, not Sam. The hair was too bright, not classy enough, and she reeked of cheap perfume.

"What are you waiting for?" Brock took a step closer, the challenge in his posture obvious. "Indulge." He gestured impatiently. "Dig in! Enjoy! Bon appétit!"

I shook my head and started to set the unknown woman back onto her feet.

"Take. A. Drink. Kyle." Brock bit every word out.

When I made no move to the woman's neck, a growl reverberated through his chest.

"What's wrong?"

I met his gaze and shrugged. "Nothing. Just might need a clear head rather than get drunk tonight."

"When you're offered blood, you take blood." He spoke through gritted teeth as he indicated the woman I still hadn't let go of.

She giggled sleepily, releasing warm, alcohol-laced breath over my face. I grimaced and turned away.

"Where are your instincts, man? We're vampires. Take the blood. Your instincts are to take blood." He grabbed the woman's arm and yanked her toward him. "Those should be *your instincts*." He lowered his face over her neck, trailing his tongue up the path of her jugular.

I glanced away then back at him.

Slowly, he turned his head until he was looking directly at me. "I've heard the Baton Rouge King takes his blood from a bag. We know that only Duponts do that. Blackbloods, *my* people, take from the vein." His words were a direct challenge, and his eyes narrowed to show he knew that. "Only Duponts don't obey their instincts," he said again, his voice dangerously quiet.

He wanted me to prove myself to him. Right here. Right now.

Well, shit. I was dancing dangerously close to blowing my cover, and I couldn't let that happen.

"Fucking new pussy king," I growled as I drew the woman toward me again.

She laughed and flung her arms around my neck. "Well, hello," she purred as she threw her head back, exposing a long column of neck.

So much fucking neck.

Endless neck…

Tempting. Torture.

I bent down, just smelling her skin. Her pulse beat wildly, and I could *hear* the blood rushing through her veins. My gums ached, and I shook my head slightly to clear it. I could maintain control here. I *had* to maintain control. But my fangs burst through my gums unbidden, and I inhaled at the unexpectedness of it.

Then as I rested my fangs against her skin, I looked Brock direct in the eyes. His pupils dilated but he grinned and nodded approvingly.

I nearly heaved at his obvious pleasure at what I was about to do, but I swallowed against it and tried to force myself to focus. If I could just concentrate on something else. Or pretend. If I could make Brock *think* I'd taken blood, I'd be just fine. Yes, that was a plan. I'd fake it. Then everything would be okay.

But instead I bit down, and I watched that grinning bastard the whole time.

Blood flooded my mouth, and I groaned while adjusting my grip on the woman to get a better angle.

"Yes," she murmured, and my cock twitched.

No bagged blood tasted like this. It was the perfect temperature, the perfect sweetness, the perfect consistency sliding down my throat. I gulped and gulped again. It was just the most amazing thing…

*Camille.*

Her face flashed into my mind.

So pale. So still.

Because I'd killed her.

I wrenched my mouth from the redhead's neck and thrust her to the floor. I couldn't be here. I couldn't do this.

I ran from the house and even the closed gate didn't prevent me from leaving.

I scaled it and I ran. I just fucking ran. Could still taste the sweetness, still smell the copper scent of the blood.

I craved.

Holy hell, I *wanted.*

I stopped and doubled over, gasping for air. Heaving in every breath like it might be my last. Or like it might save me.

Then I glanced up.

Oh, fuck no.

My hands tightened into fists.

I was in trouble and outside the very last place I should ever be.

# Chapter 10 - Sam

I was awake and it was sudden. The sound of my breathing filled my ears as my heart beat rapidly, and I blinked in the dark. Something was different. Someone was… here. I moved so quickly I startled myself, squashing against the wall as I tried to take up less space in my narrow twin bed.

I'd found the broken frame next to a dumpster and carried it home piece by piece because Esmé had only provided a mattress on the floor. But I was probably lucky for that much.

I widened my eyes, not even blinking as I tried to stare into the dark. But it was soft and muffled and messed with my focus. Someone was there, hiding in the shadows, breathing softly. And it wasn't Esmé. She would have just put the lights on and shouted at me. She didn't hold back, and she never watched me sleep.

"Who's there?" I whispered the words so quietly even I could barely hear them. Fear had paralyzed my voice.

The shadows in the room changed and shifted with the way the wind pushed the clouds over the moon. My curtainless window created the shapes on my wall, but when a shaft of moonlight finally permeated the dark, I sucked in a desperate breath.

A figure moved forward, and my heart rate ramped up to something painful as it hammered against the inside of my ribs, knocking so hard it almost rattled my teeth as well.

"Shit." The word was little more than a squeak.

Red eyes glowed in the dark but there was something familiar about the way the man held himself. Something that had my defenses lowering at the exact time I should have been walling myself up without access to a door so I could keep him out.

"K…Kyle?" I stuttered his name out as a question.

I was pretty sure it was him, but he had never looked at me with those eyes — not the ones I was used to seeing when Esmé wanted to feed. But there was something more in Kyle's gaze, an answering desire rushed through me, tightening my core and pulsing between my legs.

But no. He wouldn't want this. Wouldn't want me. Not someone else's thrall. What we were doing was merely play. It was a ruse only because Esmé had told us to act that part.

Only… oh my God… It suddenly felt like I could have every single thing I wanted. Kyle was here, wasn't he? He was pretty much offering himself on a plate. There were trumpeters trumpeting, and the written invitation was in the mail.

Still. I couldn't just let him do this if he thought it was necessary or something else was responsible for his behavior. What if he didn't actually want me? That thought was mortifying, but I needed to make sure it wasn't the case. I sat up and clutched my ratty blanket to me, trying to ignore the mix of known and unknown stains my movement revealed on the mattress.

"Kyle?" I tried again, my voice stronger. "Kyle? Why are you here? Is there a problem? Is something wrong with Esmé? Brock?" I spat that man's name out. I hoped there was a fucking problem with Brock.

But Kyle didn't speak. He just moved slowly closer, almost gliding toward me, like the alpha predator he was.

I closed my eyes for a beat as my chest tightened. Shit. I'd seen Esmé in this mode. It was either going to hurt or feel really, *really* good. And Kyle being a guy… I had my money on really good.

His fangs glinted as moonlight poured into the room again, and I grew wet, reacting to the promise of venom and the unfamiliar suggestion of sex. I almost reached for him, but instead I sat frozen against the wall, watching him move slowly closer.

When he reached me, he leaned forward, his eyes meeting mine. I didn't flinch away at his proximity. I wanted this. I *welcomed* it. Hell, I'd been waiting for it. Just never thought I'd get it.

I dropped my head slowly to one side, revealing my neck in invitation, and he growled low, the noise rumbling through his chest and adding to my excitement. Maybe I should have been scared. But I wasn't. Something about Kyle tugged me toward him despite the danger he posed. Like the danger was an extra aphrodisiac — not that I needed it.

He brought his fingers to trace the outer curve of my neck, and I moaned softly at the gentle touch, closing my eyes again so I could soak up the sensation of his skin against mine.

He gasped a little, just the smallest inhales of breath, and power filled my chest. I affected this giant of a man, this immortal being, and he wanted me.

It was like no one else had ever wanted me… And if they had, they no longer mattered.

Something soft touched my neck, and my eyes flickered open as Kyle's lips pressed against me again, as his tongue swept out and drew goosebumps. I shivered, and he cupped my breast with his hand.

I let loose an exhale at the answering prickle of desire that ran through my body, and when his thumb swept over my hardening nipple, I leaned closer to him, pushing myself into his hold.

Shit. I'd taken part in the odd fumble but nothing that did this to me, nothing that led to me offering myself. I wanted to be taken. I wanted to gift wrap myself, a present for him to open. I wanted to be that good... for *him* to want *me*.

But even as those thoughts crowded into my head, I tried to push them away. I needed to be transactional about this and not get caught up in the fake romance of it all. This was an experience I'd always wanted. That could be enough.

It *would* be enough. I could die with this damn virginity thing ticked off my bucket list.

Kyle pressed closer, his kisses moving up my neck to my jaw and along to my mouth. I was eager for him, ready, parting my lips when he reached them and covered them with his. And he kissed me like he really meant it as his tongue teased against mine, the slow caresses expert and teasing me to want more. I answered him, matching his kisses with the kind of confidence I'd never known.

Where my breathing had been ill-timed before or I didn't know what to do with my hands, now everything worked. I didn't even think about each breath. Only Kyle existed as I tugged him closer, drawing him to lie against me on the bed. My fingertips clutched against his scalp, smoothing over the scar there.

He threw a leg over me, anchoring me to the mattress, and his erection jutted against my hip as he ground against me. I wanted to work my hand between us, to take the bulge into my palm, but I didn't dare. Kyle wasn't mine to touch that way. Not really.

But he touched me again, running his hand up my thigh underneath the fabric of the oversized T-shirt I'd thrown on to sleep in, and my breath hitched in a harsh gasp. He didn't seem to be stopping.

"What are you doing?" I whispered.

For a moment I thought he might not reply. Then…

"This." And he didn't stop.

I relaxed a little beneath him, using his distraction to move my hand to his waist. I stopped there, warring sensations of desire and fear playing within me. I wanted him to complete his slow journey to between my legs. Not even trying to hide my eagerness, I parted them for him.

But I also wanted to hold him in my hand, to feel the weight of him and the heat as he throbbed with the need to be inside me. That was what I wanted to discover there, anyway. That his desire matched mine.

He moved, shifting his weight down my body, and I clutched at his head, not finding a grip on his close-cropped hair.

My throat dried. "What are you doing?" It was the same question as before.

"Minding my own business." His words gave nothing away but then his fingers gripped the outsides of my thighs, and he moved my body as he wanted it.

I closed my eyes and threw my forearm over my face, hiding suddenly, as he settled between my legs and kissed me in an intimate way I couldn't have imagined. My whole body heated at the realization of where his head was… where his lips were. I released a breath as his tongue toyed with my clit, lapping against it before he sucked it into his mouth.

The next breath I released was a soft moan, and his arm snaked up my body until his hand held my breast, pushing against it almost roughly, but I wanted more. More touches, more pressure, more pleasure.

As if he could sense my need, the hand on my breast moved, and his finger probed at my entrance instead. He pushed it inside me gently before pulling back and pressing forward again, each slow movement agonizing when I wanted him all the way, as much as I could take.

Then I gasped as he touched something inside me that sent out a wave of heat that short-circuited my thoughts. He touched it again, pressing harder, and my muscles tensed. I bit my lip, trying to stem another sound of pleasure as I writhed gently against him, my hips moving on their own.

Every time he touched me, another bolt of desire coursed through me. It was like he'd known a secret about me even I hadn't. Like he'd unlocked something no one else would have known was there.

He moved again, and the sound of a zipper being drawn down filled the room, the teeth parting noisily before the rustle of fabric followed and the sound of his pants hitting my bedroom floor.

I held my breath as he moved over me, the hard heat of his erection dragging over my thigh as he crawled back up my body.

"Hello." My voice was just a breath, but he didn't reply.

His lips were on mine again, something desperate, urgent, as the weight of him dropped between my legs and he nudged the head of his cock against me as though he was seeking permission.

Yes. *Fuck, yes.* He had that permission. I parted my legs farther, eager to feel him inside me. When he pushed forward, it was slow and short before he pulled back and forward again a little more. So slow I almost wanted to sink my fingers into his ass and stop him from pulling back, but he was careful and he was gentle with me, and where I'd been told to expect pain, there was none.

There was only pleasure.

None of the gossip I'd heard had spoken of the simple pleasure of just having a man inside my body, but each movement Kyle made spilled another gasp or sigh from my mouth, and I wanted more. I tilted my hips up to meet him, and his breathing came faster.

My eyes had been closed like I was still hiding, but I opened them now, and our gazes met. The heat in his eyes was still red. But he hadn't moaned or murmured my name. He'd been almost silent, his breathing a little heavier, but it was like he was concentrating, totally focused on our bodies.

His eyes were like hot coals, and desire heated me again, skittering underneath my skin like a shower of sparks. That was definitely a look I knew, and I offered him another invitation, rolling my head to the side and exposing my neck.

The next breath he inhaled was shakier, and I wasn't sure he was going to take from me. But I wanted that venom, and worse, I wanted Kyle. I wanted his cock inside me as he drank from my vein.

"Please," I whispered. "Please do it, Kyle."

He groaned as I said his name, and the tip of one of his fangs grazed my skin before he moaned again and sank them both into me.

My pleasure spiraled quickly, taking me to heights I'd never known before. It was like being on a runaway train, a complete loss of my control as the noise of Kyle drawing my blood filled my ears and his body moving in mine created an entirely new friction.

My muscles all clenched and pleasure pulsed a fast beat, tightening my body around Kyle as he released a muffled moan against my skin. He moved a couple more times, slow and steady… like he was teasing himself before he pressed a last soft kiss to my lips and shifted his weight from me.

The loss of him was unexpected, and I wrapped my arms around myself to try to combat it. I moved from basking in his warmth to trying to control my shivers.

He retreated to the shadows and even though the red color in his eyes had died away, I could still track him. I pulled my blanket back around myself and sat up again, trying to control the cold permeating my whole being now. It seemed to sink in, bone deep. Perhaps right to my soul.

Except, no. There was something else there, where I would have expected my soul to be. Something warm that reminded me of Kyle. Something I'd never gotten from any time Esmé had fed from me. It was like he'd embedded part of himself within me — more than just the physical evidence of what we'd just done.

He watched me, but he didn't speak, and another shiver rippled through me.

I wrapped my arms around my knees and made my body as small as possible, trying to conserve what little heat I had left. My core temperature had plummeted. "What's going on, Kyle?" I sounded tired, but I didn't have time for male crap. This was more than just rolling over and going to sleep.

He was so distant that he'd actually moved away, and the gap between us was filled with emptiness and frigid air.

He didn't speak, and I patted the mattress beside me.

"At least come and sit down. I know we didn't exactly plan this, but it happened. We can't take it back, and you standing over there in the naughty corner won't help anything." I stopped speaking.

Had he really found it that bad? Like standing in the shadows avoiding me was going to help somehow? Like he could unimagine it all or just pretend it hadn't happened?

"I don't need to sit down." His voice was gruff, still thick from him speaking around his fangs.

I lifted my head, jutting my chin out. "Yeah, you do. We've apparently got some stuff we should discuss."

"No!" He blurted the word. "Like you said, it happened. We didn't plan it, but it happened anyway. Let's just leave it here."

I nodded like I was considering his request, but what the actual hell? "Sure, let's just leave it here." I took a deep breath. Time to try to shock him into communicating with me. "Let's forget I was a virgin until about ten minutes ago and now I'm not."

He sucked in a breath, and I waited for him to say something, but the only sound I heard was his quiet, regular breathing.

"Okay." I pushed harder. "If that's the way you feel, you should just leave." My finger shook as I pointed in the direction of the door, so I pulled my hand back to my side.

I wouldn't be anything but confident and in control right now.

"If you aren't willing to talk to me, don't ever bother talking to me again." It was a bold declaration. And maybe I was stupid for calling his bluff... but I wanted to know more.

Why had he come here tonight? What had just happened? That was more than playing Esmé's game... More than just pretending to be my boyfriend. He'd made me feel alive and like I mattered for the first time in months.

He breathed out like he didn't know what to do. I couldn't tell whether it was disappointment or relief, actually, and I ended up not caring because he emerged from the shadows but only to grab his pants from where they were balled up on the floor. He shoved his legs into them, his movements rough and jerky, and the noise of the zipper fastening didn't sound near as seductive as when he'd drawn it down.

He dragged his boots back on and backed his way toward the door. I couldn't tell if he tried to speak, but maybe he did. It pleased me to think he might have spoken to me or wanted to, anyway.

The door clicked softly closed behind him and I sighed heavily. Well, shit. That hadn't ended exactly like I'd hoped. But even that thought couldn't steal the experience from me. I still had all of my memories of how Kyle had felt over me, inside me, and I closed my eyes as I allowed myself to remember his kisses and his touch.

I wanted those thoughts to transport me far away.

I'd just started to relax and sink back toward sleep when my door burst open, and my light clicked on. I sat up abruptly, ripped from my memories as Esmé stormed toward me. She stopped and her nostrils flared as she inhaled.

"What. The. Fuck." She breathed in again and her eyes became red with fury.

She grabbed the rickety table I kept by the door and threw it at me, the things that had been on top of it spilling in all directions across my room.

"What the fuck? Like seriously?" She grabbed a book from the floor and launched that at me too as I lifted my arms to protect my head. "You are *mine*, Sam. I own you, remember? After what you did, you owe me. And I'm going to collect everything you owe… but slowly. Slower now." The smile she flashed my way promised pain, and metal bands of fear wrapped around my chest. "Other vampires don't drink from you. You're no one's bloodwhore but mine."

I winced as her words slapped against me. I hadn't been a bloodwhore tonight. *I hadn't.* Kyle hadn't used me as that.

"No other vampires." Esmé's eyes gleamed as she advanced toward me. She stopped suddenly, her nostrils flaring wide and her eyes filling with hate. "A mate? A fucking *mate?* After you condemned me to a lifetime without one? How fucking dare you." She raised her arm and swung it back.

I held my hands out, trying to ward off the blow she was about to deliver as she ranted illogically. She could clearly smell the sex. There was no reasoning with Esmé when she was like this. The best I could hope for was preventing her from spiraling into a full bloodlust state and to minimize any damage she might do to me.

"No other vampires," I repeated, but she smiled at me, her expression filled with malice.

Then she flew a me, her hands twisted into claws, her cheekbones prominent and sharp. Esmé was a monster. She hadn't held back, and she could kill me now. I almost laughed. At least I was no longer a virgin, right?

I flung myself out of her way and prepared to fend off her attack, my position defensive, but she was too strong.

She ripped me from the bed and held me tight against her as she lowered her head toward my neck. I screamed, suddenly afraid of the end. *Not this way.*

A roar of rage filed the room, and Esmé's grip on me disappeared as Kyle pushed her halfway across the room until she hit the wall opposite me and crumpled to the floor.

Kyle. Holy fuck. Kyle had come back for me.

Esmé stood, each of her movements wobbly, and she bared her fangs at Kyle as she laughed. She lunged at him, raking her hands in front of her, her extended nails slashing at his face. He danced backward then grasped her wrists in his hands and spun her, so her back was to his chest.

He leaned forward, his lips against her right ear. "Off you go, Esmé," he murmured. "Run along." He released her abruptly, thrusting her forward as he did, and she snarled before speed-walking through the open door.

Kyle turned to me, and I tried to grin, but my mouth wobbled instead, and I covered it with my hand as I fought not to cry. I'd been through too much in this house. I couldn't cry because one person did one nice thing for me. But kindness was always worse than pain.

He strode toward me, and for the second time in my life, he lifted me against his chest and cradled me there. Then we left the house, and I closed my eyes as the front door banged shut behind us.

I'd been wrong before about freedom.

*This* was it.

# Chapter 11 - Kyle

Fuck. Actual *fuck*. The door to Sam's slum of a home closed behind me and I bent over, my hands on my knees as I shook my head. I needed to get away. Far away. Because… fuck.

I nearly sank to my knees.

She was my… My… I'd known it from the very moment I pushed my cock inside her body. I shook my head again. Fuck.

I started to walk away. I had to get out of there.

Sam wasn't just a thrall, a *human*. She was my fucking mate.

I didn't want a mate. I didn't need one. I'd seen Nic and Sebastian take their mates and it had screwed everything up. Humans were bad news for vampires. Human *mates* were worse.

And I'd just screwed it all up myself. So. Fucking. Much. She'd been a virgin. I'd taken her in a haze of bloodlust, and she'd been a virgin. I couldn't give that back to her. I'd taken her first experience and I hadn't made it special, and I couldn't fucking give that back.

There wasn't a do-over for Sam to lose her virginity at the right time, in the right way.

To the right fucking guy… And that right guy would never be me.

But guilt gnawed at my gut and my fangs ached with desire at just the thought of her.

A scream pierced my awareness and I turned toward the sound before I even thought about making the movement. Sam… she needed me. I couldn't ignore her.

Every impulse in my body urged me back toward her and I couldn't deny it.

I needed to rescue my mate. Her sheer fright vibrated every molecule in my body and there wasn't another thought in my head. Only Sam.

I sped back to her room. The door was already open, and I roared my fury as Esmé bent her neck, lowering her fangs toward my mate.

*My* mate.

*Mine.*

I ripped Esmé away and flung her against the nearest wall. She looked like a broken doll as she folded in on herself and lay quietly on the floor. But I didn't care about Esmé—only that she was away from Sam.

Then Esmé stood, a threat to Sam once more.

I positioned myself in front of her, and she bared her fangs at me like that sort of behavior would scare me. Holy shit. I wasn't the best at guessing the ages of other vampires — I didn't actually care — but Esmé looked like she'd still been in diapers while I'd been fighting in the great war.

She took advantage of my perusal of her, advancing forward, her hands slashing toward me as she displayed her claws, but she hadn't thought her actions through. I backed away, taking the space I needed to defend myself, to regain the aggressive advantage.

I grabbed hold of her wrists — I was faster than she was, and I took her by surprise. Then I whipped her around, my arms tightening around her body so she couldn't escape. Every fiber of my being was aware of Sam behind us, but I needed to eliminate this threat before I could go to her.

But shit. I couldn't kill Esmé. My entire mission depended on this fucking woman, this woman who I'd watched abuse Sam. Abuse my mate.

I leaned in, so close my fangs almost brushed against her ear. I vibrated with my anger, and her teeth rattled in response.

"Off you go, Esmé." I could barely contain my rage enough to keep my voice down. "Run along." I pushed her toward the door before turning to snatch Sam into my arms, where she belonged.

She relaxed against me, and I almost folded myself over her, protecting her as best I could with my body.

I couldn't leave her alone with Esmé again. Maybe I couldn't leave her alone at all. I could protect her as long as she was with me.

I hurried through the disgusting rooms of Sam's house, needing to get her away, to my place. I almost laughed. My place was no better. More disgusting rooms. She deserved to live somewhere like Sebastian's house — fuck that, somewhere better — but I couldn't go anywhere. My mission depended on maintaining my cover.

It seemed ridiculous, though, that Sam's best chance at safety, that the safest place for her, was with *me*.

But I knew it was. She was my mate, and it was my duty… my *intense need* to keep her safe.

And with me.

***

The streets between Sam's house and mine were quiet — that same *too quiet* I was all too used to around here. But I needed that quiet tonight as I sped along at vampire speed, an unfamiliar desperation to get from point A to point B spurring me along.

I climbed the rickety steps to the apartment, cradling my precious cargo. So precious, so fragile, and with the ability to bring the entire house of cards I'd just built for myself spinning down to the ground.

The front door stuck in the frame as usual, but I shouldered it open, pushing into the dank room beyond. In that moment, I was so ashamed of this place. It was only ever meant to be a place to hide out in, for fucking *Kyle Durg*. Never somewhere for me to bring my mate. She deserved so much more.

I lowered Sam to the sofa that looked like it had been rescued from an actual fire and wished I had something better to offer her. But she'd never been part of the plan.

She looked up at me, her eyes wide and almost vacant. Like shock had set in.

"You'll be okay," I murmured, hoping those words were true.

I really had no idea how she'd be. She was a human pet, in thrall to another vampire, and I'd already stormed my way through all of the etiquette in the situation, breaking every protocol and putting myself — and any other Dupont loyalist who wandered too close to my carnage — in danger.

But unusually, that didn't seem to matter. Where was my desire for control? My usual self-restraint? The mission was suddenly second.

Second to Sam.

"Can I get you something to eat?" I asked as I ran the back of my fingers down her cheek, the touch fleeting, just enough to get her to focus on me for a moment.

But she merely looked at me, her green eyes still wide, horror lingering there. She parted her lips like she might speak but said nothing. And then she started to shiver, the shudders uncontrollable, like someone had inserted a core of ice into her body.

I cast about for a blanket, something to wrap around her and preserve what little heat her emaciated body could generate, but there was nothing in this room I wanted to touch Sam. Instead, I removed my hoodie and helped her into it, a small part of me finding just as much pleasure in the fact that her scent would blend with mine as the idea that I could do something practical to help her.

"I should get you something to eat," I muttered as some overwhelming desire to provide for her took root in my chest. "You need to eat."

But my kitchen offered a fat lot of nothing. I didn't even need to check the cupboards to know that, and thralls didn't drink blood. They weren't vampires. I grimaced as I took in the almost pearlescent sheen to her skin. There was no way she was properly nourished. Esmé's antagonism towards her made no sense at all. Not to the degree to where she'd essentially starve her own source of nutrition to death.

It was like she was actively punishing Sam.

My chest tightened at the thought of someone harming her on purpose. Not on my watch.

What the hell was the restaurant called that she'd liked before? *Mario's? Mann's?* I couldn't make her anything here — the lack of food was the biggest issue but not my only one. The kitchen looked like it was waiting for health inspectors to come in and condemn it.

I slipped my phone out of my pocket. I couldn't exactly order in, but neither could I allow my newfound mate to go hungry. Not now that I knew who she was and the feelings she stirred in me.

Even Camille had never made me feel so protective, and I'd loved Camille.

But this was… This was more.

"S'up, dude," Jason answered on the first ring, and I turned away from Sam, half shielding my phone with my hand.

I cleared my throat. My contacts weren't really supposed to be used as delivery boys. After all, that was a role I hated being forced into. Just random errands? Try some other shmuck... I was a trained soldier. Yet here I was, about to ask the same of Jason.

"I need a favor." I looked at Sam and knew she was worth it.

Jason made a noise that could have been annoyance or acknowledgment, and I plowed on. I hated asking for help. I kept to myself and didn't need anybody else.

Not until today, anyway.

"I need a delivery."

"Hmm." He made another noncommittal noise.

"I need take-out from that diner I can't remember the name of. The one in the train car."

"Manny's?" He suddenly seemed interested.

And why the hell *wouldn't* he be interested? I was a vampire, undercover in a group of dangerous vampires, requesting food that none of us would eat.

"Can you do it?" I waited for him to make another noise. "Grab a pen and I'll tell you what I need." I recited Sam's order from the other night.

It was like I could still taste what little of the bacon cheeseburger I'd eaten on my tongue. Even that night, even though I'd told myself it was for appearances and just so Sam didn't fucking die the next time Esmé fed, something had felt… different. I'd told her things about myself. Things I'd wanted to share, wanted her to know.

I ended the call and checked on Sam again. She looked tired, but I wanted to keep her awake so she could get some food. For the shock she'd had as much as anything.

"Are you okay?" I walked over to her but hesitated to touch her as she turned her attention to me. "Are you in any… pain?" I gestured uselessly down her body.

I hadn't meant to take something I couldn't give back.

She shook her head—but slowly, like it took effort. "Nope."

We remained in awkward silence, her sitting rigidly on the sofa, me leaning against the wall, which was either damp or just really cold. I didn't want to guess.

The knock on the door didn't startle me. I'd sensed Jason and smelled dog long before he made a sound, but Sam flinched, and her fearful eyes grew even wider.

"It's okay. It's someone I know." But shit, I hadn't thought this through at all.

Sam would meet Jason now. That put him in danger while she was still so close to Esmé. She was my mate, but I couldn't exactly trust a thrall — even though that admission to myself pained me.

I opened the door and Jason stepped inside. "What's with your strange impulse to eat?" He bit the question off abruptly as he reached the end of his sentence when his gaze fell on Sam. "Oh, shit."

I nodded. Yeah. *Shit* about had it covered. "She's hungry." I only spoke the two words and he nodded as his nostrils flared. Then he turned his gaze on me, his eyes narrowed.

"Kyle?" He filled my name with a million unspoken questions — many of them which didn't even need an answer, and I brushed him away with a quick gesture.

"No comment, Jason. But Sam needs to eat."

"I'll say." He stepped forward and offered her the paper bag and chocolate malted shake I'd requested he pick up. "What's going on, dude?" He spoke to me as Sam tore the paper bag and the aroma of curly fries and meat drifted into the room.

She made a noise of pleasure and bit into her burger as I took Jason's elbow and led him away.

"She's a thrall."

He glanced over his shoulder as I spoke. "I can see that."

I hissed my displeasure at his assessing gaze on my mate.

"She's also my mate," I clarified.

"Oh, I know that too."

I sighed. Sure, he did. Any vampire who came in contact with Sam now would know she was a vampire mate, and that I'd staked my claim.

"Looks like you just made your mission a helluva lot more complicated."

I cast my most scathing glance at Jason. "At least I don't smell like a dog."

He laughed. "That's the best you can do?"

I opened my mouth to add another insult, a better one, but my phone buzzed from my pocket. "Saved by the bell," I muttered.

"Mmhmm." Jason didn't sound convinced.

I glanced at my phone screen, expecting a name but just seeing a number. I'd forgotten I was doing this whole fucking burner phone thing.

I showed it briefly to Jason. "Want to guess?"

He squinted a little. "Can only be Temple or Seb."

I didn't want to speak to either of the other two guys. There was too much going on here now, especially with the Sam complication, and I'd definitely created a complication.

My greeting was little more than a grunt, and Sebastian didn't introduce himself, which was good etiquette for the mission but was more likely due to his anger, given the rapid way he launched into talking.

"You dick!" He didn't even pause to take a breath. "You intercepted my latest shipment and stole from me."

I sighed. "Orders from the boss."

"That was expensive stuff."

I rolled my eyes. I hadn't expected anything less.

"And you left two of my men for dead."

I hadn't, but I wasn't about to have that conversation like this. I rolled my eyes again as Sebastian reiterated what my *little stunt* had just cost him.

"Cool." I interrupted his rant. "I'll keep you updated." I didn't have time for this shit. I was doing my part, and if Sebastian was annoyed that I was sticking to the plan to infiltrate the Blackbloods, that was on him.

I ended the call, and Jason whistled. "Balls that clank," he said then chuckled.

That earned him another glare. "Well, if Sebastian will behave like a prize prick," I muttered.

"And that might be my cue." He stood from where he'd managed to make himself comfortable on a rickety dining room chair that he'd dragged out from some dark corner of this hovel. "Sam——" He turned to her and nearly offered her a fucking bow. "It was nice to meet you."

She just nodded vaguely but her eyes were thoughtful as she watched me. "Nice to meet you, too." But she didn't look at him for long, like she wasn't quite sure if she could trust him.

Before I shoved the door closed behind Jason, he melted seamlessly into the shadows, even smoother than usual, like he was picking up bad habits off those damn wolves. Then I propped the chair he'd been using under the handle. It wouldn't stop a vampire from gaining access if they wanted to get in, but it would provide a little warning.

"So." Sam's voice was quiet but commanded my immediate attention. "What do we do now?" Some of her color had returned and all the food was gone.

I didn't know if Jason had helped himself to a couple of her fries. They held no nutritional value for him, but it was the exact kind of thing he'd do anyway.

But yeah. What would we do now? I rubbed my hand over my head, unwilling to tell her that I hadn't thought any further than keeping her with me, *saving her.*

"Kyle?" She spoke my name like a plea, like I had all the answers.

And I should have had those answers for her. I'd removed her from her home and brought her to mine. Only a fool would put her in that much danger without a plan.

Turned out I was such a fool. I sighed and shook my head. "I don't know."

Her mouth pinched a little at the corners, and I rushed on.

"But I'm not letting you go back to Esmé. You can't go back there. She'll kill you." I withheld my shudder afterward, even though the idea of Sam's death had a visceral effect on me.

When she smiled, it was sad, and her eyes glistened. "But I have to go back."

I shook my head, refusing to believe her words. That was a load of crap. *I* had her now. I'd found her. She was my mate. Mine.

"I do, Kyle." She used my name again and a small part of me melted.

I never fucking melted. I shook my head again, denying her words. Like I could change them by simply believing them not true.

But her sad smile returned, and she shrugged, the gesture despondent. "The lack of venom will kill me. And

Esmé needs to feed. If she can't have me, she might kill me, anyway."

A growl rumbled through me. I had no fucking time for this logic.

"That's not going to happen. You're staying here, with me, where I can keep you safe. Esmé's not the only vampire in town." My gums ached with the need to bare my fangs.

"Oh my God! You bloodsuckers are all alike!" Sam screwed her hands into fists and stood from the sofa, my hoodie far too big on her small frame. "You all want to control me and keep me with you. But you know what?" Her eyes flashed with green fire. "We might have had sex and everything, but I don't owe you anything at all. You don't get to tell me what to do. I can make my own decisions and I certainly don't belong to you. One night in bed together doesn't mean anything — even if you're playing the big bad rescuer now." She huffed her punctuation as she finished talking, and I stepped back, suddenly calm.

"Yes, it does," I said. "The sex means everything. You're my mate."

# Chapter 12 - Sam

A laugh burbled out of me. What the hell? "And what's that supposed to mean?" I shoved a hand through my hair, snagging my fingers on the tangles in the ends. "A *mate*? I don't think so." I shook my head as I still worked at my hair. "It was just sex."

All of these vampires were crazy.

I was a thrall. There was no way I was anyone's mate. Certainly not this guy's… This hot, hot guy who I'd willingly given my first time to… He was a vampire. I couldn't stand vampires. One of them was slowly killing me — and enjoying every fucking second of my death.

"Sam?" When he spoke, my voice held a question. A whole lot of questions, but I didn't have any answers.

"That's crap." The words exploded from me. "I'm no vampire mate." There was no fucking way. "I've seen vampire mates and they're —" I paused. "Well, duh! They're *vampires*. Or they wanted to be one."

Like Sean. He'd have willingly given his life to join Esmé for eternity.

He *had* given his life. Only not in the way he'd intended. And now I was giving my life instead. As well. *Something.* Involvement with Esmé had killed both of us.

I turned away from Kyle. Maybe this was even more cruel because I was Esmé's thrall. No one would actually want me, and to tease me about it, or to joke or whatever this was… Well, it was just unnecessary.

"No, Sam." But he sounded gentle, and he barely made a sound as he approached where I was sitting. He crouched down beside me. "No, Sam," he said again. "Vampire mates start off as human."

"Well, duh," I said again, my irritation ringing out loud, and nearly fell into his brown eyes as they softened despite my harsh mood. They'd never held so much expression before, almost liquid with a plea for my understanding. "Humans with a screw loose. I'm a thrall. Not just any old human. I'm not a mate…" But I stopped speaking.

Well, damn. What if there was a genetic connection? First Sean, now me? How the hell hadn't I considered it before? Not that it would have mattered. I hated vampires. Or at least I did now. Being a mate wasn't something I would have ever wanted to consider or explore.

"My brother," I mumbled.

"What about him?" Kyle lifted a hand like he might stroke my cheek. Then he sighed and dropped it. "I didn't know you have a brother."

"Had." I sighed. "It's a long story." I shook my head. "Except, no. It really isn't. Esmé took a shine to him. Said he was her mate. I'm the reason he met her." I shrugged. It also meant I was the reason he'd died, but I always screwed that guilt up as tight as I could and shoved it somewhere dark and deep inside my head. "He's also the reason we're still tied together like this. I saved Esmé after she failed to save Sean in the attack that killed him. And now she hates me for the fact that she's still alive." I expected Kyle to defend me somehow, to tell me what a bitch Esmé was, but instead he sucked in a breath then remained quiet for a moment like he was working out the best way to say something.

"Losing a mate can send even the most stable vampire crazy. It…" He hesitated and rubbed his fingers over his scar, like he seemed to do when he was stressed or frustrated. "It explains a lot about her."

"I lost my *brother*." I couldn't keep the annoyance from my words. "My family."

He nodded. "I know. And I'm sorry. I'm… Two mates in one family. You're unusual."

I shrugged and my lips moved into a stiff smile of resentment. "Yeah, what are the odds?"

"Sebastian's mate was a human witch before he turned her. And Nic's — the king's," he clarified like I wouldn't know he meant Nicolas Dupont himself. "Both Sebastian and Nic mated recently."

That much I knew — Esmé had spoken of it at length in the most bitter and loathing of terms. She hated mated pairs with a passion.

"What will she do to me?" I didn't need to clarify which *she* I meant.

"Nothing." His reply was immediate. And abrupt as he rose to his full height. "You're with me. I'll take care of you."

Take care of me… The idea sent a thrill of excitement through me, warming me in places that no longer warmed, no matter how many layers I wrapped myself in.

But I didn't want to be turned… Did I? I didn't want to be a bloodsucker. That much, I knew. I didn't want Esmé to be my maker. But Kyle…

I looked at him again, trying to study him discreetly. There was something about him… something that drew me. But maybe it was his kindness and the fierce way he'd taken to protecting me when he really didn't have to. It had been a long time since anyone had done that for me. No wonder I was attracted to this guy. It was like Stockholm syndrome in reverse or some shit, right?

Still, an unexpected shiver of something… anticipation? Desire? Worked through me. It was like my body had decided this was something I wanted — Kyle to turn me, without any input from logic.

I tried to look away from him in case he caught sight of the desire, which I didn't understand, lurking in my eyes.

But he met my gaze and sucked in a breath anyway. "Do you… do you *want* me to turn you?" He sounded more hesitant than I'd ever heard him, suddenly unsure of himself, like my answer really mattered.

"Would I… would I survive it?" I never thought that would be the first question I'd ask, but I hadn't ever considered the idea of being turned, either. I'd only ever discounted it as something I never wanted. But I didn't even need to ask whether Sean would have let himself be turned. Esmé would have done it for him.

I didn't know the ins and outs of their relationship, and I hadn't known their future plans or what they were waiting for. Sean had always seemed as head over heels as Esmé, but maybe he'd been reluctant because of Mom, because of me. Maybe he'd struggled with the idea of vampires. Who knew?

But if Esmé had already turned him before the night of the attack, would he have still been with me now? I almost didn't want to explore that question.

As much as I hated what she was doing to me now, Esmé had never done anything but love Sean. His death had destroyed her, and because I'd condemned her to life without him, she hated me with equal fervor. The same passion that would have driven her to make Sean immortal, their love eternal, had doomed me.

I hadn't answered his question, but Kyle spoke again — without answering mine, either.

"I can turn you if you want," he said. "I can do that for you." There was a strange undercurrent of eagerness in his voice. "But first I have to complete my mission. I need to get rid of Brock. Get rid of Esmé. And not just for Nic anymore. They're dangerous to you, and yes, they're dangerous to all vampires and the Dupont reign. But they could end your world as you are now, a human thrall, or endanger your life as a vampire."

"Esmé?" I whispered her name.

It seemed almost unreal that Kyle wanted to kill her. That Esmé could really die. I couldn't imagine that. She was vengeful and a force to be reckoned with… a vampire. Beings like that didn't just roll over and die.

"It has to be done. Otherwise, you'll be hunted your whole life. You're her thrall, Sam. She'll never just let you go. Just like you need her, she needs you."

"One of us is going to die. It's the only way to end it." I nodded, certainty in my tone as I spoke. And it looked straightforward now. Either Esmé would kill me, or I could somehow help Kyle to kill Esmé because even if I left her, I was going to die from the shock of withdrawals, anyway.

I hadn't expected Kyle's help to be offered like this. I'd planned more of a business arrangement or begging, but something about the situation just felt right, and I didn't want to question it.

*** 

We sat quietly for the next few hours. Well, I sat quietly as the sun rose. Kyle puttered around his apartment. There was nothing here for him to putter with, and I hadn't taken him for a fussy guy, but he busied himself straightening shit and fixing things and bothering over where a chair was placed in the room.

I drew in a breath. The air was dank in here and it sat in my chest like something wet and itchy. But it didn't smell as bad as where I lived, and it didn't burn my throat like I was choking on someone else's puke.

Eventually, Kyle began to slow his movements, as if reluctance had crept into him. Then his mouth set into a grimace. "I need to head out." He didn't quite meet my eyes, and apprehension strummed at my consciousness.

"Where are you going?" I had no right to ask, and I certainly had no right to sound so suspicious.

What Kyle did was very much his own business. But that didn't explain my sudden irrational fear that he might not come back.

"Brock's." He only spoke one word, and he made it quiet, but it filled me with dread.

Just that man's name had the power to frighten me. I tangled my fingers together, working them into painful knots of paper-thin skin and knobbed bone.

"I'm not sure you should go." My voice came out thin too.

He smiled slightly, and it was almost reassuring. Then he shrugged. "I don't really have a choice. I have to go — for appearances' sake, right? It's not like I can stay away today without him sending someone to look for me. It looks more suspicious not to show up to work, right?"

I nodded. Yeah, I got that. He needed to still be the good little soldier, one of Brock's enforcers. But Brock trusted Esmé more than Kyle. If he trusted anyone at all.

But he'd take her word over Kyle's in a heartbeat.

"What about Esmé? What if she gets you in trouble or she tries to get her revenge?" I didn't finish my sentence. None of the endings were pretty, but Kyle nodded as if he'd filled the rest of the words in, anyway.

He didn't need me to spell it out for him. "You don't need to worry about me." He covered my tangled hands with one of his. "I've got this. I can take care of myself." He chuckled, but it wasn't entirely humor.

I didn't doubt his survival skills, so I nodded. There were no words for me to say, and I closed my eyes as he pressed a soft kiss to my temple, like I was concentrating, trying to absorb as much of him as possible through my skin.

After Kyle left, the place was too quiet. I needed to get out of there, but where could I go? I only knew my home, and Esmé was there.

Except I didn't only know my home now. I had somewhere I could go in the Quarter, even if I had to technically pay for the privilege of spending time there.

Naomi.

Getting back to the shop could be risky, but I'd had enough practice sneaking around and losing Brock's goons. And after spending time with Kyle, I was kind of feeling up to a challenge.

I stuck to the shadows like a rat scurrying down a sewer pipe, but I reached Naomi's little shop fairly quickly. *Lettie's*. The name was worked in cursive script on the sign. The bell rang as I entered, and relief washed over me that I was somewhere safe.

I couldn't explain it, but right here felt *safe*.

Naomi glanced up from where she was writing on a clipboard by the register, and a broad smile took control of her mouth.

"Hi, Sam. I'm glad you came back. Your ring is ready." She walked to the door and flipped the sign like she had the first time I'd visited. Then she locked the shop and looked at me expectantly, her eyes bright and friendly. "Come in the back and we'll finish that tea we didn't get to."

I wrinkled my nose and she laughed.

"I'll make a fresh pot." She pushed the curtain aside and gestured for me to follow her. The room back there smelled the exact same as it had the first time. Like magic and spells and potions and *promise*.

She waved toward the table, and I sat down, my gaze darting all over again, taking in the herbs, the books, and the black range, as I relaxed in the warmth of the space.

"You been doing okay?" She lifted the same pot as before onto the range then walked to a dresser of shelves and drawers before opening one of the smallest drawers at the top. She pulled out a small paper bag and slid it across the worn surface of the table to me. "This is your ring." She cocked her head and looked at the small package, her eyes narrow, her tone thoughtful as she spoke again. "It should help with your cravings." Then she poured hot water from the boiling pot to steep the tea, and the fragrance of the leaves filled my nose.

I inhaled again, drawing the rich scent deep into my chest. I missed simple things like this, but maybe Naomi could give some of my old life back to me.

"I also added a protection spell." She glanced over her shoulder at me. "Should help with any vamp that wants to put you under a compulsion." Her smile was wry this time. "Figured you might need it with the type of company you're forced to keep."

I tried to smile at her, but my stomach dropped away. I didn't have the money to pay for extra spells. "I don't think

I can accept —" I started. "I mean, that's very kind but I can't…"

"There's no charge for the things I *choose* to do," she said, her tone firm as she placed a mug of tea in front of me.

I wrapped my hands around the thick clay, warming them. "Thank you," I whispered.

More acts of kindness from people I didn't really know and who had no reason at all to be so good to me.

"Sam, you don't deserve what's happened to you. If I can help in any way, let me know. And if you see a way out, grab it and don't let go." Then she changed the subject. "Have you always lived in New Orleans?"

"My whole life," I answered and smiled, although the movement of my mouth felt tight.

"Oh, yeah? I moved here when I made connections with the local witches." Naomi nodded thoughtfully. "The Midwest always seemed boring compared to tales of the shadows and roaming ghosts of NOLA." She chuckled and the sound was full of memories. "Man, from a small rural farm town to… To this. To magic." She still sounded in awe.

"And did you know about the… other stuff?" I meant supernaturals, although I was pretty sure I didn't have to say it.

She wrinkled her nose and shook her head. "Nope. I might not have come if I had." Then she shrugged. "But enough about them."

I nodded. Somehow, we'd circled back around to vampires, shifters, and the whole dark underbelly of New Orleans as if that was the only thing that existed.

"You like much music?" Naomi tried a different tack.

I shrugged and my own chuckle was regretful. "I used to. Haven't listened to much recently."

Naomi patted my hand. "Well, maybe we can change that for you." Her gaze softened. "I hope we can. I'm going to see what I can do." She laughed, her tone changing. "And how about some clothes first? We might be about the same size?" Her nose wrinkled again, this time a tell that she was probably lying to be kind.

Everything I wore these days hung off me.

But a conversation about clothes was nice and it was normal, and I really needed normal when everything just seemed to have upended.

After I took the last mouthful of my tea, I reached into my purse and drew out some of the money I'd withdrawn from my bank account.

"I need to pay you for the ring." I pushed the money across the table, my movements awkward. If Esmé found out what I was doing, my life would be hell, and surely, I couldn't always rely on Kyle for rescue? I swallowed my anxiety with a convulsive bob of my throat.

"Try the fit." She smiled at me and nodded toward my hands before she even so much as glanced at the bills.

My hands trembled as I slid the ring from the paper bag and slipped it onto my finger. Electricity shimmered through me, and a sense of calm followed the buzz. I breathed out a soft sigh.

"It works?" Naomi clapped her hands in sudden joy, then she chuckled. "I mean, of course it does, but I always worry right up until I know for sure."

"Thank you so much." I looked at the ring on my finger. She'd managed to make it unobtrusive but pretty too. I never wanted to take it off. I pulled her into a hug, surprising myself. I didn't ever seek out the comfort of others. Kyle's was the only recent touch I hadn't hated.

"Thank you," I said again.

"Any time," she said as she met my eyes. "I mean it. You come back here any time at all."

"Thank you." I appeared to have run out of other words, but my repeated appreciation would have to do.

I stood from the table and Naomi grinned before she pushed the curtain aside and led the way across the small shop.

She held the door open, the little bell above ringing a melodious note, and I left quickly, wanting to be back at Kyle's place when he returned home. I glanced at my new ring again, admiring the way it caught the sunlight.

Suddenly, there was a muffled scuffing noise behind me, and I half turned as someone threw a fist into my face. Pain radiated across my cheek as I focused on the two guys, their big bodies penning me against the wall. Brock and Esmé's goons. I heaved in a breath, ready to scream, but one of the men clamped a meaty, smelly palm over my mouth.

"What's this?" One of the guys grabbed my hand and splayed my fingers before one of them ripped my new ring from my finger.

It clinked as it hit the paved ground at my feet, and tears burned the backs of my eyes at its loss.

Then the men wrenched my arms behind my back, and I lost my footing as they dragged me toward an idling car. I scraped my shoes against the ground, trying to find a foothold as my shoulders pulled and ached. Then they shoved me into the backseat of the waiting car, and the second goon slid in after me, ramming my head against the opposite door and forcing me to bend the wrong way to accommodate him.

The car squealed as it pulled away, and my breaths came in rapid pants of fear.

# Chapter 13 – Kyle

I walked up to the closed gates of Brock's compound-style home, adrenaline fueling every step I took, no idea what I would find inside. I could very well have made myself *persona non grata* by stealing Esmé's thrall if she'd already gone tattling to her maker.

The little camera whirred slightly as it focused on me, and I pressed the button on the intercom then stepped back as the huge gate began to slide open before anyone even spoke.

The yard inside was deserted, everywhere quiet, but Brock was leaning against the wall of one of the outbuildings I'd noticed before. The ones where it looked like anything could happen — the outbuildings I didn't particularly want to be inside of, if I was honest with myself.

When Brock smiled, it was with malevolence, his ever-present fangs pressing against his lower lip. I glanced at the main house, but the blank windows gave nothing away. The rest of the Blackblood soldiers could have been watching from inside, or they could all have been asleep and dreaming of brightly colored flowers and white fluffy clouds.

Brock shouldn't have been expecting me, though, so the very fact he was waiting like he was suggested he had more eyes on the street than I knew about. I'd have to be more careful still going forward and tell Jason the same.

"What time do you call this?" He made a big show of checking his watch like we'd had an appointment.

I shrugged. "I'm awake." I grunted the words but made it clear I felt like *I* was doing *him* the favor.

His eyes narrowed and his shoulders tensed but then he nodded and stepped away from the wall. "We're taking things to the next level."

I didn't say anything. Silence was always my advantage.

"Against the Duponts," he clarified before confusion flickered through his gaze like he wasn't used to clarifying things for his subordinates.

Still, I waited. He hadn't given me any information to respond to. I stood at ease before him, my hands clasped behind my back, my feet apart. At ease could still quickly become *on attack* but for now I was his good little soldier, and I wanted him to be confident in that.

His grin widened before he spoke next. "We're going on the offensive and taking out the so-called king's crew."

His words sent a chill through me, but I braced my muscles and stood still, my expression neutral. This morning wasn't about Sam at all, but whether Brock knew it or not, he was still about to test me.

"In fact, we've already started leveling up. Got our first volunteers already." He chuckled darkly as he pushed the door open to the building.

The interior was dark and like everywhere else in this city, it smelled of swamp. The air was warm and wet, and for a moment there didn't seem to be anything in here. An empty outhouse. I readied to run — perhaps I'd walked straight into a trap. But then there was a movement in the corner and as my gaze sharpened, I looked straight into the faces of four vampires.

Four vampires I knew very well.

My soldiers.

Men I'd trained in their techniques. Men I should have been disappointed in that they were now sitting in Brock's makeshift prison, their wrists and feet bound with silver chain.

Men who could fucking give me away with a single word or wrong look now that they'd seen my face.

They all wore gags, though, which made it easier to trust they wouldn't say anything, but their eyes widened as I stood in front of them, and each man went still. I could almost see their minds turning, wondering if I was here to be their savior or their angel of death.

The shuffling and fidgeting stopped, and one by one, each man went still, as if they were waiting for orders from me, which proved at least that I'd trained them well. It wasn't the response I wanted from them right now, though. They needed to continue fearing their situation if they weren't about to give us all away.

"Well, well…" Brock swiveled his gaze to me, something hard in his expression. "What did you just do to them?" His eyes narrowed again like they always did when he seemed to be considering exactly who I was. "This is the quietest they've been. It's like they're waiting for you to speak, *soldier*." He stressed the last word, sarcasm evident in his tone.

I didn't say anything. One wrong word and one of my men could give all of us away. I couldn't even look at them in case they saw my fear. And I was still disappointed in them. Fuck it all. I thought I'd trained them better than this, and now look at them. I didn't even know if I could save them. I couldn't do anything to jeopardize my mission. But neither were my men just disposable.

They'd put me in an impossible position. Their presence here could kill us all.

Brock shifted his weight and folded his arms over his barrel chest. "Kill them all." His words were stark and without inflection… and directed at me. This wasn't an emotive issue for him. "I need to send a message to the Duponts. Sebastian Dupont needs to return to Baton Rouge. New Orleans is ours now."

That was all this was to him. A message. I couldn't fault his tactics. But my position had just gotten worse.

My men. How could I just kill them? And they were clearly thinking the same. They each watched me, their eyes widening. A couple of them even shuffled backward, but the more trusting ones stayed exactly where they were. Those men didn't believe I'd kill them, and that ripped at my insides, because even I didn't know what I was about to do.

The mission to take down the Blackbloods had to come above all else. So much rested on it. I owed Nic everything, and he was depending on me to help secure his reign here. This mission was vital. Critical to the future.

But *my men*.

The door burst open behind us and Esmé entered in a whirlwind of white-blonde hair and some sort of gauzy dress. She moved so fast she was almost a blur, and she growled as she crossed the space toward the imprisoned vampires.

I flipped into a battle-ready stance. There was no telling what she'd do now that she was here, or whether she'd tell Brock about Sam. Maybe I'd need to fight both of them off to get out of here. Well, whatever she was about to do, I was ready.

Except she reached my men, and they cried out as her clawed fingers flashed through the air in front of them, and blood spurted from them, covering us all in the warm, copper-scented fluid. I hadn't expected that.

I wiped my face and let the drips fall to the dusty concrete floor. The rich red splotches shone wetly in a shaft of sunlight that fell through the high, narrow windows.

I was torn between rage and relief. Esmé had killed my men.

But *Esmé* had killed my men. I no longer had to. The job was done.

Rage nearly won out, though, when she finally stopped her frenzied movements and turned to me, a vindictive smile curving her lips. I wanted to tear her apart and seek vengeance for the lost lives of men I had trained and lived with. For the violence.

She sidled closer to me, nearly touching my ear with her mouth as she murmured words meant just for me.

"That was for Sam." Then she whirled away again and ran a hand down Brock's arm. "We have bigger problems than just a few captive vampires," she informed him, and my stomach clenched.

She could say anything now. The mission could be over in a moment, and I could join the vampire corpses Esmé had just left on the ground. If she told him.

I clenched my fists, working on looking as neutral as I could. Brock couldn't be allowed to see that I cared about what Esmé had just done — or that not knowing her next play made me uneasy. I tamped down my rage. I just needed to wait. I couldn't plan for what I didn't know.

Brock covered Esmé's hand with his own, stopping the movement up and down his arm, although I couldn't tell if it was an affectionate gesture or a threatening one when he squeezed her fingers and her lips parted on a hissed breath. She looked like the kind to enjoy pain.

"What's going on?" he asked, his smile thin and fake.

"The Duponts have found your warehouse. They've stolen the alcohol." She flashed me a glance like I must have been the one who'd led Sebastian to his wine and spirits, but this new development was as much a surprise to me as it was to Brock, and I let that surprise show.

Brock needed to see it, needed to see my loyalty to his cause.

A low rumble sounded from his chest. And he turned abruptly, striding from the building. Esmé hurried after him, trying to catch his arm like she might be able to draw him to a stop. When he finally faced her, his cheekbones were prominent, his eyes glowing a dull red. "Get that carnage in there cleaned up," he roared as he pointed to the door of the outbuilding. "Then come into the house. We have a lot to discuss." He crooked a finger at me. "You come now. You just got extra clearance."

Esmé slanted a glare at me, and I allowed myself a small shrug. It was dangerous to piss her off right now, but I couldn't help but poke that bear as I pondered my new status with Brock. I hadn't done anything but be in the right place at the right time. I wanted to find out what my new status meant, but Brock was already stomping up the steps to the deck. I followed him, concealing my amusement as he shouldered roughly past the armed guys who'd materialized in their usual position at the top of the stairs.

He led me to a room that was almost a mirror of the one I'd seen at Esmé's house. The walls were plastered with pictures of locations and people, and luckily Jason wasn't here, either. He and I appeared to have had a very lucky escape regarding attracting the kind of attention that would have made my infiltration into the Blackbloods impossible.

Brock strode around the room, jabbing his finger against various pictures. "This needs to be taken care of," he muttered. "And this," as he indicated a picture of Temple. "He's always right in the thick of things. He needs to be stopped."

He turned a circle and laughed before ripping a picture of Nic from the wall and tearing it into pieces, which he let flutter to the floor at the side of him.

"Total destruction," he bellowed. "We're all in. It ends tonight. We take out as many of them as we can."

I sat in one of the chairs, watching him as I did. He was buzzing with an energy I'd never seen in him before — but he seemed totally out of control. I was more used to a Brock who at least appeared to think things through and have his tactics planned out.

"I thought we were starting small… Inconveniencing them?" I kept my tone casual, like I didn't care either way.

He glared at me, and I shrugged.

"I mean, whatever, man. It's your war. But this is a big change in tactics." The escalation worried me. Being organized enough to steal liquor from a container ship was one thing. Taking on an entire army was another. And Sebastian had an entire army at his disposal, which Brock should have known on the back of all of this surveillance.

But Brock had surprise on his side, and that was enough to concern me, even with Seb's army. Sometimes surprise was enough. I'd seen battles won on less than surprise and enthusiasm.

And Brock had both of those things today.

Damn Sebastian. If only he'd trusted me enough to let things play out rather than storming in and taking back his toys. I sighed quietly. But this wasn't Sebastian's fault. To sit quietly on his hands and be seen to do nothing would have aroused far more suspicion and made the Duponts look far weaker.

He'd only reacted in the same way he would have done whether I was here or not, and I probably would have been right at his side reclaiming the stolen alcohol at any other time. No one knew how delicately this mission was all balanced, and it certainly seemed especially delicate right now.

Brock didn't even seem sane as he paced and muttered to himself.

I watched him move while I tried to figure out what I needed to do next, and how I could do anything without being discovered. Esmé would probably think nothing of taking me out now that I had Sam, no matter what her agreement with Temple was.

Temple. Shit. I'd need to warn him what Brock was doing.

As I made my own plans. Brock had pulled out his cell phone and clamped it to his ear. He was still ranting and raving, although now it was instructions as he summoned all his vampires to the house.

Soon, the meeting room was full of his ill-trained soldiers, their hoots and hollers as they hung off his every word a far cry from the way my men accepted their orders in silence.

At the thought of my men, my stomach churned at the way Esmé had ripped through the four who'd been captured. But I couldn't afford sentimentality over them right now. They'd died as soldiers — in a war.

I needed to focus on Brock's plans, so I had something to report to Temple or Jason. Jason was probably my best contact as he still seemed to be unknown, although I risked exposing him when I reached out.

Brock stepped back toward his pictures and thumped his fist against photographs of Nightfall and Sebastian's mansion. "We attack tonight," he announced as if he hadn't already told everyone that several times. "And we're going where they'd least expect us. The Regent's house." He laughed and it was a cold, cruel sound. "We know what time the club closes and we know what time they should all be tucked up at home in bed."

Dread formed a small ball in the pit of my stomach. They were going after Sebastian and Kayla. Sebastian and Nic didn't always see eye to eye, but the murder of his brother could bring Nic down.

I had to get word out somehow. My mind spun, and I almost started to stand, but Brock's gaze suddenly met mine.

"You," he said, the word boomed around the room. "You're with me tonight. You're my shadow, my second. You don't leave my side."

I lifted an eyebrow.

"You beat Demon," he clarified. "You earned it."

Which was great for running interference but… How the hell was I going to warn everyone who needed to know about the attack when Brock had just shortened my leash right to *heel?* There was no way I'd get to Temple or Jason without him wondering where I'd gone, and I'd find it hard to even make a call on my burner.

I drew a breath. Somehow, I'd keep Brock from doing too much damage to my family. I'd have to wing it and hope that Sam would manage to keep her head down and stay safe.

Brock's side was the last place I wanted to be now that I'd found my mate and my family was in danger.

Unease trickled through me, icing my veins. Being at the center of a Blackblood mission right now was deadly. If Esmé blew my cover, Brock could kill me, and Sam —my mate—would be left all alone, without my protection, I controlled my shudder at that thought. Esmé would torture her to death.

***

We walked down Sebastian's quiet street in Brock's preferred battle formation, and I glanced at the men taking up their positions along the sides of the buildings, melting into the shadows like they might really make it as trained soldiers after all. More soldiers had climbed onto nearby rooftops, and others were ready to do the same at the mansion.

I took note of their positions. I'd need to be sure everyone was where they were supposed to be so I could raise the alarm inside the mansion without alerting the Blackbloods to being a traitor to their cause. Really, I just needed to slip away from Brock, but he kept leaning close to discuss strategy with me, and there was only so much misdirection I could throw out there.

He continued beckoning to men and pointing to where he wanted them to position themselves right up until we reached the gates of the mansion, a small band of Blackblood soldiers on our heels.

He drew us to a stop and pointed to some of the men. "You, you, and you," he said. The guy didn't even know their names. "You take first-floor windows." He looked at me. "I want you to go in the back. I'll take the front and we can meet inside. Destroy anyone you come across on the way. I have no use for Dupont loyalists."

I nodded. Thank fuck. I didn't need to try to slip away — Brock had just instructed me to go. There was an alarm panel in the kitchen I could use to sound the panic alarm. I needed to make sure Sebastian and Kayla would be okay — although I wasn't naïve enough to believe I could save everybody. With Brock and his men in this mood, there would be some death tonight. Collateral damage.

"Got it." I started to move away.

I needed to get inside before too many of Sebastian's men got taken out by Blackbloods or simply noticed us here and attacked first.

Damn fine balances.

I crept toward the door that led into the kitchen, and the feeling of coming home washed over me, but a figure stepped out of the corridor.

"What the…?" The guard's tone was one of disbelief. "Kyle?"

Well, shit. I hadn't come this far to be given away. I leapt onto him and choked him until he passed out. To anyone else, he'd look dead long enough for me to at least warn Sebastian what was happening.

I crept to the alarm panel and pressed the panic button. Immediately, the siren rang through the house, and my walkie crackled at my hip.

"Shit," Brock's voice ground out. "We must have been made. Where are you?"

I silenced the walkie and headed to the back stairs. I didn't have long to reach Sebastian. Brock would be even more desperate now his mission was in peril, and I couldn't guarantee if he'd follow his plan or just start trying things out and issuing new instructions.

It was tempting to turn my walkie back on, but as much as it would allow me to listen in, it would also give away my position to anyone else who could hear it.

The plush carpeting was familiar underfoot as I rushed to Sebastian's wing. Hopefully knowing the layout of the house gave me an advantage but I had no way of knowing which of Sebastian's men were also on Brock's payroll. Any one of them could have given away or sold valuable information, and we'd need to thoroughly clean house after all of this was put to bed. There was no room for traitors in our group.

I pushed the door open to Sebastian's bedroom and barged in. A loud roar of anger filled my ears, and something landed on my back, sharp fangs grazing my neck.

"It's Kyle." I spoke hastily, and the person released me.

"Shit, Kyle." Kayla dropped to the floor next to me. "I nearly took you out."

Before she'd finished speaking, there was a blur of motion and I was knocked to the floor, a pair of red eyes close to my face.

"Seb," I said. "It's me."

Kayla grabbed his arm. "Get up," she muttered. "It's Kyle. We need to listen." Then she looked at me. "Why are you here? What's going on?"

"The Blackbloods are attacking. You need to get everyone to safety." I glanced at the door.

I didn't have time to fuck around telling them the whole story. Sebastian grasped the urgency first.

"Panic room," he said to Kayla, pointing toward their closet, which led to the secure room. "Go in there and stay inside until I tell you it's safe to come out."

"Nope." She lifted her chin. "I'm not some weak human you can order around. I'm going to fight."

I sighed. We fucking didn't have time for some sort of marital dispute right now. "Guys."

"Panic room," Sebastian repeated. "I can't lose you."

"No," Kayla said again. "I stay at your side."

"Guys." Frustration laced my repeated word. "We don't have time," I hissed. "Argue later." Brock was on his way.

He'd given up on a quiet entry and was yelling orders to people as they approached the bedroom.

"Look. They're coming. Preserve my cover by knocking me out or blow my cover and stay and fight with each other instead of against *your actual enemy*." I hissed the last words.

Sebastian grimaced. "I still need you on the inside," he said. "We don't know enough yet. They're still too powerful."

I shrugged. "Okay. He's out of control and we need to stop him. He's coming for you and for Nic."

Without warning, Sebastian sprang toward me, and he snarled. He whipped me around, taking hold of my wrists and dragged me out into the hallway. "You're going out the balcony doors," he murmured into my ear. "Might even make you a new scar. The fall won't kill you, but it will make a good show for anyone who still isn't sure how we handle our enemies."

I sighed then relaxed, signaling my agreement with his plan.

Sharp pain crashed over the back of my skull and the world went black.

# Chapter 14 - Sam

After about ten minutes, the driver pulled the car over, and I groaned as my head bashed against the hard plastic of the door again.

"Restrain her," the driving goon barked from the front. "We need to get her in the trunk."

"What the fuck, Evan?" the vampire alongside me whined. "Why don't you do some of the work for a change?"

"I'm fucking driving, Tommy, you dickwad. Or do you need me to do everything?"

Rope wound around my wrists, Tommy's big hands clumsy as he tried to bind them together.

"She's too small. Hold her still for me." The whine was still present in his tone.

The fucker. I wasn't even moving. But Evan sighed in the front and got out of the car then slammed his displeasure shut with the door so hard that the whole vehicle rocked.

He opened the door by my head and dragged me roughly out, letting me fall to the ground as he yanked on me. "It's not that hard. Look." Then he bent down and expertly bound my ankles as I lay still for him, winded from the drop.

There was no point fighting back right now, anyway. These were vampires. They could kill me in a split second, or they could bleed me dry. I had to wait for them to take me to the second location. Maybe I'd have more luck there.

Evan bent and lifted me into his arms before slinging me over his shoulder.

"Jesus Christ, this one's all bones," he complained. "It'll be like fucking a wooden plank with nails left in it."

He walked around his car and popped the trunk before dumping me inside. Then he slammed it shut again and the engine started a short moment later.

The rope chafed against my wrists, and I rolled around a lot more back here, banging and scraping myself on the usual shit people kept in the trunks of their cars. Everything was damp back here, and it smelled old and dead, so clearly these two fuckers kept things in their trunk that most people *did not*.

The road was mostly smooth, and the low-level rumble of the engine soothing, although the potholes we occasionally hit prevented sleep, which I was glad for because I needed to be alert. They were vampires, but I needed to try to escape. I couldn't just surrender to my fate.

I'd survived Esmé for this long, so I wasn't about to roll over now.

An image of Kyle floated through my mind, and I tried to brush it away, but I couldn't. I wanted to stay alive now. I really wanted to live, and a big part of the reason was him. It didn't make any sense. I'd been resigned to my fate for so long, and I'd never let a man affect my reasoning like this... But somehow, Kyle did. He made me want more. He made me want him.

Life suddenly seemed like the better option. For so long, I'd been resigned to my death, but now I was prepared to fight. Something about Kyle made me want to fight.

I struggled against the ropes at my wrists, looking for something to rub them against. And I needed to bust out a taillight, right? Right? That was still a thing? Signal to a car behind us or something.

Panic clouded my thoughts as I scuffed my feet over the interior of the trunk, looking for the right spot to kick. This was bad, so very bad.

The more the car lurched, the more disoriented I became. I rolled over as we went around a corner and my breathing come in spurts as I tried to catch enough air in my chest.

My thoughts seemed to slam into my mind, dizzying me, I couldn't catch hold of those either.

The car began to slow, and I had no idea how long we'd been driving. After we stopped completely, two doors slammed, rocking me as the car swayed from the impacts. I held my breath as footsteps moved closer. The trunk opened, and I blinked in the sudden light. Rough hands grabbed me. It was Evan and Tommy, although I could barely see them as they stood backlit by the sun.

Panic burned the back of my throat. and my flight-or-fight response gave way to complete submission. I was frozen with fear.

They lifted me between them, and it was like that action reawakened my thoughts.

I still hadn't thought of a concrete plan, so I went with kicking and screaming but it was a poor method to save myself. They quickly pinned me so that I remained still again, the hand that Evan wrapped over my mouth and nose was callused and smelled of motor oil.

The smell here was different than the city — a smell of something green and fresh and growing. Like life itself. Frogs croaked somewhere nearby, and the air was full of the sounds of crickets and birdsong.

This thrall wasn't in Kansas anymore… and as much as fear thrummed through me, relief trickled in that maybe Esmé wouldn't be able to demand a feed. But that led to anxiety because I'd need a fix of venom, and I didn't exactly want to offer myself to either Evan or Tommy.

I stopped trying to wriggle and fight pretty quickly. It was hotter here, and the weight of the air made unnecessary movement exhausting. I couldn't see my hair, but I could feel the frizz, like my hair was moving and shifting into a bigger ball of fuzz with every passing second. My clothes grew damp and stuck to my skin, and the moisture-filled air was thick in my lungs.

I was hanging over Tommy's back now, bouncing along like he was toting Santa's sack or just some regular garbage, and I twisted to try to see where they were taking me.

A cabin with more gaps between the planks of wood than windows stood at the end of a path, and I sighed. Another hovel.

I couldn't beat against Tommy with my fists as he walked, since my hands were behind my back, and I didn't waste my energy screaming — we were in the middle of nowhere, and I needed to preserve what little energy I could.

Evan pushed the door to the shack open—because it really was only a shack. Wind blowing in the wrong direction could bring it down in a heap of firewood. Once we were inside, Tommy dumped me into a chair with unceremonious lack of care, and I winced as my shoulders pulled at my awkward landing and inability to break my fall.

They watched me for a moment.

"What the hell?" I started, but Tommy just smirked. "Where have you brought me? What am I doing here? What the hell…" I paused, thinking over what I'd just been about to ask. It wasn't wise, but I went with it anyway. "What the hell will Esmé say?"

Evan snarled and smoothed his already greased back hair, but Tommy just laughed again, the sound unfriendly.

"Who do you think ordered this?" he said.

"Yeah, this was Esmé's idea." Evan was quick to interject his own statement, and he smiled smugly as he spoke.

Tommy cut him a glance like Evan needed to keep his damn mouth shut and let Tommy handle the talking.

"What?" I frowned then automatically rethought and tried to smooth out the crease in my brow, so it didn't stick. It was a habit I'd picked up from Mom.

"Esmé told you to tie me up, put me in the trunk of a car, and drive me to the middle of nowhere?" I mean, it probably didn't sound so far-fetched, but… Yeah, I still didn't understand why she'd go to these lengths to get me away from Kyle. There were places in New Orleans where she could hide me, surely?

"Maybe not in those exact words," Tommy muttered, and there was a gleam in his eye that suggested he and Evan had carried out Esmé's instructions in the way that most appealed to them.

It didn't surprise me. They were a pair of sadists and wannabe gangsters, both of them. I was lucky they'd only tied me up. Brock really was building an army of monsters.

"But why?" I knew why, but I needed to hear them say it.

Evan arched an eyebrow. "Because it's naughty to run away," he cooed.

I nodded. Yep. That was what I'd thought. Esmé had just reclaimed her pet and put me in timeout. But now the idea of belonging to someone burned bitterness and resentment through me, where before there had been mostly acceptance of the way my life would end.

"Don't forget the fight." Tommy looked at Evan expectantly. "We're supposed to keep her safe during the attack." He brushed my hair back from my face, and I shuddered.

Yeah. There was safe and there was *safe*… Their ideas of the what the word meant probably didn't align with mine.

"Oh, yeah?" I tossed my head to dislodge Tommy's fingers. "What's going on?" I did my best to sound casual, like I didn't really care.

But it wouldn't have mattered how much I wanted to know. Tommy was so eager to tell me about it, he looked like a kid at Christmas. It wasn't information he would have withheld just to fuck with me.

"The Duponts. We're going after the Regent." His smile grew wider, and his fangs descended as he rubbed his hands together, unable to conceal his glee at the idea. "We're going to take him out."

"Oh, yeah? And you two are here, missing out? Who did Brock take?" Again, I aimed for casual. After a small jab at their pride, of course.

Evan snarled again. "That fucking new guy."

My chest hollowed, cold tricking through my torso. Kyle? He was the only *new guy*, right? If he was going out with Brock, he could be in danger.

"Hey." I sat up as straight as I could and fumbled for the ends of the rope around my wrists. "Hey, if you let me go, I can help Esmé. She'd want that." I nodded emphatically as I spoke, agreeing with myself as I willed them to agree with me too.

But Evan laughed and shook his head, and Tommy cackled along.

"Stupid thrall," he grunted.

Then almost as one, they turned and walked to the door. The freaks.

As the door closed behind them, I remained sitting on the uncomfortable chair, my chafed wrists aching and the low glow of an old orange bulb doing absolutely nothing as it swung gently above me.

I rolled my ankles to try to keep the circulation in my legs going. They hadn't strapped me down here, but what was I realistically going to do? Bounce all over the shack like some kind of deranged Tigger and enable my own escape by pogoing through a window?

There hadn't been the noise of a car engine starting, so the guys were still outside somewhere, lurking in the bayou. Hopefully, they wouldn't get hungry anytime soon. For all I knew, I was the only human in a fifty-mile radius.

Night had long since fallen and I'd just started to work at moving my hands to stop the numb feeling when apprehension tickled the back of my brain. Something was off. Something I couldn't quite place. I looked at the door and froze as the prickle grew, stealing my breath.

This was weird. I was nervous about being in this shack with two vampires of exact whereabouts unknown outside the door, but this wasn't that. The apprehension was foreign. Almost like it didn't belong in my body. Almost like it belonged to someone else.

I shook my head, trying to dislodge it, but my chest tightened, and I struggled to breathe. There was certainty now — certainty and a degree of acceptance. I sucked in a breath as a wave of pain crashed over my skull, and I shrieked.

The door handle rattled, and Evan burst inside.

"What are you screaming at, woman?" he barked.

I screamed again as my head continued to ache. Was I dying? Was this it? A brain tumor? An aneurysm? I sighed, releasing a long breath. Maybe this was the better way. Maybe it was the quickest, kindest death.

My head throbbed like it might explode.

"Get her off that chair," Evan ordered as Tommy ran toward me. "Lay her on the floor. We need to find out what she's doing."

"Esmé's going to kill us," Tommy groaned, his voice close to my ear as he lifted me from my seat and laid me on the floor.

"Well, fucking untie her!" Evan shoved his hand back and forth through his greased hair, ruffling it so it stood up in sharp spikes.

"Oh, shit, dude." Tommy leaned over me and his movements were rough and careless as he jerked the ropes free, dragging them over my already sore skin.

I clutched my head as soon as the rope disappeared. The screams didn't stop coming. I could barely draw breath. If this truly was death, it couldn't come quick enough.

Shock caught my breath again and the feeling of being out of control, and then darkness claimed me.

***

My scalp still hurt. It burned like someone was ripping the skin clean off, and I squealed.

"Wake up, bitch." Esmé's voice permeated my confusion, and I forced my eyes open.

I reached to grasp Esmé's hand where she held me by my hair, then slipped my fingers down the strands to try to stem the pain by holding closer to the roots.

"Esmé, stop." I forced the words out, but her eyes glowed deeper red. "You're hurting me."

She bared her fangs, and her snarl filled the small space. "I should do more than *hurt you*."

I shrank away and winced as my hair tugged again at the movement.

She leaned closer to me, and her breath was hot against my face as she spoke again. "You're mine. There is *no room* for anyone else. Especially not that infiltrator, Kyle *Durg*. It was never supposed to be real." She emphasized his surname like it was a dirty word, and I flinched as she drew so close to revealing his deception in front of Tommy and Evan.

Her eyes glinted with knowing — she wasn't stupid. She'd throw Kyle under the bus in a heartbeat to keep me in line.

I began to nod but Esmé stood, her grip still strong on me as she lifted me higher into the air before she drew her arm back. I swung like a pendulum before she released me, and I crashed into the rough wood wall opposite. My arm throbbed and I crumpled as I slid down to the floor.

She approached me, a growl on her lips, and I froze as I watched her. Not even a breath moved in or out of my chest as she almost glided across the space between us, her movements sinuous, a smile of seduction on her lips.

Only there would be no seduction. This was punishment.

"I would rather kill you than let Kyle have you," she whispered as soon as she drew close enough for me to hear her. Her foot connected with my ribs first, and the impact forced a sound of pain from my lips.

The next kick was to my head, and soon I lost track as she struck me again and again and bent low to pummel me with her fists as well, landing strikes on my face and arms as I tried to protect my head.

Then everything stopped and my world hung, the silence almost painful as I waited for what was next.

Esmé swooped low, her mouth wide, and I closed my eyes, dread filling me instead of anticipation.

Pain burned through my whole body, using my veins and arteries as conduits as Esmé's venom coursed down each of them. Nothing about this felt good, and I clamped my lips against a scream.

I knew exactly what it felt like to experience euphoria from a bite now, and I'd gotten that from Kyle. Never

Esmé, who only inflicted her bites to hurt me in the same way she believed I'd already hurt her.

I lay back and let the venom drug me to sleep, hoping to somehow find Kyle in the darkness.

# Chapter 15 - Kyle

"Fuck!" I yelled the word and jerked forward, awake in an instant.

New Orleans scenery whistled by outside the windows, and I sat up on the rear bench seat of a truck.

"What's going on?"

Brock glanced over his shoulder from the driver's seat. "What the fuck do you mean, what's fucking going on? I'm five fucking men down."

I rested my head back and released a quiet sigh. "Five?" I ran my hand over the back of my head and winced as I skimmed the lump that Sebastian had created. Luckily, he'd opened the French doors before launching me from the balcony or I'd have been picking chunks of glass from my flesh before I could heal.

He slammed his fist on the steering wheel. "Fucking Duponts. We had to retreat." He shook his head and thumped the steering wheel again. "*Fucking* Duponts."

He pressed his foot on the gas and the truck roared as it picked up speed.

Pain flashed like fire through me, and I bent double in the seat, groaning. What the hell? It burned. Goddamn, it burned. Then Sam's face was in my head, and her scent surrounded me, and she was all I could focus on.

Only Sam.

She was everywhere around me, inside me... and in so much pain.

Holy fuck. *Sam's* pain.

"Stop the truck," I choked out. "Sweet Jesus, stop the fucking truck." I had to get to my mate.

Brock glanced at me again. "What? What the hell?"

"It's my mate," I ground out. "She needs me."

I reached for the door handle and Brock swerved to the side of the road.

"What the hell, man? What mate? You're a soldier —"

But he'd barely finished speaking before I threw the door open. We were close enough to a stop when I leaped out and started running. My whole body still burned. Sam was in pain. She was in immense pain. I stumbled and nearly fell, but I couldn't afford to be distracted from my goal.

Sam.

I just had to get to her.

Instinct drove me forward, pushing me to take turns I didn't even consciously know to make. I could feel Sam somehow, her pain pulsing between us, her vitality waning.

Her screams echoed in my head, growing quieter with each moment that passed. Someone was hurting her, and someone would have to pay.

How the hell had they even found her? I wasn't running in the direction of my apartment. I kicked my speed up a notch, trusting whatever force inside me was guiding me the right way. It was like Sam and I were connected, like a thread stretched between us, although it was growing thin.

I'd never moved so fast. I pounded the miles, barely seeing the scenery as I dodged around trees and splashed through swamps. I leaped over twisted roots and ducked under low-hanging branches. Nothing else was as important to me right now as getting to Sam.

Nothing else had been as important ever.

The trees started growing closer together, and the air was filled with the sounds of the bayou. Water lapped softly in the distance somewhere, and night insects chirped and clicked. Creatures scuttled in the undergrowth, moving out of my way, and I paused to assess my surroundings.

Her screams had stopped completely now, but instead of being relieved, fear took control of my limbs and I began to run again, pumping my legs and arms as hard as I could. What if the worst had happened? But no... surely, I'd know?

The connection would be gone entirely. Yeah. It would be gone. Sam was hanging in there, and I needed to get to her. Urgency replaced my fear, giving me another burst of speed.

A small building appeared at the end of the path. A cabin of some sort. Barely a fucking shed. And I knew without a doubt that Sam was in there. My gums ached as my fangs pierced them. Someone was hurting Sam and they were right inside that building. I'd kill them for laying hands on my mate.

I threw the door open, and two vampires stepped forward, both looking more like hired muscle than they shared a brain cell between them. I roared my anger at them as they crowded me, preventing me from moving forward into the room.

I raked my claws down the first guy's chest before plunging my hand through his ribcage and ripping his heart from his chest. It beat for a moment before I threw it to land wetly on the floor.

The second guy stepped forward before he threw a bewildered glance at the heart between me and the corpse. He tried to run but I let out another roar and grabbed his head, twisting it so hard that I unscrewed it from his neck like a pop bottle cap.

Bloodlust hung heavy in the air, and I inhaled the tang of copper, bringing with it the familiar scent of my mate. Esmé sat hunched against the wall, Sam limp in her arms as she fed. Sam's blood trickled from Esmé's lips, dripping, wasted to the floor.

I took two strides and grasped Esmé's hair, ripping her lips from Sam. She screamed at me, the high-pitched sound maniacal as she cackled and spat her mouthful of blood in my face. For the second time since I'd known Esmé, I lifted her and threw her at a wall before watching as she slid down the rough wood. And for the second time since I'd known Esmé, she picked herself right back up from that action and turned to face me, still laughing.

"You're going to have to do better than that," she taunted, as she launched herself at me, her eyes bright with madness but her strength gifted from my mate's blood.

She was fast now, faster than I'd ever known her, and she darted toward me, slashing at my torso and face.

I danced for a while, weaving backward, evading her slashing claws as she reached for my face.

"Now, now, Esmé," I muttered as I let her swing for me and connect with my ribs as I moved into a better defensive position.

I had to protect Sam, and that meant keeping Esmé's focus on me.

Esmé darted forward again, and I stepped aside before smashing my elbow into her back and sending her to sprawl on the floor. She lay still for a moment, winded, and my gaze landed on Sam. She was so pale, and her chest barely moved. How much fucking blood had Esmé just taken?

I shook my head. I already knew… too fucking much. Even one drop was too much. No one would ever drink from my mate but me.

She was no one's pet.

Esmé raced at me again, but I was done playing and dancing. I grabbed her and held her tight to me, before twisting her neck and listening for the snap that would incapacitate her but not kill her. It would give us long enough to get away, and I couldn't kill her just yet in case it set off more repercussions with Brock. I glanced at her one last time, checking she was truly down, and she glared back at me, her eyes angry, but she couldn't manage any more than that.

Keys… I'd seen a car out there. Shit, I needed keys. I looked at Sam, still and quiet on the floor, but I could feel her inside me still, so she was still alive, even if barely. I needed to get her away. Back to safety.

I was her safety. As long as she was with me, she'd be safe. That much, I knew.

One of the guys I'd slaughtered when I arrived must have the keys in his pocket. I patted both of their waists until the second guy jingled, and I grabbed the keys before scooping Sam up and striding from the shack. I'd won many, many victories in battle since I'd been turned, but this was possibly the sweetest of all, leaving the scene with my mate in my arms.

I pressed the fob button to open the car, then pressed it three more times before the lights finally flashed in recognition. Fucking piece of junk, but I only needed it to get us back to my apartment then I was taking it and dumping it in the nearest swamp, anyway.

Sam moaned a little as I lowered her carefully onto the backseat. It was the first noise she'd made, and I couldn't tell if that was a good sign or a bad one. I glanced around for a way to make her more secure while I drove, but there was nothing immediate and I didn't have time to waste. I'd just need to drive carefully.

Well, shit. *Of course* I'd drive carefully. I had very precious cargo.

I jumped into the driver's seat and rammed the key into the ignition before turning it, fingers crossed as I waited for it to start. The I squealed out of there, my foot pressed firmly on the gas. I only had one objective now — get Sam home.

***

I grimaced as I laid Sam on the couch, wishing I had something better to offer. This was worn in patches and, to be honest, didn't smell great. It hadn't mattered so much when this place was only ever meant to be a base for me while I focused on infiltrating the Blackbloods and bringing them down. Well, my mission was well and truly disrupted now, my focus divided, but I still needed to end the Blackbloods and whatever Brock thought he'd started. That objective was even more important now — now that it meant keeping Sam safe, too.

I tucked Sam's blaze of hair behind her ear, worry gnawing at me due to the pallor of her skin. She was so pale. Almost white. Fucking see-through. Esmé had taken too much blood.

I concentrated, listening for Sam's heartbeat as my gaze tracked the spot on her neck where I should have seen her pulse fluttering.

It was too slow. Too fucking slow. And I never panicked, but there was an unfamiliar flutter inside me that rose and threatened to turn into cords and vines that would strangle me and crush my insides.

I touched her skin and snatched my hand away at the icy coldness I found there.

I only had one way to save her.

*Turn her.*

Surely, I couldn't.

But instinct moved inside me again, like something ancient waking up. *Turn her.* My internal voice was insistent.

And she needed blood. She needed blood so badly. Esmé had very nearly succeeded in killing her, but I couldn't let that happen.

Before I could think it through any further… *overthink it…* I ripped my fangs through my wrist and blood sprayed out, painting the wall in ruby red splotches before I got the wound to Sam's mouth.

At first, she gagged and resisted my offering, my *gift*, but then she latched on and began to suck, accepting the life I was giving to her, accepting *me*. My cock twitched as I watched her, and she moaned, which only aroused me more.

I needed to complete this, though, if she was going to live. Being with a mate was always an erotic experience, but we had plenty of time for all of those in our future. I just had to get this part right.

Anxiety chased away my earlier panic as I leaned toward Sam's neck. Color had returned to her cheeks, and her pulse was more evident now. I'd always wanted to share this moment with my mate properly, but this was very much an emergency situation.

It was a long way from the candles, soft light, and quiet words I would have wanted for Sam. The sharing, the tenderness, and the knowledge of giving and receiving. But this moment wasn't about that. I didn't have that luxury, although love had never struck me as a luxury before. This moment, this action, was about preventing Sam's death.

I could save her. I *had* to.

I pressed my fangs into her vein and blood rushed into my mouth and down my throat, closing our circle and creating our bond. Energy flowed through me unlike anything I'd ever felt before.

It was actual ecstasy on my tongue, in my throat, in my veins as Sam consumed my blood and I consumed hers. It was like nothing ever before. Truly nothing.

*Camille.* Her name came unbidden. But this was nothing like Camille. I'd loved her, but she had never been mine.

My attempt to turn her had been misguided. Selfish. Wrong. And I hadn't known any better.

Everything about this, with Sam... With my *mate*. It was right. As things needed to be.

My mate needed to be with me. We belonged together, and it was always a vampire's duty to turn their mate so they could experience eternity as a pair. We lived for this — to find the other part of our soul and keep them with us.

Nic had done it, Seb had, too... and I hadn't understood why. But now I knew everything, and I understood. Nothing could be better than this.

I relaxed my sucking, just enjoying the teasing trickle of Sam's blood. I didn't want to take too much. Memories coursed through me alongside fresh energy, memories of when I'd been turned.

Truthfully, I usually shoved those memories to the deepest corners of my brain. It had been violent and it had been bloody, but it had led me to this, so now they held value. My whole journey held value because it had brought me to this moment, to Sam.

When Nic had found me, he'd changed everything about my life. I'd nearly died of consumption, been turned by a rogue who ripped through the hospital, and I'd killed the only woman I'd loved in a haze of bloodlust. I'd tried to turn her, but it had been too late. I'd gone too far.

But I'd also heard plenty of stories about human bodies that rejected venom, and as I drew away from Sam, I looked her over carefully. Would she be all right? Both Leia and Kayla had survived, although the transition had been harder for Leia, according to the things Nic said when he told that story, and the way he still paled when he recalled those days at Leia's bedside.

I shuddered. I didn't want that for Sam. I wanted her to join me as a vampire without a struggle. I couldn't imagine a life without her. Not now.

She appeared peaceful as I sealed the bite marks on her neck, healing them with a soft swipe of my tongue.

When she appeared to be sleeping quietly, I stepped toward the small kitchen and pulled out my burner cell. I'd sworn never to call this number, but I needed to talk to Nic. It was an emergency.

"It's me." I grunted out the words as soon as he answered.

"Hmm?" Even though he sounded distracted and not at all invested in our conversation, I knew I had his full attention. He hadn't been expecting to hear from me, so he'd be on alert — especially if he'd already spoken to Sebastian, which he almost definitely had.

"I... Uh..." I didn't know how to tell him all the stuff. "I've found my mate." Well, there it was. I'd just needed to blurt it out like a fucking goon.

"Wait... What? You have? In New Orleans? In the Blackbloods?" Nic reeled off questions.

His last question caught me off guard. Was Sam a Blackblood? "Not really?" I sounded like I was guessing.

He chuckled softly. "You didn't really find your mate?" He teased me over the answer I'd given to his initial flurry of questions.

"No. Yes. Yes, I did."

He chuckled softly. "So which part is the *not really* part?"

"She's not a Blackblood." I made it more emphatic now. "But I did just take her away from them. She was the second's thrall."

Nic whistled, the sound low. "Risky business, then." Then he sucked in a breath. "Jason has told me some of this, but I'm interested to hear it from you."

Nodding, I rubbed my hand over my head, my fingers automatically finding my scar. "You don't even know the half of it. Esmé nearly killed Sam. Sam's here now, with me."

"At that rathole Temple organized for you?" He sounded disbelieving. "You've taken your mate there?"

Something akin to shame burned my cheeks. "I'm on a mission." I shrugged. "I have no choice. I need to work but Sam needs to be safe, and she's safest with me. Don't you think?" I added the last part when he didn't say anything right away, and there was a note of pleading in my voice that I rarely used.

"The mission." Nic sighed, the release of air from his chest bridging the gap between us.

"Yeah," I confirmed as I glanced over my shoulder at my still sleeping mate. I pulled my hoodie from the chair where I'd slung it, and draped it over her, my movements gentle.

"She's sleeping now, but I've started the turning process." I brushed strands of hair from her forehead as I gauged the color in her cheeks.

"Okay." Nic sounded entirely focused now. "Okay, then we need to get things moving. No more pussying around. We need to show those Blackbloods that the Duponts own Baton Rouge *and* New Orleans, and that our way is the only way."

"I've got this, Nic. I don't want you to worry." I'd volunteered to infiltrate the Blackbloods, so I'd see it through.

"I'm not worried. Do I sound worried?"

Shit, yeah. He kinda sounded worried. That or genuinely distracted now.

"Listen, I'm getting in touch with Ben. I'm going to have him oversee everything here, and I'm going to fly out to join you guys in New Orleans. Maybe I need to be present for this, you know?"

"You don't need —" I started.

"I think I do." His voice was commanding, definitely my king in that statement, and I pressed my lips closed. "Now that you have a mate you need to take care of, we need to bring this Blackbloods shit to an end as soon as possible. I'm coming out there."

"Yes, my king," I murmured before he ended the call.

I slid the phone into the back of a drawer in the kitchen. I tried not to have it on me too often. Although it was a burner and held only other burner numbers, it was too risky to get caught with.

Then I turned and rested my ass against the edge of the counter as I watched Sam. Shit, I was so out of my depth now. Nic coming out was actually a relief. I could handle all of the military shit with the Blackbloods, the mission, infiltration, subterfuge... That was all fine. A walk down Easy Street, even.

But I didn't know what to do with a new mate, and I didn't know how to get her through her transition.

I sighed and rubbed my hand over my head as adrenaline started to course through me, readying me for the next stage of battle.

The Blackbloods needed to start their prayers. The Duponts were coming.

# Chapter 16 - Sam

My head ached, the pain burrowing into my skull, and I clutched my hands over my hair, pressing like I might be able to squash the pain away. But maybe I'd never been so awake as I was right now. Straight from sleep to awareness — smells assaulted me immediately.

Damp and the lingering odor of salt-filled sweat.

My eyes sprang open, and I sucked in a breath as I stared at Kyle's sleeping face, inches away from me across the pillow. I'd never been in his bedroom before, and I didn't remember coming here now.

Something was different in my body. A feeling of being alive that hadn't been there for a very long time. Something vital. I wasn't on a slow march toward death anymore, and I didn't know how I knew that.

Energy teased me, spiraling and twisting through me, pressing upward under my skin like it almost couldn't be contained. My gums were full, and there was pressure behind them that didn't ease when I ran the tip of my tongue over the tender area.

I was vampire.

The thought was both foreign and innate. Something that shouldn't have been possible but also something that couldn't be denied. I just knew it.

Sometime between being inside that shack in the bayou and waking up here, Kyle had turned me.

I was vampire and I was fucking *strong*.

Oh my God, nothing had ever been like this. Total awareness of everything — dust motes in the air, the thread count under my ass. The sound of Kyle's breathing.

But where was the pain? Any rumors and stories I'd heard always spoke of pain — burning worse than an unwanted feed or agony while the body shifted and reshaped itself, becoming new and different… and undead.

Esmé had sometimes spoken in scathing terms about the humans who were too weak to make the transition or the humans who didn't come through it for days on end. Although, perhaps if she could have guaranteed I wouldn't make it, she'd have tried to turn me herself.

I didn't feel weak, though, and I was still here. I wasn't lost in some sort of private hell like Esmé had described seeing — humans who wouldn't reawaken right away, or had fevers, hallucinations and dreams akin to night terrors. Those humans were the ones that good vampires watched anxiously over.

Presumably, Esmé had never kept that kind of watch over anyone. Would she have watched over Sean? In my heart, I knew the answer was yes. If Esmé had ever loved at all, it had been my brother. That had been undeniable.

And she would have gifted him this if they hadn't been attacked. Perhaps I shouldn't have saved her, but I hadn't known any better, and I hadn't known what destruction to my own life my actions would bring.

I stretched and yawned, the movements habitual. There was no lingering sense of sleep anywhere in my body. Instead, there was the fizz of excitement for a new day. Something that had been missing for a very long time. There was something exciting about just being *alive*.

As I watched Kyle, his eyes opened, the deep brown still those melting pools of chocolate as he looked at me, appearing to see right inside me and search my soul in the very first glance.

He touched my cheek, merely grazing it with his fingertips before brushing some of my hair from my face and tucking it behind my ear. I wriggled around to face him more fully, leeching some of his warmth from the space between us. I was in Kyle's bed. That revelation wasn't lost on me.

But somehow it felt natural — like there was nowhere else I belonged. He closed the space between us and kissed me gently, little more than a soft tug on my lips before he drew away again.

"How are you feeling?" His lips pinched at the corners in an unfamiliar indication of worry, and he caressed my cheek again.

I didn't even need to think about it. "Pretty good," I said, and his eyes narrowed. "Amazing, actually," I amended. "I haven't felt like this since…since…"

"Never?" Kyle supplied, flashing a small grin.

I stopped and considered. Even before Esmé, I hadn't felt so… aware. Colors had never been so vivid, sounds so loud.

"I don't have that undercurrent of want," I murmured. "There isn't that niggle in the back of my mind telling me that I need something, that something is missing."

"The venom?" It was a quiet question, but I nodded.

"Yeah. I don't need it anymore." That realization was life-changing. I wouldn't be ruled by an urge I couldn't control anymore.

Esmé couldn't control *me*.

"Maybe this is how I used to feel." I shrugged. "I can barely remember."

Kyle wrapped his arms around me and drew me closer against his body, and I lay my head against his chest, my arm thrown over him as we melded together.

"I can finally breathe," I said.

He chuckled. "Not that you need to. That's just an old habit your body will continue for now."

I giggled at the idea something as vital as breathing was no longer necessary. "How much do you know about Esmé?"

He stiffened, his muscles tensing beneath me as his hold tightened. "Other than the fact I could cheerfully enact her final death?"

I sighed. "She wasn't always that way. She knew love once. Had a mate."

Kyle huffed. "I think you said. And her mate was your brother?"

"That's right." I glanced up, taking in his face.

He had a beautiful face, and I loved to look at it.

Particularly now, like this. There was something relaxed and unguarded about this moment, like I was seeing something that would usually be private, and he was sharing it only with me.

He looked at me, the angle forcing him to press his chin to his chest. "I can still hardly believe Esmé loved your brother."

"Yeah. Sean." I moved to rest my palm on his chest, able to feel the thud of his heart through his skin. I could hear it too, that old remnant of humanity, and the steady beat comforted me. There was something reassuring about being so close to life, and the presence of another person, and the intimacy that brought. "He was there the day we were attacked." Sudden tears filled my eyes, and I blinked.

Goddamn. I'd been so numb for so long, I'd forgotten about rushes of emotion. I cleared my throat and blinked furiously. I wasn't ready for the weakness of tears yet. That would make me too vulnerable — which was ridiculous given we were lying here nearly naked, wrapped together, but my self-control was the last thing I had. It was a protective coating over me. Like armor. And I wasn't ready to shed it. Not yet anyway.

Esmé had pretty much stripped my self-control away completely, but now it was back, and I was glad for it.

"Before, you mentioned an attack?" He was still looking at me, but I shifted my position and looked over his chest at the wall opposite as I doodled my fingers across his skin.

Being so close to a man and being allowed to touch him so casually was still such a privilege. I didn't want to look at him as I spoke, though. It was easier to tell this story and not let him see all of me.

"Yeah. Esmé and Sean were a thing. He loved her like he'd lost his mind. We spent a lot of time together, the three of us. When I met Esmé, she got me a job at the bar where she worked, and we were really good friends." I sighed at the thoughts of those days. "Best friends. I didn't know what she was. Then I introduced her to Sean and that's when everything changed. Where it all went wrong, I suppose. I didn't know what she and Sean had planned — she didn't tell me until later."

And then she'd told me many times as she'd raged at me for not letting her die, for condemning her to a life without her mate.

"I lost Sean, too," I whispered. "It wasn't just her, and I couldn't lose them both that day, so I saved the only one I could. I didn't know it would lead to… all of… all of *this*."

Kyle nodded, the movement big enough to feel. "Who attacked?" He kept his tone light, but I could tell he was assessing, and his mind was working, information gathering.

"The Blackbloods. I don't think Brock expected Esmé to be caught up in the attack. She'd helped orchestrate it, but she and Sean had a change of plans or…" I sighed. "I don't know. It's all a blur. But she nearly died, and I saved her, and she's never forgiven me for that. I don't think Brock would have cared if she died, but I did."

My last words were vehement. Back then, I hadn't known I was saving the woman who'd come to hate me more than anyone else in the world. I hadn't known I was signing my own death warrant.

"And you bound yourself to her." It was Kyle's turn to sigh.

"I didn't know that would happen. The whole thing was such a shock. First, my friend, my brother's girlfriend, was a vampire… I didn't even know you… *we* existed. Then Sean was dead and Esmé was dying, but I could save her, you know? So, I did. I saved her." I used to feel pride at that statement, but no longer. "I let her bite me and I let her take as much blood as she needed."

My life would have been a whole hell of a lot easier if I'd just let her die that night. But maybe saving Esmé had kept me alive long enough for Kyle to find me. Perhaps everything had worked out just as it needed to.

I glanced at his face again, meeting his eyes, loving that zing of connection. "Thank you for right now."

He chuckled. "For what?"

I shrugged, the movement small. "I know I'm not the best you could have picked." Hell, this guy must have had serious options. Better options than me, anyway. "And I feel lucky to be here with you." I shrugged again. My words didn't say enough really, but they'd have to do while I thought of more.

"No thanks are required. You're the only one I will ever want." Fervor shone in his gaze, even though his voice was soft.

I nodded and resumed staring at the wall, still stroking his skin, relaxed and happy against him. "I don't want to go back there, you know. To the Blackbloods. I don't want to belong to Esmé."

He made a scoffing noise. "You will never belong to that woman. You'll never belong to anyone again."

"I can't go back."

Kyle's arm tightened again. "You won't ever need to. I'll protect you with my life."

I nodded, reassured by his words, feeling his intention echoing between us. He meant what he'd said. He'd protect me. I'd be okay now.

"What are you hiding down there for?"

His sudden question surprised me, and I met his gaze once more as confusion made me slow.

"Come up here and kiss me."

My confusion deepened. I hadn't known he wanted kisses. Hadn't really expected him to. But hell, *I* wanted kisses.

I grinned as I moved, bringing our heads level. And before I could overthink it, I pressed my lips to his.

What started slow and questioning quickly became deeper and more passionate, and I pushed closer to him as his tongue swept into my mouth. His hand clutched at my thigh as my T-shirt rode up between us, and he urged my leg across both of his until I lay on top of him, my knees resting either side of him on the bed.

He still had his underwear on, but I couldn't resist grinding a little on top of him, and he sucked in a breath.

"Naughty," he murmured against my lips, and I laughed.

"Not at all." I pressed against him again. "I think you're feeling quite naughty yourself."

His erection pressed against my inner thigh, and my breathing quickened. Never had I wanted my panties to melt off more.

"I think we're wearing too many clothes." Kyle echoed my thoughts, and I laughed again.

"You think we're wearing too many clothes?"

"Oh, definitely." He reached around and his hand brushed over my ass before he plucked at the waistband and began to inch the panties down.

He groaned when my position prevented any further movement and I moved.

"I'll take them off."

"Get naked," he half growled, and I chuckled at the ridiculous instruction but complied anyway as he removed his own underwear.

I retook my position over the top of him and clashed our mouths back together as his hands clutched my hips, and he tilted me so that I could feel his cock nudging against me. I sucked in a breath that was little more than a whimper of need.

I wanted this man, and I wanted him inside me now. My nipples rubbed over his chest as I moved up and down against him, trying to coax him closer, to thrust deeper, and my breathing was more audible.

Shit, this man made me wanton.

I broke our kiss. "Kyle." I whispered his name.

"Yes?" A crooked smile played at his lips, and he quirked an eyebrow.

"You're teasing me."

"Yes," he agreed as he resumed nudging against me, the movement both titillating and disappointingly useless.

"But I want you." The words were somewhere between a moan and a whine as frustration coursed through me.

"I want you too." He brushed the pads of his thumbs over my nipples, and I arched my back as pleasure lit sparks through me.

"Then stop teasing me."

"But I know you like it." He grinned again and I moaned as he moved against me, hitting just the right spot.

I couldn't exactly deny that I liked it when clearly, I did. But I liked everything he did to me, and I shivered as he trailed his fingertips down my back to rest on my ass. He pressed his mouth to my neck, and I whispered my pleasure as I tried to encourage his cock into my body, but he angled himself away, and I groaned.

Then without warning, he flipped us, and I landed flat on my back, Kyle above me.

"Is it better to tease you from here?" He lowered his mouth back to my neck, sucking and licking the skin there.

"Don't tease me," I begged.

"You are very distracting," he murmured. "Very distracting indeed." He moved his hips and his cock probed forward between my legs until I sucked in a breath as he entered me just a little way.

I whimpered as he stretched me before withdrawing and entering again. Each of his adjustments forced another breath of pleasure from me, and I reached my arms above my head as I looked for something to hold and anchor myself to. I turned my head, unable to look at him during such an intimate moment, wanting to hide.

"Sam." His quiet voice was a command and I glanced back, my top teeth worrying my lower lip even as I tilted my hips, offering more of myself to him as he slid farther inside me. "Look at me."

As I met his gaze, his pupils dilated, and I almost fell into his eyes to drown. The connection was intense and so intimate. He began to thrust in and out of my body, the movements regular and smooth, each one stoking the desire within me into warm flames that licked my insides and lapped over my skin.

His scent swirled over me, and he was everywhere. Around me, inside me, and consuming my thoughts. Only he existed in this moment.

He changed his angle, sweeping over my G-spot again and again, and my toes curled at the pleasure of it.

His eyes widened as he watched me. "I'm close," he gasped, and I nodded.

I couldn't speak, but it was getting harder to breathe and everything was starting to move faster with that loss of control feeling.

Kyle buried his mouth against my neck and his fangs sliced through my skin, pushing my pleasure over the edge, and my body pulsed around him as I moaned. He released me, lapping his tongue quickly over the marks before pressing his neck to my mouth. Instinct took over as my fangs descended and I punctured his skin.

He didn't shout his release, but his ragged inhale was like an aphrodisiac. My body tensed as he came inside me, an extra jolt of pleasure bursting within my body. I held myself still as his breathing slowed and he bent to take my lips in another tender kiss.

He supported his weight above me for a moment before rolling to one side and gathering me against him, his body warm and comforting as I rested in his arms. My eyes drifted closed as he held me, and his protection and emotions exploded through me, as if I was aware of Kyle and his feelings, too.

Everything was suddenly right with my world. I'd never been as safe. Not even as a child at home with my family. It was like my whole life had been waiting for this very moment right now.

I drifted to sleep, not scared or anxious for the first time since Sean had died.

***

The chinking of mugs and plates disturbed me, my eyes open in an instant. I lay there, staring at the ceiling and taking in all the cracks and imperfections in the paintwork up there.

Fantastic hearing, excellent eyesight. These were clearly not curses of the vampire condition.

But neither told me what the hell Kyle was doing in the kitchen, because it sure sounded like he was in the kitchen. Vampires didn't eat, right? I mean, they didn't eat, *really*. Only for appearances… And Esmé and Brock didn't even bother with that.

Kyle had, though, and that memory warmed my heart. He'd eaten on our date. Enough to look human alongside me and allow me to imagine we could really have been dating for real.

And now here we were — mates. It was almost unbelievable. I pinched myself and discovered another vampire quality — strength.

I sat up and glanced around. One of Kyle's black tees hung, discarded over a chair with three legs that was balanced against the wall. I removed the shirt and slipped it on, lifting the fabric to my nose to inhale as much of Kyle as I could.

I hadn't walked as a vampire yet, but there was something almost fluid about my stride as I padded from the bedroom and across the pokey living room to the kitchen. Pokey was a kind way to describe it. It was dank and dark too, but compared to where Esmé had made me live, Kyle's place was a virtual palace.

I just didn't know how long I could stay. Esmé would make it her mission to take me back. Apprehension shivered through me, and as I entered the kitchen, Kyle turned around.

"What's wrong?"

"Nothing." I shrugged.

"I can feel it… you're scared." He looked at an ancient coffee machine again.

"It was just a thought about Esmé." I walked up behind him and changed the subject. "But what are you doing?"

He huffed a sigh and clunked a handle. "The previous resident left this contraption, and I was trying to make you some coffee because I know it's what you like to drink in the morning, so I assumed now is a good time?" He grinned as he glanced over his shoulder at me.

I slung my arm around his waist and rested my head on his shoulder as we both looked at the machine. I had no idea how old it was, or even how sanitary it was, although that probably didn't matter now if I was immortal.

"Did you forget?" I asked.

"Forget what?" He dropped a kiss onto my hair.

"You turned me yesterday and now I'm a vampire just like you. I don't think I need to drink at all, at least not coffee, and I definitely don't need the caffeine fix for energy anymore." I gave him a mischievous grin and brushed my hand across the front of his boxer-briefs.

He chuckled and kissed my temple this time. "I see that. I just wanted something normal for you. You know, so you didn't think I'd made you into a monster like the others."

I nodded. That kind of made sense. "Yeah. I never wanted Esmé to turn me. I hate everything about the way they live. I didn't want that as my eternal damnation."

He winced at my harsh words a little before he spoke. "You know, sometimes I still do the things I enjoyed most as a human. I kind of hope it helps to keep a piece of my humanity tucked into me." He shrugged like it was no big deal, but his cheeks pinked. "I've never told anyone that." Then he focused even harder on the coffee machine.

"Kyle?"

When he looked at me, I stepped forward and lifted myself onto my tiptoes to give him a kiss. He responded immediately, his arms encircling my back as he held me to him.

Eventually, I drew away. "And as much as I would like to kiss you all day, it looks like I've got some coffee to make."

It looked kind of like the model of coffee machine my gram used to have, and I'd watched her make enough coffee on enough Sunday mornings before church that I should have been able to operate this old thing in my sleep.

"Let me try it?"

"Sure." He stepped back but rested his hand on my ass as I bent over for a closer look.

I leveled a mock glare at him over my shoulder. "I need to concentrate. Did *I* distract *you*?"

He shrugged. "You're always distracting."

I liked this Kyle. This emotionally available one.

I liked the other Kyle, too. The man of few words who just looked imposing and untouchable.

But this Kyle, this man in front of me, was very definitely mine.

I returned my attention to the coffee machine and wiggled my ass slightly as I did. Kyle's fingers tightened and he groaned quietly.

I grinned. "See… You just want to press this button here, make sure the mug is in place like so…" I reached and adjusted the position of the mug. "Flip this switch and…" I waited until the machine made a lazy chugging noise, spluttering to life for the first time in God alone knew how long. "Voilà! Coffee is coming."

He caught me to him.

"Is coffee the only thing that will be coming this morning?" I caught my breath as I dared ask him the overly bold question, then determinedly looked him in the eye so I could style it out.

He chuckled. "Hmm… Now there's an idea that hadn't occurred to me."

I pressed against him and wound my arms around his neck. "You're having an idea?" I shifted against him. "Wait… You carry your ideas in your pocket? I think I can feel it."

He laughed and shifted away. "Well, you should probably drink your coffee, but we do need to stay in, although I don't want to wear you out."

"Are we staying in to hide from Esmé?" A sizzle of fear flickered through me at the thought of Esmé in a rage. I probably wasn't strong enough to deal with that just yet.

"Mostly to make sure nothing changes with you, really." He kissed my forehead.

"But I feel great." The words were the truest I'd ever spoken.

Behind me, the coffee machine hissed in either relief or satisfaction as it finished brewing my coffee. Could also have been a sound of defeat.

"But you might not always feel great." Kyle's mouth formed a grim line, and a flicker of fear flashed in his eyes. "We don't know if your body will try to shut down."

"Wait… that happens?" It made no sense. I'd never felt better.

"Yeah." He rubbed a hand over his scar, tracing it back and forth. "Yeah, turning is risky. I've…" He hesitated. "I've gotten it wrong before."

"You've… you've turned other people?" My throat dried even though *of course* he'd turned other people. It wasn't like he was a monk before me.

I reached for my coffee, my movements deceptively casual, and took a sip after saying, "You had a mate before?"

Kyle spluttered like he was the one who'd just taken a drink. "What? No." His denial was so shocked, so emphatic, that I didn't deny it.

I watched him over the rim of my mug, so I didn't need to talk. I didn't know what to say.

"No. I mean, I loved Camille, but she wasn't my mate. I thought... I thought I loved her, anyway. But I... I fed too much. And when I tried to turn her, she... it... didn't..." He floundered. "It didn't work, or her body rejected it. I've *seen* bodies reject the change. Nic's mate, Leia, he didn't think she'd make it through. I've —" He gestured at me. "I've never seen this."

I laughed. "This? You mean me?"

"I've never seen someone do this well. I don't... I don't..." He shook his head.

I took his hand, placing my mug on the counter before I moved to stand next to him. "You know what? I've been a thrall for a while now. And it's not like Esmé has been the most careful owner. I've been chock full of vampire venom for all that time. Maybe I've built up a resistance to it? That would make sense, right?"

He shook his head. "I don't know." His stubble rasped as he scratched his jaw. "I've never dealt with —" He stopped again.

"A thrall?" I supplied. "It's okay to say it."

"But you aren't a thrall," he said. "You're my mate."

Those words sent a sharp spike of pleasure through me. "I know." I rested my head on his shoulder. "But I was a thrall and that means I might be making the transition easier than most, right?" I put a new mug under the coffee machine spout. "Coffee for you, too?"

He nodded. "Sure. Look, I'll ask Nic about the venom resistance thing. Maybe you're right. Maybe your system already knew how to handle it. But Nic will know for sure, or maybe he can find something in his Book of Gray. That's like a lore or history thing. I don't know. I don't have one."

As his coffee started to perfume the air, he told me a little about Nic and his family. About how their long history meant they had a wealth of information to draw on.

"Nic was even a born vampire," he finished as I handed him his steaming mug.

"Can you tell me more about them in bed? We can take our drinks in there?" Sitting curled up to him and listening while he talked seemed like the perfect way to spend our day together, especially if Kyle wanted to keep as close an eye on me as he said he did.

He glanced at me and winked. "Sounds great to me."

# Chapter 17 - Kyle

My phone was loud the next morning, but my eyes snapped open at the same time as I reached out to grab it. A number flashed on the screen, and I squinted at it as I tried to recall which of my contacts it was. Jason, most likely. Temple would try to stay out of contact because it would be dangerous for us to have any sort of connection.

"Yeah?" I never answered with anything that would identify one of us in case the wrong person had the other phone.

Any wrong person.

"Hey." Yeah, it was Jason. "Everything okay, dude?"

I pulled the phone away from my ear and looked at it before speaking into it again. "You calling for a cozy chat now?"

"No." He chuckled but sounded awkward. "It's just I… I spoke to Nic, and he said…"

"Yeah." I glanced at Sam. "We're done." Even I sounded disbelieving. "I think we're all transitioned."

"Really? That's great news. I'll let Nic know."

I spoke quickly before Jason could hang up. "But I don't know what to do. I need to see Brock today to find out what they're doing and make sure I don't lose my in. But how can I leave Sam here? It's too dangerous to leave her unguarded. She's too new."

Jason inhaled.

"Can you come and get her?" Damn, I hated when I sounded so fucking needy. I never had to ask any of the others for anything, and that was the way I liked it.

Only now that I had Sam, I'd ask and keep asking, and I'd ask some more if it meant keeping her safe. That realization hit me square in the chest like a ton of lead.

"What's the plan?" Jason sounded thoughtful, and I glanced at Sam before tucking a lock of hair back from her face.

Some of the vivid red dye was leaching away now, leaving a softer red in its wake.

"I hate the idea that I need to leave her here while I go and make nice with the fuckers who made her life such a misery. They nearly killed her." I stopped and lowered my voice.

"I know." Perhaps Jason had intended to be reassuring with his interjection, but nothing would reassure me.

Not until I knew Sam was somewhere safe.

"No, you don't know," I snapped then immediately regretted my tone. "Sorry, man. I just mean —"

"You're worried. I know. What can I do to help?"

"Can we get her to Leia and Kayla? Keep her safe?" I had a feeling Sebastian wouldn't have kept Kayla around New Orleans if he could help it after the attack at his house. If I knew him, he would have convinced her to go back to Baton Rouge with Leia — although she was strong-willed, so there was no guarantee she would have gone anywhere.

Jason laughed. "Will Sam handle being shuffled out of the way that much better than Kayla did when Sebastian tried it?"

I shook my head a little and smiled. "I have no idea. I hope so, but I can't risk anything happening to her."

"Okay, but Nic's arriving here, so Leia and Kayla will be at Seb's place. That all right?"

I pressed my lips together. It wasn't ideal. I wanted Sam carefully wrapped for her own protection and stored as far away from New Orleans as possible, but she'd be safest with Nic's and Sebastian's mates. They wouldn't be left unguarded. I blew out a sigh. "I guess."

"Okay, then this is what we're going to do. Remember the old witch, Lettie?"

I started to nod. "Yes. I mean, yeah, I do."

"Her shop is still kind of a safe place for us. The woman who runs it now, Naomi, is an ally. If you can get Sam to the Quarter, to Naomi, I can do the rest."

"Great." Relief lightened the weight in my chest. "I'll get her there ASAP."

If I needed to, I'd strap her to my back and run her there. Hell, I'd run her all the way to Baton Rouge if it guaranteed her safety.

I ended the call and Sam was suddenly awake next to me.

"Good morning." She sat up and pressed a kiss to my cheek. "When are we leaving?"

I glanced at her. "What?"

She gestured toward her ears. "This vamp hearing is amazing, right?"

I laughed as I pushed the comforter off me. This bed was about the only clean thing in the whole place, and I enjoyed the rustle the fabric made as it moved.

"I'm taking you to a shop we know in the Quarter," I said, and she laughed.

"I think I know the one. I've been there." She lowered her voice as she slipped her jeans on and fastened her bra. "It's actually where Brock's goons grabbed me from the other day."

"What?" I stopped what I was doing and turned to her. "They took you from a Dupont safe location? The storekeeper sold you out?"

She shook her head. "Naomi? What? No way. No… They saw me go in and grabbed me on the way out, I think. Those guys have followed me around for a long time, now. Always in my business. I should have suspected something, really. I got complacent, I guess."

We were both dressed, and I followed her out into the living room, my chest lighter than it had been in a long time. Sam radiated vitality now, and she half turned to look at me, flashing me a grin before she opened her mouth as if to speak.

But she froze and her eyes widened as the sound of glass shattering filled the room, and four bodies leapt into the space. The vampires' mouths were pulled back into snarls, their descended fangs on display.

I leaped in front of Sam as the first vampire in my apartment reached for her, and I hissed my anger, my vision reddening. "Get out!" I roared, the volume of my voice shaking the window frames.

But the vampire who'd reached for Sam just laughed. "We've come for the thrall. And Brock knows you're the traitor, so we'll be coming for you, too, soon enough."

They'd come for Sam. I'd expected some sort of move but not like this, and fury drove me forward, my nails forming claws as I slashed indiscriminately at the vampires who'd busted out the windows to make their dramatic entrance.

And perhaps that was all it was, showmanship, because the first two folded like cards. I was getting tired of taking out Brock's men now. It was almost too easy.

I glanced toward Sam. The fourth guy had approached her, and she screamed as she lashed out at him, her fighting style unskilled but enthusiastic. When she screamed again, the instinct to protect my mate surged inside me, and I grabbed the guy I'd merely been toying with and ripped his head from his body.

Nobody touched Sam.

I reached her side in a burst of speed and thrust my hand into the vampire's chest before he could grab Sam. The squelch noise of ramming my hand into his body sickened me, but there was triumph in clutching his heart as it beat its last thump. He'd endangered my mate, and now he was dead.

Ultimate justice.

I left the mangled heart in his chest and extracted my hand from the wet, glistening hole I'd made. There was no point making more of a mess on the floor by dumping the unwanted body parts there, although it probably wouldn't have been noticed alongside the four corpses.

I fought to bring my breathing back under control before I turned to Sam. I also didn't want my features to scare her. "You okay?" I reached out to take her hand, relieved when she nodded.

She was pale, green eyes darker than usual, her expression a little haunted, but she nodded again, more firmly this time. "Yeah, I'm good."

"Did that guy get you anywhere?" I scanned my gaze over her, looking for injuries and a fresh reason to be glad I'd ripped his heart out.

She started to shake her head then held out her arm to reveal the soft inner flesh above her wrist. "Just a scratch here." As she spoke, the shallow wound began to knit back together, and she drew in a breath. "Holy shit, that's cool," she murmured. Then she glanced at me, excitement dancing in her eyes. "That's cool, right?"

I chuckled, suddenly remembering the first time I'd seen my own body heal. "Yes, it's very cool." I felt almost indulgent as I joined her in her awe over her new body and its abilities.

But I couldn't imagine how she must have felt to have lived in the broken shell of a thrall for so long. My anger at Esmé ramped up again, but the thought of her reminded me of Brock and galvanized me into action.

"We can't stay here." I sped through the tiny apartment, throwing the few things I still wanted into the small duffle bag I'd arrived with. "I need to get you safe."

I couldn't go to Brock now, either. My cover was blown. I'd probably blown it myself when I took Sam, but there was no point going over the details of what I'd done wrong — in reality, I'd hardly done anything right. My mission had been a bust from the moment I'd met Sam.

From that very first moment, then.

"Come on." I held my hand out to her so we could get the hell out of Dodge. "Time to introduce you to my family."

# Chapter 18 - Sam

I sat in a small parlor-like room and glanced around. It was something out of Regency France. Kind of, anyway. The furniture was delicate, and I couldn't imagine a big guy like Kyle sitting comfortably in any of it.

It was entirely different than how Esmé decorated. Or how Brock decorated, anyway. And it was only the first indication these people were different than the vampires I was used to. The house was quiet for a start. No thralls, blood slaves, or bloodwhores hanging around, desperate to donate, or sleeping off a high in the corner.

And the people I'd met here didn't seem feral, either. There was even a fucking butler, like something out of a stately home in England.

"How are you finding things?" One of the women smiled at me as she spoke, and I smiled back, hoping my expression was suitably bland. I didn't want to seem too impressed, even though I totally was.

"It's…" I looked around again and failed at my attempts at being casual. "It's a lot," I admitted.

The second woman — Kayla? — laughed. "I'll say. But at least you already knew vampires existed, right? Leia didn't even now that much before she met one. And what a one to meet — the king."

I grimaced. "I knew. Maybe not the right kind of vampire, though. I knew about monsters more than anything else."

Leia nodded. "The Duponts aren't monsters. Nic sees to that." She sounded so sure of her mate that I smiled.

Weirdly, I felt the same way about Kyle. That I could trust anything he did and all of his intentions.

"Has Kyle told you much about us?" she continued as she tucked some of her hair behind her ear and leaned forward like I might impart some excellent gossip.

"You're the mates of the Baton Rouge King and New Orleans Regent." I stopped there. He'd probably told me more, but the finer details of things he'd told me when I was still a thrall were lost in that haze of venom lust.

Kayla nodded. "Yep." Her bright smile said everything. "And we were both human, just like you."

"*Just* like me, though?" A small sliver of shame cut through me. I hadn't just been human. I'd been a thrall. Something disgraceful and not spoken of. Something humans aware of the world avoided and vampires seemed to despise, despite the fact that thralls were a food source.

Leia shook her head. "Not exactly the same, no, but we were humans with lives and a certain degree of ignorance of the supernatural world, which you must have been once, too?" She shrugged. "Kayla knew more than me but even now things can surprise her."

I nodded. It all seemed like a very long time ago. "Kyle behaved like turning a human is really difficult." I didn't want to tell his stories for him, so I left it there.

Leia nodded thoughtfully. "It was hard for me."

"Sebastian said Nic thought he'd lost her. The men seem to panic." Kayla imparted information like it was all precious nuggets of knowledge, her expression serious and knowing.

Leia appeared to agree. "I had quite a hard time with the transition. I remember some of it."

"But is it rare to turn, though?" I pressed. "Kyle made it seem like it might be."

Kayla pursed her lips. "I guess it might be? I mean, I'm pretty sure the whole finding true mates is a rare thing in of itself."

"That's right." Leia pitched back in. "Nic's sister is happy with her vampire mate, many of them are, but they don't bring the power and connection of *true* mates... like we are." She glanced between Kayla and me. "There's something special about us, I think."

"But why is that?" I didn't understand any of this.

Leia shrugged. "I don't know. But Nic is head of the Dupont line, and he's a born vampire. That might make his House extra powerful right now."

Kayla shifted a little like she was growing bored, but she'd been more of a fidgeter than Leia, anyway. Leia seemed more regal, but she was the actual queen, if Nic was king – although both women seemed so down to Earth.

There was something just amazing about being around other women and not feeling as if I was less. Well, no less than usual social anxiety. It was as if these two would understand my journey. Well, most of it, anyway, and certainly this last part and my introduction to their men.

"Let's show her to her room?" Kayla glanced at Leia.

Leia nodded. "Sure, but it's Kyle's space, right, so it's a little…" She waved her hand briefly. "A little sparse?"

I laughed. "Yeah. He seems to travel light."

"Tell me about it." Kayla rolled her eyes. "And he's the exact same at Nightfall. An office of cardboard boxes of files rather than comfortable furniture. It's like he's never quite ready to put down roots, like he's always waiting for the next mission, the next destination or location."

"Hmm…" Leia eyed me thoughtfully as she stood. "Maybe that will change now, right, Sam?"

My cheeks heated. I couldn't imagine influencing Kyle's behavior to that degree. I wasn't sure I even wanted to. I liked him as he was.

Kayla led the way up a beautiful staircase with a sleek, polished banister that finished in a perfect closed spiral at the bottom. At the top, she pointed briefly left. "That's Sebastian's and my wing. But this way—" She walked out of a door and onto a bridge outside. "This is where the guest rooms are."

I glanced over the side and into the small garden courtyard below. Sebastian's home was all fenced in, but not in the way that Brock's compound looked like a prison.

"There are more guards here now," Leia sad. "Nic brought some more with him from Baton Rouge, and they're all on high alert since the attack by the Blackbloods."

Kayla stopped by a plain door. "This is Kyle's room."

"And Nic and I are just down the hall." Leia pointed vaguely down a hallway to the right.

Kayla smiled but it looked grim as she swung the door open. "I haven't decorated in here, and like I said, Kyle's taste verges on utilitarian."

I almost laughed at the sight of the bed and nothing more than other essential furniture. "It's perfect," I said, meaning it. "I've never known anyone like Kyle before and this is exactly him."

"So, what's your family like?" Kayla sounded curious as she stepped inside the bedroom.

"Oh. There's only Mom now. She doesn't know about vampires, though. I didn't until we lost my brother in an attack."

Leia caught her breath. "It's better that way. Vampires don't play nice when they can use family as leverage." And something about the expression in her eyes suggested there was far more to her story than that sentence could sum up, but my head was full of thoughts of Sean and Mom.

"We've both lost people, too." Kayla wrapped an arm around my waist, and I leaned my head against her shoulder in an uncharacteristic gesture of trust and affection. I'd only known these women for a few hours, and already they felt like family, like we had a bond between us.

"Esmé nearly killed me," I whispered as a single tear found its way from the corner of my eye.

"Some of them are monsters," Leia agreed as she laced her fingers with mine. "But we've got you now. You're safe here with us."

We stood for a little while, three women who used to be human and now plunged into a new world, until Kayla moved away.

"We should leave you to get some of your bearings – or whatever good hosts do when they don't want to overcrowd their new guests. I'm sure Kyle will be back soon, and you'll want some time with him, too. This is a lot to get used to all at once."

After a flurry of see-you-laters and unexpectedly warm hugs, they left, and the room fell silent. I breathed out a sigh and sank onto the foot of Kyle's plain bed, smoothing my hand over the comforter.

There was a knock at the door, and I glanced over as it began to open. Kyle walked into the room, carrying two mugs, and I sprang off the bed and almost tackled him to the floor as he laughed.

"Whoa, Sam. Don't spill it." He held the mugs out of my reach, but the aroma from them tantalized me, and my gums ached.

"Mine," I growled, and he laughed again.

"I've never seen you look this fierce." He dropped the volume of his voice. "It's very sexy."

"Mine," I blurted again, almost not sure what I was asking for, but whatever was in those mugs, I wanted it.

The coppery tang hit me again and I inhaled deeply, my body almost fizzing in response.

"Blood? Is it blood?" Where I should have felt only revulsion, a roiling, gut-clenching nausea, there was only temptation… desire to consume and never stop.

"I brought us a drink." He held one of the mugs out to me and I snatched it from his hands before slamming it back like the world's biggest shot.

I didn't even chug. I just emptied the contents right down my throat.

Then I grabbed the second mug from Kyle's hands and put that one to my lips. He moved to take it back, and I growled, the sound surprising me. It wasn't one I'd ever made before.

"Hey!" But he laughed good-naturedly before backing away, his hands in the air, palms toward me. "I see your need is greater."

I nodded but had more self-control this time and sipped at the drink. He dropped onto an uncomfortable-looking wooden chair and watched me. I really was lucky that Kyle had found me, that I'd been his mate. If another vampire had found me… could they even have done that? A small stirring of a memory in the back of my brain suggested that yes, another vampire could have found me first if they'd realized what I was.

Luckily, the Blackbloods had only ever seen me as a pet. Kyle was sane and trustworthy. I just *felt* that knowledge. I just knew. We'd known each other for such a short time, and I knew it anyway.

Before Kyle, I'd only seen the bad side of vampires, the darkness. But now there was something else. The House of Dupont was different. They were family. And now that I knew there was another way, it doubled my resolve that I never wanted to be anything like Esmé or Brock or the other Blackbloods.

Kyle shifted and cleared his throat. "There's going to be a meeting soon."

I drained my cup and focused all of my attention on him, and it was like I could see every fine detail of everything in the room, hear even the smallest sounds of fabric settling. It wasn't as good as taking Kyle's blood directly from his vein, but it obviously worked, and they obviously had an alternative to bloodwhores.

"What will the meeting be about?" I had plenty of time to ask Kyle about the intricacies of feeding.

He leaned forward, resting his elbows on his knees, steepling his fingers below his chin, watching me intently.

"Nic's here now, and we're planning to stop the Blackbloods once and for all."

"We?" Did the word include me?

If it did, what possible use could I be? But at the same time, how could the word *not* include me? There was no way around that, and I'd just decided I didn't want there to be. I was one of them now and happy to be here.

"And it's dangerous." I didn't mean to protest, and it wasn't what Kyle seemed to have expected to hear because he sat back in the chair again and just watched me, his expression curious. "Now, I know you know how to fight…" I paused, my mouth suddenly dry.

He narrowed his eyes, although his mouth quirked into an amused grin.

I sucked in a quick breath before I continued. "Brock is a *monster*." I spat the word in a new vampire hiss I seemed to have developed. "He's a monster and he's horrible and he's strong. He won't give up. What if someone gets hurt? What if that someone is *you?*" My vision reddened as I looked at him, and he chuckled.

I'd probably never felt as strongly about anything. I couldn't lose Kyle, and I especially couldn't lose him to that bastard Brock. He and Esmé had already taken so much of my life. I couldn't let them take my future, the future I was only just grasping, as well.

"But I've been alive so long. And I've fought in war after war after war." He sounded weary. "I know how to fight, and I know how to take down arrogant fuckers like Brock Saxton."

My emotions were all over the place, out of control like I'd never known them. As a thrall, they'd been dulled. As a human, I'd been quietly controlled, but now it was like I couldn't even see straight.

"I know what you say about your wars and the way you've leveled up and learned." I remembered every word he'd said in Manny's like he'd etched them directly on my brain. "But Brock doesn't care about any of your military skill, and he certainly doesn't care about the rest of his clan. He would throw each and every one of them under the bus, sacrifice them all, to come out as top dog in New Orleans." I was on a roll now, passion carrying my speech. "And I'm afraid... I'm afraid that I can't help you because I can't fight. You saw me with those goons in the apartment before. I couldn't fight." Shit. I shook my head. I hadn't been able to fight. I'd been useless. So useless.

I couldn't even save myself. How the hell would I be able to help Kyle and his family?

But he was already shaking his head. "No, Sam. Whatever you're thinking, stop right there. You're new. You're a fledgling, and you're staying right here. You're right. The fighting isn't safe for you."

I just watched him – I couldn't exactly disagree. But I didn't want to be apart from him either.

"Two guards will wait with you," he said, but my mind was already skipping forward.

"What about Leia and Kayla?" Would I wait with them? I liked them, and I wasn't sure I wanted to be all alone.

He shook his head. "Leia has been training with Nic for a while now. She's been a vampire the longest out of the three of you, so she's ahead on learning to use her vampire strength and abilities. And Nic must have confidence in what she can do, or he'd never allow her to join the battle." He looked thoughtful for a moment.

"And Kayla?" I prompted.

"She's a witch. She has some unique abilities that she's been honing to be useful in a fight. Being a vampire seems to have gifted her extra talent, which she's been refining."

"Oh." Well, shit. I was the only useless mate here.

A burden, really.

But Kyle stood. "I can feel that."

"Feel what?" I smiled to show I was okay, but it was fake.

He wrapped his arm around me and drew me into a hug. "You don't need to worry or be unsure or doubt yourself. We were all fledglings once. We know how this part goes. We know how to protect you and what you need and a lot of what you can and can't do." He pulled away a little and smiled down at me. "Really don't worry."

Then his breathing changed, and his eyes reddened slightly, sending a thrill of excitement through me.

"Don't worry?" I questioned.

"Well, maybe worry a little bit. Turns out I might be dangerous." His lips were on mine before I could process that thought.

"What were we talking about?" It was a half-teasing question. I wasn't sure I cared any longer.

He shook his head. "Doesn't matter. I'm distracted."

I laughed against his mouth. I could get used to distracting this man. Then his lips roved hungrily over mine again, as he cupped the back of my head with his hand, urging me closer while his tongue slipped inside my mouth.

I kissed him back. Damn, I wanted this man. My hands were already at his waistband, playing with his belt, searching for his button and zipper.

He cupped my left breast and I gasped at the unexpected tingle of awareness as he brushed his thumb across my nipple. I wanted to drag my shirt off, I wanted to push his pants down, and I didn't know which I wanted to do first.

But Kyle solved my problem when he drew my shirt up and over my head. I unfastened his belt in reply, and the jingle of the buckle only heightened my arousal. I wanted him inside me right now. I'd probably never wanted anything more.

If he went into this battle and I lost him… I pushed the thought from my mind as I focused on the two of us, right here, right now.

I finally pushed his pants down his thighs, and they dropped to the floor as he was working on mine, struggling with the tiny zipper. I laughed before pushing his hands away.

"I've got it." As I undid my pants, Kyle unhooked my bra with a quick flick of his fingers, and it fell away, revealing my breasts to him.

He cupped them and I backed away from his hold. "Uh-uh," I taunted as I tapped the hem of his tee. "You are overdressed for this moment."

He grinned then whipped the tee over his head. "Not anymore," he said as he stepped out of his pants and strode forward, his feet already bare.

I gasped as he pushed me gently and I bounced onto his mattress before he crawled up over my body, dragging my jeans down the rest of the way as he did and allowing them to tumble to the floor.

Then my panties were gone as well, and the cool air rushed over my clit. It throbbed in time with my need.

"I want you," I whispered, trying to keep my desire quiet, but he heard, and he grinned before slipping his hands between my legs.

"Yeah, you do," he agreed and grinned wider.

My cheeks heated with both embarrassment and amusement. Apparently, this man got me wet in minutes.

"Nope," I whispered and pushed his hand away, playing with him. "No, it's like the Sahara down there."

He grinned wider and shook his head. "You're so wet for me," he murmured before leaning his head forward and kissing me again as he rolled my clit under his finger, the pressure light but firm as I angled my hips toward him, silently asking for more.

"Inside me." I offered myself to him again, lifting my hips.

He quirked an eyebrow. "You sure?"

Hell, yes, I was sure. I nodded, and he positioned himself above me, probing with his cock before he slid inside just a little and I sucked in a breath as he stretched my body with his.

This was what it was all about. Not the hokey pokey after all. This moment right now with my mate inside me, the two of us joined.

He shifted away then pushed farther in, and again, each time making me catch my breath in sounds of pleasure. I moaned a little at his steady rhythm, and moved against him, trying to capture more of him inside my body, always wanting more, always greedy.

I slipped my hand between us to touch myself, picking up where Kyle had left off, and I moaned as pleasure sparked through me as Kyle moved at the same time.

Kyle groaned above me as my fingers nudged against the base of his cock. "Yes, Sam," he whispered, and his approval accelerated my pleasure.

I gasped as I started to hyperventilate, my breathing coming faster and faster as I maintained my rhythm and Kyle's increased. He stroked me on the inside, and I stroked the outside and the combination of sensations started the tightening of my muscles. I surrendered myself to the sudden feeling of floating, hanging there before everything in me pulsed.

Kyle inhaled suddenly as my body clenched around him, and he drove forward harder until he drew in another harsh breath and stilled.

Then he moved a couple of extra times and dropped a kiss to my forehead.

"Thank you." The words pressed out of me.

He chuckled. "Why are you thanking me?"

I stretched my arms above my head. "Because I liked it." I smiled, but the movement was lazy, and Kyle chuckled again.

"So did I."

# Chapter 19 - Kyle

I stood at ease as Nic presided over our meeting. None of us were seated, instead, we were all slightly on the defensive, despite the additional guards. It seemed too comfortable, too complacent, to be any less aware of our surroundings, given the attack Brock had just launched and I'd been able to prevent the worst of. Thank fuck for that.

My blood heated at just the thought of that filthy Blackblood stomping through these hallways like he had a right to be here. He no longer had a right to even walk this planet. Not after the damage he and his group had caused in various cities and now New Orleans — and the things he'd let Esmé do to Sam.

"I think our best plan is to ambush Brock. We react swiftly and take him by surprise. There's no point spending weeks planning. He already knows I'm here, if his spies are any good, and we can capitalize on their lack of discipline and preparation if we move quickly." Nic spoke with purpose and the air of command from his place at the other side of the room.

I considered Nic's words, but Sebastian directly questioned his brother.

"Are you sure? I thought we were gathering information and making a plan. Wasn't that why we sent Kyle in undercover?" He slanted me a quick glance like maybe he disapproved of how things had turned out.

But Nic merely shrugged. "Plans change. Mates make a difference."

Surely, that was something Sebastian understood? Maybe he did because he didn't say anything further.

"I think if we go in like we did with Francois and do what we need to do then get out, we'll be good. We're a well-oiled machine. It worked before, and you know, if it ain't broke…" Nic shrugged.

I grimaced. Francois's mansion, tucked away from most of Baton Rouge, was a very different battlefield than Brock's compound in the city of New Orleans.

"There are too many innocents who could be hurt," I said, "and Brock won't care."

Sebastian glanced over this shoulder. "That's the old soldier in you talking, Kyle."

Nic met my gaze. "We'll do our best to minimize damage to innocents — we always do."

I nodded. That much was true. And maybe Sebastian was right. I still preferred the old ways — a deserted battlefield somewhere where men met, and the war was waged and won.

"Okay." I stepped forward, ready to tell them everything I knew about Brock's compound. The main house and the outbuildings. It wasn't as much information as I'd wanted to glean when I started this, but it was the best we had. More than we would have known if I hadn't infiltrated in the first place.

I picked up a dry erase marker and walked to the board on the wall. "This is what the compound looks like." I drew the basic shape of the house and yard, and I indicated the outbuildings with rough shapes alongside. "There are always armed guards posted here, up the steps by the house. These gates remain closed and are covered by at least one camera." I kept the marker moving as I spoke, filling in all the things I was mentioning. Then I faced Nic. "The inside of the house is largely empty of belongings. The Blackbloods don't seem to hoard or have collections."

Nic nodded. "Less clutter helps."

"I don't know where Brock will be, though." He was usually at his stronghold, but I couldn't guarantee it, and if he'd been warned ahead of time, he could be anywhere. "He puts his men through training, but it doesn't match our level. Too many of them are fledglings, but they do have enthusiasm."

Sebastian nodded this time. "Yes, we saw that the other night," he said. "They shouldn't be underestimated."

I spoke a little more — just details on the vampires our teams might find inside, Demon in particular, but there wasn't a lot else to say and after a short time, Nic drew the meeting to a close. He didn't want to waste too much time or daylight.

We divided into our usual units, Nic and Sebastian each keeping their mates with them, and traveled to Brock's compound in SUVs. But not all the way — no point in announcing ourselves by roaring up to the gates in a convoy.

After leaving the trucks about a mile away, we started to head in on foot.

"This isn't all the vampires in his army," I said to Nic, "but Brock houses a good portion of them here from what I can tell."

"Doesn't really matter." Nic glanced at me. "All we need to do to end this is get Brock. The other vampires will fall in line once they have a new leader."

Jason chuckled from his position where he'd joined us at the drop point. "That's a very alpha way to think, Nic. I'll have to let Conri know you're becoming more like a wolf."

Nic hissed fake displeasure then I broke away to start directing the different units to their missions.

We were close to the compound, and I wanted us all on a different building, a different entry point. Scaling the fence wasn't really an issue — Brock was living in a fantasyland if he thought his security measures would keep highly trained, highly skilled, disciplined vampires out. His armed guards wouldn't succeed at that either, but maybe it was preferable that he lived in faux-safety rather than having the sense to truly keep himself and his army protected and secure—although only good training would do that.

Each of our units entered without a problem — just as I'd known we would. We cleared our areas and arrived at the large training yard where I'd fought for Brock when he'd been testing me. Brock stood there, flanked by Demon and more of his men.

As soon as he spotted me, he spat on the ground and his fangs descended. "There's the traitor scum." His laugh afterward was malicious. He threw a look over his shoulder. "Let this be a lesson to you, boys. If any of you are found to be traitors, you will be dealt with." At a lift of his arm, his entire group surged forward.

But what they had in enthusiasm, they lacked in skill. They roared their intentions and signaled many of their moves before they even made them. They were no match for the men I'd trained, or for Leia and Kayla, and blood spurted high into the air after Brock's men started to fall, one after the other, until corpses littered the ground like discarded children's toys.

Bloodlust colored my vision as Demon stepped in front of me and smiled, his fangs showing.

"Traitor." He greeted me and nodded his head in mock acknowledgment, the gesture out of place for the large man who didn't appear to have a brain.

I didn't bother replying to him. Instead, I acted before he could even move. His faux politeness had been his weakness as I clawed across his face then gouged his jugular, slitting it and working the new ends out like a frayed wire.

His eyes and mouth went wide, and he clutched his neck, but his ginormous body swayed to the side, and he leaned at an awkward angle for a moment before he crashed to the ground, sending up a plume of dust and blood spray.

I hadn't just gone to the mountain. I'd brought it to the ground.

Flexing my fingers, I scoured the area for my next target. Then I glanced around until I found Nic. He could handle himself, but I wanted to watch his back. He'd saved me from a life like Brock's. I was so lost I could have been a Blackblood if I'd stayed on my path of destruction after I'd killed Camille.

I owed Nic my life and I was sure as hell going to protect his. Except, my king didn't need my protection. He was fighting with Brock, and Brock was strong and like a wall of muscle, but Nic was old and powerful. He'd fought alongside me many times in more recent years, and he'd honed his moves while killing many, many enemies.

Brock was his enemy now.

But their battle was far less than extraordinary. Brock looked lumbering and slow around Nic, like he usually had the others do his fighting for him and he was out of practice. He stumbled as Nic feinted, and that was all it took.

Nic looked down at him, his claws already in Brock's chest. Brock grasped Nic's wrist and looked up at him. Around him, the fighting was already dying down, my men starting to mill around as they killed or captured Brock's soldiers, subduing as many as they could.

I couldn't tell which vampires were dead and which were just incapacitated, though.

Something a hell of lot like fear flickered through Brock's eyes as he parted his lips to speak, like he was about to plead for his life. Stupid fucker.

But Nic drew back. Just a tiny amount, maybe imperceptible to anyone else, but I saw it. I knew him. He was relenting. His principles were overriding his common sense. Damn him.

Damn fair king with an overinflated sense of right and wrong. His moral code was almost unshakeable. I shook my head. He'd let Francois live, too. Francois who'd kidnapped his mate and killed her father... None of us really understood that. I mean, Francois had been on dead man's blood, but still. Nic had overridden his instinct to kill the man who'd wronged his mate.

*Overridden.*

Fuck, Nic was one strong guy. He'd gone against an urge that must have nearly ripped him apart, and now he looked like he was about to show mercy to the man who'd tried to take his throne.

After a quick check that the rest of the yard was truly under control, I focused my attention on Nic. This could all go bad very, very fast.

"Mercy," Brock croaked out, and I scoffed. "Let me live. Have mercy, The New... Orleans... King. The old... King..."

Well, fuck. Brock was invoking Francois, too. But would Nic's earlier act of leniency count against him now? Would it be seen as a weakness? I was ready if Brock was about to try anything.

Nic nodded sharply, just one swift movement. "You can live. But it won't be as a free man." He intoned the words with the weight of justice.

It was *his* justice. As King of Baton Rouge and New Orleans, his word was law.

He had dungeon cells in Baton Rouge where it looked like Brock was about to be housed.

Nic had everything under control, and I directed two more of my men to help secure Brock. Now that he was still alive — I grimaced again as the full weight of Nic's decision hit me — we needed to be sure that Brock couldn't endanger anyone else.

When there were enough vampires around Brock to take care of anything he could dish out, I looked to the rest of the yard and the clean-up and sighed. This was the worst part. *Always* the fucking worst part.

So much wasted life, so much wasted opportunity.

It was bad enough when it was humans, but at least their corpses on a bloody battlefield didn't risk vampire discovery.

I beckoned to Jason, and he jogged to my side, his face grim.

"Clean-up?" he asked, but he already knew.

He'd handled clean-up for Nic for years, knew the best methods and the best places.

"There are a lot of them to dump at once." He sucked air between his teeth like a tradesman quoting a price on a big job.

I didn't say anything, falling back on the silence to do the work.

"But I think I can do it," he finished.

"As usual," I said.

He grinned, his eyes lighting with warmth for a moment. "Yeah, as usual."

I clapped him on the shoulder and moved behind him, signaling to the nearest men to follow me into the house. "We need to see if there's anything in here that's useful." I directed them inside. "Work through methodically, turning out drawers, emptying cupboards and closets. Be careful of survivors. They could act against you in fear, or they could act against you out of belief in their cause." I issued my instructions on autopilot.

This wasn't my men's first rodeo. They didn't need to hear how to do their jobs.

I stepped back out onto the deck to send more men into the outbuildings, unsure what we'd find. The last time I'd been inside one, it was a makeshift prison.

Somewhere nearby, Brock cackled, and I turned toward the sound, watching as some of my guys dragged him over the ground so they could arrange his journey to Baton Rouge. They weren't sparing his pain, but he laughed again anyway, and then he raised his gaze to me before beckoning with just his forefinger.

I scoffed and shook my head. He thought he had that much power over me? Then I chuckled. Hell, what did it matter? Brock was pretty much a condemned man. Damned to spend the whole rest of his fucking immortal life at Nic's pleasure.

I could listen to a few last words. I sauntered in his direction — in no hurry to get there and wanted to make sure he knew it.

He laughed again as I neared him, the sound setting me on edge. He really was one unbalanced motherfucker.

"Kyle? It *is* actually Kyle, right? No false name for your false story?"

I pressed my lips together and looked past him. I wasn't here for a friendly chat.

"Where's Esmé?" He was asking *me* that question? That made no sense.

She was his sireling.

Then every one of my muscles tightened at his words, and I felt for my bond with Sam. The adrenaline of the fight must have drowned her out, and now she was almost too weak to register.

Weak and scared.

Everything in me chilled, and I took off running, Brock's laughter echoing through my head and the rest of the yard.

# Chapter 20 - Sam

Well, shit. I'd stared at the four walls of this room for what felt like actual hours. And the guard posted here with me too. I knew every pore on his face, how many breaths he took per minute, even though he didn't need to, and exactly what he sounded like when he sighed in frustration when I asked him for the time. He'd made that noise countless times now, and I was pretty sure it was ingrained on my eardrums.

I'd looked at the guard outside the room, too. He hadn't endeared himself to me any more than this stern guy.

But damn, if I didn't wish I'd had a hobby of some sort. At least then I'd be able to distract myself or something with... Hell, origami? Crochet? Cake decorating? I snorted. Like that would work, anyway.

I was way too antsy to even watch the TV anymore, even though it was droning away on the wall. And reading wasn't an option unless I wanted to read the same paragraph over six or seven times. But maybe I wasn't onto a complete loser with the cake thing. I could totally head to the kitchen and bake something, if Sebastian kept it stocked. And not that I wanted to eat the cake. Just keep myself busy making it. I could gift it to some nearby humans, or something. Make nice in the neighborhood.

It didn't really make sense, but that was okay. Keeping busy was my real objective. Anything to keep my head free from the fears of Kyle dying or getting killed in a vampire battle. Or my whole life falling apart or imploding or whatever eternal lives did.

I shook my hands, trying to get rid of the low-level of adrenaline that seemed to be flowing through me. It had kicked up an hour or so ago, and I couldn't seem to get it to drop back off. I needed to do something. Anything at all, so baking it was.

As I moved toward the kitchen, the guards fell into step behind me. "You guys like cake?" I asked over my shoulder.

The stern one curled his lip a little, but neither replied. They were both obviously the strong silent type. Or some shit like that, anyway.

But thinking of them only took my mind back to Kyle. He was truly strong and silent and gorgeous with it. And he was mine.

And he was the whole reason I was baking a cake. Because I needed to keep my thoughts busy, so I didn't think of him.

I scoured the small bookshelf in the kitchen. A lot of it was Kayla's spell books, but there was one recipe book, presumably something left over from her previous life. I pulled it over to me and flipped it open, looking at pictures of fabulous food porn that no longer made my mouth water. That part was a little sad.

I selected a cake, an easy one, and started opening cupboards, hoping to find the ingredients I needed. But did it actually matter? If I substituted all the sugar for salt, not one person would care. I wasn't making this cake to eat it.

I squinted at the package of flour, automatically looking for the best before date, although it didn't matter if it was full of weevils and mites. This was all I had, and I was using it.

"Well, pet…"

I stiffened at the familiar dulcet tone, my blood suddenly shards of ice that scraped the insides of my veins. How the hell hadn't I heard her come in?

"You're baking now?" Esmé sounded amused, flirty almost.

I didn't turn around. I couldn't. Fear froze me exactly as I was, flour in one hand, the other resting on the open page of the book. *Had* I heard something? I racked my brains, trying to remember. Had there been a footstep I'd thought was a security guard? Dammit. I'd felt too safe here. Untouchable.

But still. How the hell was she here? There was a battle going on, and she should have been with Brock. Maybe even fighting the fucking thing for him, based on what I'd seen in the past. He rarely did his own dirty work.

"What have you done, Sammy?" She lifted a lock of my hair as she spoke, and a shiver flickered across my skin. Then she inhaled, close to me, and noisily. "What have you done to my blood supply?"

I sucked in a breath, my mind racing with too many thoughts. Of course Esmé was here. And it didn't matter how she'd gotten in or past the guards. She'd do anything at all that she needed to do so she could get to me.

I was her end game.

She'd always come after me, extract her revenge for the empty life I'd left her with, and I understood some of that now. I had a mate of my own, and I was petrified to lose him, petrified that I might be without him.

I'd condemned Esmé to this life. One of loss and grief.

For a moment, pity for her welled inside me.

Then she spoke again. "Nothing to say?"

I wasn't her food source anymore. My blood couldn't sustain her. But there was no telling what else she might do to me.

I still didn't turn around, but I made my voice as hard as possible. "You need to leave, Esmé." It came out brittle instead.

"Aww… Do I?" She sounded like a lost little girl, but her grip on my hair tightened.

I spun around, surprising her, and she let go. "Yes, you do. I don't ever want to see you again. You don't belong here, and I am *not* your pet." Holy crap, saying these words felt good, and I couldn't stop them coming out. "I'm Kyle's mate, and I'm not a human any longer. I'm no use to you now."

She laughed. "You think I didn't know that as soon as I stepped into this fucking rat's nest of a house?"

I stared at her, unable to put my disbelief into words. She was seriously calling this place a rat's nest after the conditions she'd made me live in?

"Oh, I can't leave, Sam." She reached out and touched my hair again. "You're mine. Mine until one of us dies, anyway." She smiled, but it only twisted her lips. "I don't care if you're a vampire now or not, or you fancy yourself mated and in love. You're mine. You'll always be mine."

Her words lit a spark inside me and my fury erupted. My gums burst with pain as my fangs shoved through them. Vivid red colored my vision, and my nails sharpened to claws. All of this had happened when the guys had surprised us at Kyle's apartment before, but not quite like this.

I hadn't a fucking clue what to do with this new power or how to fight or use my body. My brain didn't seem to have evolved to contain the knowledge, but no way was I going back with Esmé. Or anywhere with her.

I glanced around, searching for the guards, and she shook her head.

"There's no one left to help you. I took care of them."

And I had no doubt she had. She'd always been a good fighter, and…

Quicker than I could complete my thought, Esmé was on me. She was fast and moved almost faster than I could see her. She grabbed my neck and lifted me, proving her dominance, as her fingers flexed and tightened around my throat, pressing uncomfortably against the muscles as she squeezed. I strained to suck in a breath in a reflex I couldn't control. I clawed at her hands but my attempts to free myself were useless.

She was strong, even when I shredded her skin and blood pretty much flowed from her wrists to drip on Sebastian's pristine tile floor, she didn't flinch or relax.

I kicked out with my feet, trying to connect with Esmé, trying to find a foothold against something so I could do more than hang. Nothing, just dead air, and I tried again, desperation giving me more energy.

My toe caught the end of Sebastian's kitchen island, and I tried again, stretching farther than I thought possible, pushing us both back against the fridge.

Esmé stumbled at the sudden movement and released me. I crashed against the counter and grabbed at the first thing I saw — the knife block. I yanked out the biggest, meanest-looking knife I'd seen and stabbed Esmé with it, plunging it between her ribs under her shoulder.

But it scraped against bone and my forward momentum ground to a stop. I backed away. The wound wasn't enough to stop a vampire. I hadn't hit her heart, so I wouldn't even render her incapable of movement for any time.

I grabbed another knife from the block, this one not as big but easier to handle and direct, and I stood looking at Esmé, waiting.

She gripped the handle of the knife that I'd left in her, and she extracted the blade slowly, smiling at me the whole time like she couldn't believe I'd been so stupid, like I'd just signed my own death warrant all over again.

Maybe I fucking had. Esmé's wound was already healing, her flesh and skin knitting back into place like it had never been torn apart.

She looked down at the knife and laughed, a little high-pitched, a little off balance. "Wasn't good enough, Sammy. *You're* not good enough. You'll never be able to kill me. You haven't got the balls and you're not good enough. Had any training yet? Or has your *mate* neglected you?"

"It doesn't matter, Esmé. I know why you came here, and I'd rather die than go anywhere with you." Then my self-control snapped, and my next words were almost a scream as years of frustration and hurt came rushing out. "This has all been a nightmare. Losing Sean, saving you. I never should have saved you. I wish I'd let you die that night. Saving you was the biggest mistake of my life." The windows rattled at the volume of my voice, and Esmé stilled in the way only a vampire could.

She was a predator now. Stealthy and deadly. And she was locked in on killing me.

I might have blinked. Maybe. Because suddenly she'd rushed toward me and I held out my little knife to hold her off, slicing across her arm. Bright red blood welled up, but the shallow cut healed quickly, leaving only the wet blood as evidence that it had ever been there at all.

We circled each other, although she had the obvious upper hand. She had the power and the strength. It was a game, and she was enjoying this. We were circling because she was allowing me a chance to fight back.

She launched herself toward me and grabbed my knife before throwing it carelessly to the side. There was a clinking noise as it hit the tile floor and bounced.

Anxiety was a sharp prickle along my nerves, and adrenaline focused my vision and movements. Everything I did was desperate. I wouldn't let Esmé take me from Kyle or end this life I'd only just found.

I kicked out and I hit. I would have head-butted her if she'd been close enough, but everything I did only served to make me more tired as she darted closer and away, making herself a target then retreating out of even touching distance.

My strength was waning fast, and Esmé knew it. I swung for her one last time, but she was ready, and she took hold of my arm, whipping me around as she yanked me against her.

She pressed her mouth against my neck, and I screamed as the familiar slice of her fangs tore at my skin. I went limp, muscle memory taking over as my body remembered what to do under Esmé's attack.

I didn't even scream again.

My vision started to dim. I'd always thought Esmé would kill me, but not like this. Not now that I was a vampire.

But suddenly her weight lifted. She was there one moment, gone the next, and I clutched my throat, blood gushing between my fingers from the hole she'd gnawed there.

Kyle roared, the sound ferocious. But it was also a sound that was familiar and comforting, and I relaxed as he did it again. He was here now, and I'd be safe. I slumped to the floor, too weak to stand.

He attacked Esmé, shaking her by her shoulders until her teeth rattled and the bones in her neck snapped and popped like someone was letting off firecrackers. Then he reached out and her head was on the floor and rolling away with a quick flick of his wrist. I watched her face as it appeared then disappeared with each rotation, her pale blue eyes wide in death, her impossibly blonde hair now ombre with blood.

I panted, heaving in giant, ridiculous breaths like my life depended on the oxygen, and a small pool of blood congealed around me.

Kyle rushed toward me before kneeling at my side and gathering me in his arms, cradling me against him.

He tore at the inside of his wrist until it bled and held it against my mouth. "Drink, Sam," he murmured. "Everything will be all right now. She's gone." He reached out his leg and nudged Esmé's head farther away with his boot. "Brock's under control. Nic has him."

The hole in my neck started to heal. It prickled as it repaired itself, and I touched it, running my fingers over the sensitive skin.

"It's okay," Kyle said again, and I leaned my weight against him as I leeched security from him and breathed in his familiar spicy scent.

It warmed me, and for the first time in a very long time, the safety and security surrounding me didn't feel temporary. Esmé was gone. Dead. Truly dead. She couldn't get to me anymore.

She was at peace.

I glanced at Kyle, taking in the line of his jaw. Finally, I was at peace too. I couldn't think of anywhere else I wanted to be. In his arms was perfect. The ultimate place. Where I belonged.

And now everything would be truly okay — whatever the future brought us.

# Chapter 21 - Sam

I stood in Kyle's office in Nightfall, and nearly laughed. It was exactly as Kayla had described — definitely more boxes than personality. Sebastian's office was also as I'd expected after seeing his house — decadent and luxurious while still being completely alpha within this ethereal nightclub space. He so obviously ran this business. This was Sebastian's territory.

Kyle handed me some more paperwork and nodded to a box. "That one."

"What are you doing with all the boxes? Shipping them back to New Orleans?"

It had been three weeks since Kyle had killed Esmé, and I still tried not to dwell on it. There were so many mixed feelings.

Relief was always the primary one — *always* — but I couldn't help a little sadness. I hadn't meant for Esmé to live in a world of torture, but perhaps I'd inadvertently created that for her. Maybe being without Sean had truly sent her into some sort of madness. She'd certainly been hellbent on making me pay.

And now she was gone.

There was that relief again.

Thank fuck she was gone.

I glanced at Kyle as he lifted a box, and happiness squeezed my heart. He was my savior and my mate, and now we were off for new adventures.

"No, these aren't coming with us to Baton Rouge," he said, answering my question about what was happening with the boxes. "These are going to the storage room, where Sebastian will probably never look at them again." He grinned. "Maybe they didn't need to be here in the first place, who knows? Wasn't like they helped me a whole lot with intel."

I shrugged. "Yeah, things moved pretty fast in the end there."

He chuckled, his biceps bulging against his short sleeves as he hefted another box. Made me want to touch him. No, scratch that. Made me want to *lick* him.

"I think you'll like it in Baton Rouge. And you'll get to hang out with Leia. Aimée, Nic's sister, is there a lot too. She can help you with a lot of the new vampire stuff. Nic was born, but Aimée was turned. She's fun."

That was high praise of someone from Kyle. "I look forward to meeting her," I said.

"Yeah," he continued. "I think you might like all of the Duponts."

I cast him some side-eye. Running headlong into another nest of vampires wasn't exactly what I wanted to do right now, but where he went, I went, so... Plus, he said they were good people, and I trusted him. He hadn't steered me wrong so far, and I'd liked Nic and Leia when we met — Sebastian and Kayla, too.

"You know, there is one last place we should probably go before we hit the airport." He sounded hesitant, and wariness filled me.

"Oh, yeah?" I tried to sound casual as I folded the box in front of me closed and taped it up, but my heart beat faster.

"Yeah." He sighed apologetically. "I think we should go to the place you shared with Esmé."

"What?" That was a ridiculous suggestion. "Why?"

"You have some of your human stuff there, right? This might be your last chance to reclaim it."

I sat heavily on a box behind me. I hadn't even thought of that. "Do I need it?"

He shrugged. "I don't know. But a lot of newly turned vampires start with some of their own belongings, at least."

"Do you have those things?" I didn't know a whole lot about how Kyle had gotten his start.

He shook his head. "No, but I wasn't turned…" He hesitated. "…kindly. Or for the right reasons. Nic saved me, but not until after. Not until I nearly lost myself, and by then it was too late. Nothing of mine from before probably even existed anymore, anyway."

I nodded. "Okay. We'll go. If you think we should."

\*\*\*

The driver, one Sebastian had provided, dropped us at the curb outside Esmé's place.

"We haven't got long," Kyle said as we walked up the path.

"Don't worry," I replied as my stomach about flipped with anxiety and I gripped Kyle's hand tighter. "I won't need long. Esmé didn't let me bring much. Pets don't have possessions."

Those had been the exact words from Esmé's mouth, and I should have been so much more aware then.

The door creaked open and the familiar, horrific smell hit me like a wall coming to meet me at one hundred miles per hour. It was so much worse now that I had vampire senses.

I covered my nose. "Fuck. You smelled this every time you came in here?"

Kyle smiled, but it was just the smallest quirk of his lips. "Every time," he confirmed.

"Well, shit." I glanced around. "I'll be quick. I don't have much."

"Bring whatever you can," he called as I headed to my room. "What doesn't seem important now might be what you really need in the next few weeks, months, or years."

Paused on my way through the door. "Years?"

"We have long memories."

I didn't look at him as I headed through the door. I didn't have a bag or anything, but I dumped random books and trinkets I'd hidden from Esmé on the bed and wrapped it all up in the blanket.

That was it. I'd emptied the room. I lifted my bundle and sighed. I'd lived here like a fucking hobo, and now I was leaving as one.

Kyle appeared in the doorway, his arm outstretched. "I'll take that. We should head out."

I handed it to him, glad he hadn't asked if it was everything or made me talk about it. It was like he knew that wasn't the right thing to say just now.

He took my hand in his free one and we left the house where I'd been both pet and prisoner together.

I was free now. Really free. The kind of forever that I'd always rejected before was now a possibility, because it looked like some forevers could be good.

***

"You know —" Kyle looked at me as we sat in the airplane.

It was a luxurious private jet. I shouldn't have expected anything else when Kyle had told me the King of Baton Rouge was helping him get home.

"You should probably call your mom. Tell her what's up."

I lifted an eyebrow. "Really? I don't think telling her I'm a vampire is a good idea at all." I'd been protecting her from this world this whole time, ever since Sean. "Like what? *Hey, Mom… SURPRISE?!*"

He laughed. "Fuck, no. But maybe she should know that you're going to Baton Rouge?"

Well, shit. I'd been so sidetracked with everything recently. "Oh. Of course, yeah. I'll call her now."

Kyle reached into his pocket and handed me his cell phone.

"Wait?" I met his gaze. "I can use this up here?"

He shrugged. "Voice over Wi-Fi works, and no one onboard this plane is going to say a word against you if you place a quick call to your mom." He lowered his brows into a slight frown. "I'll make sure of it."

I dialed her number and waited until her voice echoed down the line.

"Hello?" She sounded suspicious, but she always did when she got a call from an unknown number.

"Hey, Mom. It's me."

"Oh, Sam!" Her tone grew happier. "How are you doing?"

"I'm..." I glanced at Kyle. "I'm okay. Listen, I got a job offer in Baton Rouge —"

"That's great! When do you start?" She was always so enthusiastic about my opportunities, but I hesitated now.

Now that I had to tell her even more lies. "It's immediate. I'm on my way there now."

"Now?" Her happiness turned to disappointment, and I withheld a sigh of sadness.

I hated disappointing her. "Yeah. It was an opportunity too good to miss."

Kyle squeezed my hand.

"I've got to go, but I'll call you again in a few days, when I'm settled, and maybe we can arrange a visit?" I didn't know the rules on seeing people from my old life, but surely it was okay to see my mom a couple of times? I'd work something out, anyway.

I hung up but didn't talk to Kyle right away. I wasn't sure how he'd take my offer to see my mom. And if I talked, I might cry. And if I cried, he might be kind. And if he was kind… I'd fall apart.

"We can make a plan." That was all he said, and I leaned my head on his shoulder for the rest of the journey.

When the plane landed, I glanced around. The airport was tiny so it wasn't the hustle and bustle I'd expected. Kyle led the way down the short flight of stairs and over to a waiting car.

"I'd usually take my bike," he said, "but I didn't know how much luggage we'd be bringing with us."

"Are we going to Nic's house?" Leia had told me bits and pieces about it, and it sounded awesome, but I wasn't sure I wanted to live like someone's guest or employee.

Kyle shook his head. "Nope."

"Then where?" The only other place I'd been told about in Baton Rouge was Leia's old family home, but I couldn't imagine living there, either. That wouldn't feel like my home, either, with all of the history Leia had there.

"Surprise." He chuckled. "And I can feel your brain working overtime, you know. But relax. I've got it all under control."

We rode for a little while through cute neighborhoods of houses with their well-kept yards and proper American dream existence.

It was my American dream, anyway.

Kyle slowed and turned into the driveway of one of the little cottage homes. We were on a street where they were all chocolate box and pretty, but each was unique.

"Where are we?" It made sense he had other friends I didn't know about.

"Home." The word was simple. Perfect.

But it didn't make sense. "Home?"

"That's right." He climbed out of the car then bent so he could meet my gaze again. "You coming?"

I opened the car door, confusion still rearranging my thoughts. This perfect little house was my home? "It's home?" Mom's house was my last real home and so much had changed since then.

"Sure is." He wrapped his arms around me. "I bought this place for us right after you were turned. Figured it was important for you to have someplace just for you, away from the craziness."

I met his beautiful, brown-eyed gaze. "Somewhere that smells good?"

His lips twisted in a small grimace. "That too." He released me and took my hand. "Come and see the inside."

My gaze roamed over the plants and flowers I suddenly wanted to tend. "This is all mine… *ours*?"

He nodded. "Yep." And that was just the way it was. Matter of fact and to the point. He'd bought us a house. Somewhere I could build a new life with him.

Like I said… it was perfect.

I gasped as we walked inside. "You furnished it too?"

He shrugged. "Just some basics." Then he turned to me, and as we looked at each other, his gaze turned heated, and I didn't know who moved first.

Suddenly our mouths were pressed together, my breathing rapid, his hands sliding under my long-sleeved tee, my skin feverish with the heat he generated in me. He backed me against the wall, one hand tangled in my hair, as he continued his delicious assault on my lips, his tongue stroking against mine.

I gasped and cupped his face as he dropped his hands to drag my skirt up my thighs, bunching it at my waist.

"I need you." His voice was urgent against my lips, and I nodded.

I needed him too. I wasn't sure that need would ever go away. Kyle was like a second heartbeat inside me, a living part of my soul.

His belt clinked before I heard his zipper being drawn down and he lifted me so that I could wrap my legs around his waist. Then he rocked against me, teasing me with his heavy hard cock as it nudged against me.

"Tease." I grinned as I spoke the muffled word.

"Always," he murmured back. "But I know it excites you." He pressed forward again, and I gasped as he touched against me then receded.

I angled my hips, trying to capture him, wanting to feel him slide inside me, but he only chuckled.

"Not until I'm ready." He spoke between placing kisses down my neck.

"But I'm ready now." My words were little more than a plea, and he chuckled.

"I'll be the judge of that."

His expert fingers found my clit and smoothed against it, and my lips parted on a soft breath as I relaxed between his hard body and the wall, relying on him to hold my weight as he touched me.

Each stroke of his fingers spiraled more desire through me, and I moaned softly as I began to move against him.

"I want you, Kyle."

"I know," he replied, and it was like he knew everything, including exactly where I needed to be touched and how to do that as he continued to tease me, stoking my pleasure higher.

His lips were on my neck again, soft open-mouthed kisses with a touch of tongue, and his cock rested against my inner thigh. Nearly where I wanted it, but not quite.

"Bedroom?" It was half question, half instruction. I wanted better access to him. "I want to touch you, Kyle."

He heard my soft words and I laughed as he duck-walked at vampire speed to the bedroom, his jeans still around his ankles. The bed was big and soft, and he dropped me lightly onto the mattress, my skirt still in disarray, before he stripped his jeans the rest of the way off and joined me.

He kissed me again before returning his fingers between my legs. and he probed against me gently as I took his cock in my hands. It hardened further as I held it, and I squeezed my fingers gently against the warm, soft skin before playing my fingertips around the head.

His rhythm where he touched me didn't change, and I strained against him, chasing my release.

"Nearly there," he murmured, and his confidence and encouragement sent me spinning over the edge. I tilted my head back and gasped as my breaths came one on top of the other and my body throbbed.

Kyle's mouth was gentle on mine as he positioned himself over me, and I smiled, anticipating his slow side into me. I wanted this. Always wanted it.

The intimacy of his body in mine was something else. More than I'd ever read about or expected. He stretched me and filled me, and I welcomed him, wanted to share myself with him as he thrust inside me in the rhythm that would bring his pleasure.

His movements grew more rapid, his breathing changing as he neared his orgasm. I bit back my grin as he dropped his head, and I licked the pulse point on his neck.

He groaned. "Sam."

I grazed his skin with my fangs, and he groaned again, offering his neck to me. When I slid my fangs into him, his warm blood flowed into my mouth, and his thrusting rhythm paused as warmth filled the inside of me, too.

His release sent a shockwave through me, and my body throbbed around him as I released my hold on his neck to gasp. He dropped his head forward, resting his forehead against mine as he rocked inside me a couple more times, sending extra tremors through me.

"Wow." I breathed the word, and he quirked an eyebrow.

"I already made wow?"

I nodded. "I think you might have."

His voice dropped. "So, there's nowhere to go from here?"

I laughed as I looked up at him, my hand on the back of his head, my fingers tracing the ridge of his scar. "Oh, I don't know. I think we have a long time to find out."

He nodded his agreement and lowered his head for another kiss.

Forever was a very long time indeed.

# Chapter 22 - Jason

I shoved the desk drawer shut and leaned back on the squeaky office chair I'd commandeered from Kyle's old office at Nightfall even though I had nothing at all to do with the club. It just gave me a quiet space to think away from dogs.

Dogs. Hell, even after all this time, part of me still thought of the wolf shifters that way. They smelled like dogs, sometimes looked a lot like them... Dogs, right? But I liked some of them. Conri and Simon, his beta. They were both good guys.

Wouldn't have wanted to get on the wrong side of them, though.

I scanned through the letters in front of me again, spreading them across the desk so I could see them all.

Fucking hell. These had been found in the raid at the Blackbloods' compound, and if there was one thing I was grateful to Brock for, it was that he didn't appear to throw any of his paperwork away. *Now* we had plenty of intel. Or it seemed so, anyway.

I read over the next one in line. Well, shit. It was here in black and white, exactly as Nic and Sebastian had said:

'The fucking ancients had fucking awakened.'

Whatever the holy fuck that meant.

Even the phrase sent a tendril of dread to wrap around my ribs, tightening until it constricted my chest.

*Ancients.* Vampires even older than Nic. More powerful. And likely far more ruthless.

The letters in front of me detailed that they'd heard of Nic overthrowing Émile Ricard and his son, Francois and taking New Orleans. They were coming to determine his worthiness to rule.

I scoffed. It sounded so fucking ridiculous. Like Nic should be judged? Like they could really deem him not worthy? But enough doubt lingered in my gut that it made me anxious. Things might not go our way this time. After all the crap the Duponts had just put to bed, things might not go our way.

Luckily, Nic was on the case, and he wasn't taking the challenge to his rule lightly. Or at all. He wasn't just waiting for a few old guys to come and decide if he had what it took. That was the part of why I was here.

I sighed and rolled my eyes. I didn't mind being here and reading through the letters and trying to make a plan — I'd serve Nic in whatever way he needed—but I had major problems with the next part.

Francois fucking Ricard.

For some reason, Nic had believed Francois when he said the rehabilitation program had worked, that the training had made him stronger, that he'd found a new purpose. Blah, blah, fucking blah.

And yeah, right.

If I'd kidnapped Nic's mate and killed her father while hopped up on dead man's blood, I'd have found myself a new purpose pretty fucking fast, too.

I rolled my eyes. Now Nic had passed Francois on as *my* problem. Maybe because I was Nic's sireling — we had a bond of trust between us that surpassed a lot of other bonds between vampires. He was letting him step foot back in New Orleans. He should have been banished for life after everything he and his father had allowed to happen and caused in this city.

But no. I sighed again. I couldn't exactly question Nic's decision. That was treason, even for me. Probably questioning my sire's decision was worse than treason, but I didn't have to like it.

There was a knock at the door, and I didn't even look up. "Come in." My voice was little more than a grunt. I still had several more pages of these letters to work through.

"Jason!" Francois's French accent jarred against my ears. "Such a pleasure to be back here in New Orleans, n'est-ce pas?"

I shook my head. No way was this a pleasure for me. "Not so much, Francois. I'm only working with you because Nic has said that's what he wants."

"Bon." Francois sat in the chair on the other side of my desk and his booted feet landed on the surface in front of me.

I glanced up to find him examining his usual flamboyant sleeves. His dress sense hadn't improved when he came off the drug, then. Shame.

"We are agreed." He met my gaze, his eyes steely. "Neither of us likes this. We are here because we need to be."

There was a new awareness in his eyes, I'd give him that much. But full-on rehabilitation? I wasn't sure about that. I'd definitely need to keep an eye on him and report anything suspicious back to Nic.

I started gathering the letters back into a pile. "If that's all you came for…" I didn't finish my sentence as I lifted his feet to get to a letter trapped underneath them. "I actually need to go." I checked my watch, but it was for pure showmanship.

I was already running late to meet Conri, and that was because this was a meeting I wanted to attend even less than my own funeral.

"Oh." Francois pursed his lips into a coy little pout. "Am I keeping you? You have a meeting with someone more important than moi, peut-être?"

I wanted to punch that expression right off his face, but I settled for slamming my desk drawer closed instead. The force jingled the little buckles on his boots, and the sound grated over my nerves.

I swallowed my initial annoyance and forced myself to sound bored instead. "Everyone is more important than you, Francois."

"Oui. Oui. Bien sûr," he agreed, his tone amiable. "But of course. And I must allow you to attend the little meeting you appear to be late for, and you and I will see each other soon."

Damn it. How did that fucking guy know I was late? I waited for him to leave the office then followed him, locking the door behind me then rattling the handle to be sure no one without the key would be able to get in.

\*\*\*

"What's going on Jason?" Conri leaned his elbows on his worn pine kitchen table, his hands clasped beneath his chin, as he looked at me. "We were promised land and resources. Nic and I had a deal." He paused to examine his nails. "Or did the king forget?"

My stomach clenched. This was exactly the conversation I'd been trying to avoid. "The threat of the Blackbloods took priority. Surely, you can see their existence threatened *everyone's* safety?" I needed to appeal to his morals, to his principles, but Conri shook his head.

"And what does a nest of rogue vampires have to do with shifter politics? I'm sorry you guys can't tell your ass-end from your head, but that's not my problem."

He had a point, and I couldn't deny it. "Exposure of vampires is a danger for us all," I said instead. "But we've neutralized that threat now, so things should be back on track."

"Should?" He raised an eyebrow.

"Are," I corrected. "They are."

Simon never gave me that hard a time. I preferred dealing with the beta, for sure. Having to talk to Conri was harder because he was more on top of everything, and I had to talk faster to find better explanations.

I tried a different tack. "What can I do to make you happy today, Conri?"

He growled, and it almost seemed like the answer was a big fat fucking nothing.

He leaned forward and lowered his voice, all the more threatening for that. "You can tell Nic that I'm not happy."

I swallowed and nodded. "Absolutely." It was easier to let Nic sort this shit directly, anyway. He and Conri had some sort of understanding over Leia. Not exactly a meeting of the minds, but Conri had recognized something fragile in Leia that meant he'd helped Nic out when he most needed it.

It was probably better for me to let their uneasy alliance handle the weight of Conri's displeasure now.

I stood. "I'll go deliver that message."

"You'd better." The alpha's voice was a mere growl, and I strode from the room, trying to look a lot more at ease than I felt.

I left the small house he lived in on pack lands, closed the door behind me, then started down the steps that led from his porch. I'd just reached the track out front when a beautiful aroma teased me. I'd never smelled anything like it. It was soft caramel and honey with hints of vanilla. I wasn't sure if I wanted to eat it or wrap myself in it and bask for days.

I was on pack lands. I needed to just get in my car and head back to New Orleans. I couldn't investigate the source of any smells, no matter how enticing, no matter how much they called to me.

And I fucking knew all of this as I strode down the dark wooded trail, following my nose, walking into who the fuck knew what.

Water. I could definitely hear water. It lapped at a shore, and I could smell a lake, more fresh than swampy, which was unusual. But the sweet, enticing scent eclipsed nearly everything else.

I'd never wanted anything more. I rounded the corner of the small trail and stopped as moonlight glinted off the lake I'd expected to see. It illuminated a woman standing just up to the curve of her ass in the water.

My mouth dried and my eyes widened as I took in her caramel-colored hair where it stuck wetly to her back. I resisted the urge to rush into the water and join her, to scoop her up and run her back to New Orleans to be with me.

She stiffened like she could sense me, but she didn't turn immediately. As I watched her, her back straightened, and she drew herself to her full height. I wanted her more with each passing moment and flex of her muscles.

I held my breath as she turned, and a low growl echoed over the water from her. I searched her gaze for a hint of wolf, but there was nothing. The eyes looking back at me were entirely human.

Human, and they belonged to my mate.

Printed in Great Britain
by Amazon

34982764R00209